THE WEDDING WAGER

*Emma Langston has three sons to love,
but she is at that age where a woman longs for
grandbabies. Wouldn't it be wonderful if her
three strapping sons could give her three tiny
granddaughters to love?*

Gabe Langston

Rich, powerful and ruthless, Gabe may have found
his fortune, but he has yet to find his heart....

Robert Langston

A sexy secret service agent about to get
the surprise delivery of his life!

Clu Langston

A man devoted to the life of the mind,
Clu might need a little push in order to
answer the call of love....

*All Emma needs is a plan—perhaps a little wager
designed to get her brood of bachelors to the altar.
After all, she has to do something if she hopes
to get her stubborn sons to attend to*

Matters of the Heart

PAMELA MORSI

"The Garrison Keillor of romance, Morsi's stories are filled with lively narration and generous doses of humor."
—*Publishers Weekly*

National bestselling author Pamela Morsi is best known for her charming tales of carousels, country dances and the simple pleasures of an America long gone by. A two-time winner of the prestigious RITA Award, Pam lives with her family in San Antonio, Texas.

ANN MAJOR

"Compelling characters, intense, fast-moving plots and snappy dialogue have made Ann Major's name synonymous with the best in contemporary romantic fiction."
—*Rendezvous*

Ann Major has written over forty novels for Silhouette Books. She is a founding board member of the Romance Writers of America. She loves to write and considers her ability to do so a gift. She lives in Texas with her husband of many years and is the mother of three grown children.

ANNETTE BROADRICK

"Annette Broadrick's glorious love stories always sparkle with irresistible joy and grace."
—*Romantic Times Magazine*

Annette Broadrick believes in romance and the magic of life. Since 1984, she has shared her view of life and love with readers. In addition to being nominated by *Romantic Times Magazine* as one of the Best New Authors of that year, she has also won the *Romantic Times Magazine* Reviewers' Choice Award for Best in its Series; the *Romantic Times Magazine* WISH award; and the *Romantic Times Magazine* Lifetime Achievement Awards for Series Romance and Series Romantic Fantasy.

Pamela Morsi
Ann Major
Annette Broadrick

Matters of the Heart

Silhouette Books

Published by Silhouette Books
America's Publisher of Contemporary Romance

SILHOUETTE BOOKS

MATTERS OF THE HEART

Copyright © 2001 by Harlequin Books S.A.

ISBN 0-373-48427-5

The publisher acknowledges the copyright holders of the individual works as follows:

YOU'RE MY BABY
Copyright © 2001 by Ann Major

I'M GOING TO BE A...WHAT?!
Copyright © 2001 by Annette Broadrick

WITH MARRIAGE IN MIND
Copyright © 2001 by Pamela Morsi

CONTENTS

Dear Reader,

It was such a wonderful honor to be asked to write a love story that has to do with the fierce, sweet longing to be a mother. Never have the children of the world been in greater jeopardy. Never have mothers felt more under siege to protect and prepare their precious darlings to go out and make the world a better place.

I wanted children more than anything, and they are everything to me now. My daughter actually inspired this story. She has always adored children, and she wants to adopt children who need to belong somewhere and give them a home. In writing my particular story I talked to several women who have adopted children, and many who have adopted from other races and cultures. The stories these mothers told me were filled with profound love and hope.

And what a special joy it was to collaborate with two of my dearest friends, Annette and Pam, who both wrote heartwarming tales about love, marriage and motherhood.

All my best,

Ann Major

YOU'RE MY BABY
Ann Major

Dedication

To the children in the world
who need a place to call home
and someone they belong to.
My prayers go out to each and every one of you.

Acknowledgments

I want to thank the following people:
Tara Gavin, Karen Solem, Patience Smith,
Annette Broadrick and Pam Morsi

And also
David Cleaves and Mitra for telling me
about the computer business in Austin.
Kim Cleaves, who wants to save children

Steve Stainkamp and Geri Rice

Patricia Patterson
for streamlining my business affairs so I can write

Prologue

A Mother's Day in Texas

No good deed goes unpunished.

By the time Emma Langston had listened to Maura Blair rattle nonstop for more than an hour about the arthritis in her lower back, Emma's own spine ached in sympathy. Why had she talked her son Gabe into bringing his gossipy next-door neighbor home with him for Mother's Day?

"She's the bane of my existence, Mom. She's always after me to kill her pigeons, and I like pigeons."

"She's a lonely old lady, and she was my mother's oldest and dearest friend."

"There's a reason why people in Old Enfield leave her alone, Mom."

Poor Maura. She was both dear and difficult. Emma stood at her kitchen sink beside a pitcher of iced tea and four glasses, wishing she were outside with her sons enjoying the beautiful day.

Only two of her boys ever came home these days. From her window Emma could see the darkly handsome pair in the pasture with Zafir.

As usual, Gabe, who'd been closer to his father than he was to her, turned everything into some sort of competition. He had his stopwatch out and was racing the white Arabian around the ring. Clu looked pale and drawn, worrisomely bleak as he did too often these days, which made her wonder what was going on with him. Still, he smiled and pretended an interest in his brother's boyish game.

Yes, two of Emma's boys were home, but she could tell they missed those who weren't as much as she did. A lump formed in Emma's throat. Would holidays always be this difficult?

Was it only three years ago that Emma had rushed her Robert to the hospital after he'd complained of chest pains, only to lose him to an unexpected heart attack, and return to the ranch a widow? After the funeral, she'd gone numb, collapsing in her bed, refusing to get up. Days had run into weeks. People had told her she'd feel better in time, but the emptiness inside her had only seemed to expand until her youngest and most sensitive son, Clu, had put his own academic teaching career on hold and moved home.

"It's my time to take care of you, Mom," he'd said gently.

Gabe came by most Sundays, but somehow she and Gabe weren't nearly as close.

"Did you hear what I said?" Maura said, interrupting her thoughts. "My Samantha's coming home to Austin."

Emma started. "Samantha?"

"And she's bringing that rainbow brood she adopted—those four *fatherless* little girls who came from all over the world to live with her."

Emma drew a sharp, painful breath. Gabe's Samantha? Her Samantha?

No. Not Gabe's Sam anymore. Nor hers either. Sam had broken all their hearts when she'd run off and gotten married.

"Fatherless little girls?"

"You know Tom died nearly two years ago."

Emma had barely been functioning back then. "You told me, and I wrote Sam, remember?"

And dear, precious Sam, who never wrote anybody, had written her back. She'd told her about China, about the twin little girls she and Tom had adopted from an orphanage there, about the problems she and all the girls were having on their own without Tom.

Maura ran a hand through her blue hair. She had a beak for a nose and bright, birdlike eyes. "Well, her father says it's high time Sam caught herself a new husband, and I agree."

"Maybe she hasn't gotten over Tom—"

"Sam's far too clever to just come out and announce what she's up to. But Austin's the perfect city for husband-hunting. Gabe's going to have plenty of competition this go-round."

"Gabe? What's he got to do with it?"

"Everything. She was his first love, and he was hers."

"That was years ago."

"They're both single. Sam's rich, and that counts, especially to a man like Gabe. She's beautiful too. And she's fun. From what I've seen of his women, Sam's a big step up. She's going to live with me for a while. But you tell him from me, he isn't the only eligible bachelor in our neighborhood or in Austin."

"Maura Blair, if this is another of your schemes to meddle in Gabe's love life or in Sam's—"

"Who, me—meddle? But I'd have to be blind not to know somebody better make a smart move fast, or he could end up with the wrong sort. His women drive fast cars and sleep over. But with Sam next door—"

Gabe was the super-rich CEO of a computer software company. Emma knew he wasn't too crazy about Maura spying on him or sulking when he didn't help her fast enough with repairs or her yard. Would Gabe feel cornered when Sam and her girls moved next door?

"My, my, what a pretty day," Emma murmured, changing the subject to distract Maura.

May in Texas was indeed the prettiest, softest

month of the year. The sun was brilliant, the cloudless sky utter blue. The balmy air was redolent with the perfume of wildflowers—bluebonnets, Indian paintbrush, and pink, evening primroses. Beyond, the distant hills glowed lavender.

Four little girls.

Emma knew she should be grateful for her three handsome, successful sons, but sometimes she wished they were more ordinary. Maybe then they would have married, had children…had little girls. Those thoughts brought her back to Sam and her flock.

Samantha Martin had been so young when her parents had divorced. Her wealthy father, who was an international businessman, had remarried a glamorous younger wife who'd had no use for a lonely, motherless child.

Sam had spent lots of holidays and summers, even entire school terms, with her great-aunt Maura. Since Maura was a close family friend, Samantha had come to know the Langstons and had eventually fallen in love with Gabe.

Maybe her lonely childhood was why Samantha had always wanted a whole houseful of children. She'd adored Gabe, who'd been seven years older, but Gabe had been competitive and ambitious and unready for marriage.

When Sam had pressured, he'd broken up with her. Not that she hadn't quickly married that preacher fellow, who'd been as idealistic as Sam. They'd adopted those four little girls. Everybody had said they were perfect for each other. Everybody except Gabe and her father, Henry. Instead, Gabe had grown colder and seemed even more ruthlessly determined to succeed at any cost.

How Emma longed for granddaughters, granddaughters who could take turns riding Zafir.

Not that there was any chance of that. Not when Gabe was more against marriage than ever. She sensed he was lonely, but he was always quick to say that his life in the fast-paced tech industry in nearby Austin was enough challenge for any man, that he could find plenty of female companionship without marriage.

Clu, her brilliant son, the math/science professor, wasn't even dating. It worried Emma that Clu seemed perfectly content to move in and stay with her after Robert's death. Three years later, he still hadn't left.

And Rob—there was no way Rob could marry. Not with his dangerous job as an agent for the Treasury Department. Besides, as the oldest, he had taken his father's death almost as hard as she had. After the funeral, he never came home, saying his career kept him in D.C. But she knew he couldn't face her or the ranch or his memories any more than she could. So, once again he'd sent red roses and a note for Mother's Day.

Oh, how she envied him. She had to live here. She had to pretend everything was fine and that life would go on. People kept telling her it was time for her to move forward, not backward.

"You're not listening!" Maura snapped from her stool at the kitchen table. "That's the trouble with getting old—nobody pays any attention to you."

"I am too!" Emma swiped her hands across the front of her apron. Poor dear Maura.

"What did I say then?" the erect old lady demanded querulously.

"Something…something about Gabe…and Samantha."

"I didn't say a thing about Sam. I said Gabe's dating a fast girl named Vicki who sleeps over."

"I don't want to hear—"

"Young ladies didn't stay out all night at gentlemen's houses in my day."

"Gabe says you have a set of binoculars in every single window. I thought he was exaggerating."

"I watch birds!" Maura snapped. Then she began on a different track. "I've been after your Gabe all week to fix my porch light switch and to do something about all the pigeons that keep stealing food from my birdfeeders."

"I'm sure he's been busy."

"Things keep breaking. When I told my Oleta, she said the house is too big for me. Then she sent a real estate agent friend of hers over."

"Oh, dear." Oleta was Maura's bossy daughter who lived overseas.

"Oleta thinks I should think about assisted living. That's why I wrote to Samantha in the first place. That's why Sam decided to come home with her four little girls."

Outside Gabe was still racing Zafir.

Gabe hadn't ever loved another woman the way he'd loved Sam. Suddenly Emma's mind played a trick. Gabe and the Arabian vanished. Instead, she saw a field filled with little girls who were chasing each other and laughing. And Robert was there.

Emma caught her breath.

"You look like you're seeing ghosts."

Emma shook her head, but her heart beat a little too quickly as she gestured out the window to her sons. "How my boys love that horse! My Robert.... Did I ever tell you how he rescued that animal from a life of slavery on the streets of Houston?"

Emma's voice trailed off as fragments of thought collided in her brain. Samantha and those four little girls of hers needed a father. Gabe let himself be chased by the wrong sort. Rob never came home.

Again, as Emma stared dreamily out the window, she imagined she saw Zafir, his head down, plodding docilely along the lane in front of her house pulling a wagon full of little girls with garlands of wildflowers in their hair.

A hazy hope hatched in her brain as Emma watched her Gabe canter raucously over to Clu, who was holding the stopwatch as he leaned against the fence.

Granddaughters!

All her life Emma had longed for little girls. Girls to sew for, to bake for, to teach all the things her boys had never had any use for.

"Why doesn't Clu get on with his own life?"

demanded Maura now, moving on to her next target. "We all understood at first. Robert's death was so sudden and all."

"Clu was a lifesaver," Emma murmured defensively unable to admit she was worried too. Clu was too nice, too perfect to stay single.

Gabe dismounted. Emma heard her sons' laughter outside, heard their boots on the porch, heard the scrape of wood as they flung their large bodies down in wicker chairs. They sounded so much like her Robert. Almost....

For a moment the memory was so acute, she almost expected Robert to walk through the door. If he were out there right now, he'd be making them a wager, thinking up some sport, some game, some interesting prize for them to compete over.

Suddenly, Emma's vague idea jelled.

"What do you say we go outside, Maura dear, and join my boys?" Emma said almost gaily.

"I told you I'm allergic to wasps."

Emma poured tea into the four glasses anyway.

"I said I'm allergic."

Emma slapped Maura's glass on the table in front of the older woman as she swept past her.

"Your hands are shaking," Maura said, sensing drama. The old lady forgot about wasps and allergies. She forgot about that arthritis she'd told Emma about too. As spryly as a girl, she picked up her glass and chased Emma.

"That's just the ice cubes tinkling," whispered Emma mildly, but her heart was hammering with wild excitement as she stepped outside into golden sunshine.

"Mom!"

Emma handed them each a glass of tea and said quietly, "What if I made you a wager just like your father used to?"

They got up, fought to be the first to pull a chair out for her and then another for Maura.

Gabe's black brows shot upward the way they used to when Robert was alive. "A wager?"

She took her time settling in. Indeed, she waited until they'd sweetened their tea and taken a sip or two and were completely relaxed.

"I ask you both, now what does an old lady like me need with a horse like Zafir?" she asked.

"You're not old, Mom," they both exclaimed. "And...and you'd better not sell Zafir."

"Did I say sell?" Emma put an extra teaspoon of sugar in the smile she gave her two darlings and Maura. "I'm going to make you a wager."

"What sort of wager?" Gabe asked with a suspicious frown.

"It's simple, Gabe. Simple and wonderful."

Not one for sentiment as she was, he looked away.

Emma held up her glass of iced tea as if to toast them. "The son who gets married and produces my first granddaughter wins Zafir for his very own!"

Chairs flew back. Gabe and Clu were instantly on their feet. "That's not fair, Mom!"

"No! But it's delicious fun. You've been telling

me it's time to move forward, that I can't live in the past forever. Well, neither should you!''

"We didn't mean for you to go and get crazy and start meddling in our lives just like—'' Clu broke off.

"Don't look at me!'' snapped Maura, but her birdlike eyes brightened with mischief.

Emma laughed. "Maybe dear Maura did inspire me,'' she murmured. "Boys, call Rob—first thing! You tell him I want a granddaughter! Future testosterone-charged little Treasury agents simply won't do!''

Gabe and Clu stared at each other and then at her so long, Emma felt the need to repeat herself.

"Whoever has the first granddaughter wins Zafir!''

"You're actually serious,'' growled Clu.

Maura lifted her glass of tea and clicked it against Gabe's. "Samantha's coming home to find a father for her little girls!''

"He'll win for sure!'' Clu exclaimed. "Just like always.'' But he was studying his brother with new interest.

"Samantha?'' Gabe's handsome face darkened, and his low tone was stiff and unnatural.

"She's moving in with me,'' Maura said.

"I couldn't care less,'' said Gabe.

The two women smiled at each other.

"Let the games begin,'' said Emma.

"Go, Gabe!'' Clu teased, using an old family football yell back from when Gabe had been a quarterback.

Chapter 1

It was nearly midnight. Samantha Martin Tracy's eyes felt dry and gritty. Except for half a dozen other weary-looking passengers, Sam's four little girls—her rainbow brood as she affectionately called them—and her dad, Henry—as she not so affectionately called him—the luggage claim area at Bergstrom was deserted.

"Mommy! Mommy!" Courtney's thin black fist tugged on Samantha's limp, wrinkled jeans. "There it comes!"

Black braids flying, the ten-year-old little girl jumped up and down. Her voice was so piercing that Samantha had to clamp both hands over her ears.

"Thank goodness, darling," Sam murmured in a slow, soothing tone in an attempt to calm her. "I don't think I could deal with a lost bag at this hour."

"Nobody's around anyway," her father grumbled.

Courtney's huge red bag spilled out of the aluminum shoot like a clumsy caterpillar, toppling three black suitcases.

"Oh, dear!" Samantha moved toward the fat red bag like a sleepwalker. Her father followed, droning on about how his businesses were flourishing.

Sam was so tired and depressed, his words hit her in a blur. It was Mother's Day. Maybe that was what had her so down. Her own mother had run away on Mother's Day. Sam had been five.

Or was it coming home to Austin for the first time since she'd left as a brokenhearted girl that crushed her spirit? After all, this city, no, Gabe Langston had broken her heart. Or was it just that she was exhausted from crossing oceans with four lively kids who hadn't ever fallen asleep at the same time.

Bea, who was six, had lost her teddy bears more times than Sam could count. Kim and Lee, the six-year-old twins Sam had gone to China to adopt, had been more clingy than usual. Even now they refused to get more than a few inches from her legs.

Bea was Sam's blond golden child from Russia. Even though she was the same age as the twins, they wouldn't play with her. And Courtney.... Dear, hyper Courtney still hadn't gotten used to being part of "their" family. More than once she'd said Sam, who had long red hair, didn't look enough like her to be her mommy. Tall and slim, Sam's eldest was the color of rich chocolate.

"Mommy! Mommy! Grab it before that man does!" Courtney shouted again.

The passenger in question turned. Samantha avoided his nervous stare and raced blindly. When she caught the handle of the duffel bag, it was so heavy it dragged her along for a step or two. Instead of giving her a hand, her father, who'd come to pick them up, bellowed, "Even if you do have way too many kids—and they are a motley bunch, if I do say so—you're still a prize catch, honey."

Sam flinched. He meant his money was.

"Why don't you do something smart the second time around? Spruce up, the way you did to attract Gabe."

Gabe.

"Henry, please don't start in on me about Gabe. Not when I've been on planes for thirty-six straight hours."

"It shows."

"Dad!" She corrected herself. "I—I mean... Henry!"

"Honey, get out your mirror."

She'd already checked herself in one before she got off the plane. From doing so she knew her face was a waxen gray under the florescent lights, that her long red hair was dull and limp against her neck, and that her cotton blouse and jeans looked equally tired.

"This time, honey, catch a real man. Somebody rich who I can be proud of."

Why don't you yell that a little louder. Maybe then even Gabe Langston will hear....

Gabe Langston.

As she thought of Gabe again, Gabe, the boy she'd loved so desperately, her first love—was there anything so wonderful or so terrible as first love— pain lanced her heart. She gave a little shudder. The handle she'd been tugging on so breathlessly slipped out of her fingers, and she nearly fell.

Bea and the twins, along with the ever-lively Courtney, raced gleefully along after it.

Her father frowned, first at Sam as she picked herself up, and then at her rowdy girls, who were now fighting over the revolving bag.

The stranger Courtney had been worried about said, "Lady, is this your bag?"

Sam nodded, and then smiled in weary gratitude when he pulled it off for her.

When her girls threw themselves onto Courtney's bag with way too much energy, her father shot them another disapproving glance, the kind he'd given Sam so often as a child. "Think about them. If you don't want a husband, they damn sure need a father."

As if you care. Sam was too tired to argue.

"Is he mean?" Bea wanted to know on the curb as they waited beside their mountain of bags for Henry to bring the car.

"No, it's just late. He's tired. Like we are." As always she made excuses for him.

The twins touched her leg. "Is he gonna be our grandpa?"

"He's my father," Sam said shortly. "He says you're to call him Henry and his wife Mary because they're too young to be anybody's grandpa or grandma. If it makes you feel better, I'll call them Henry and Mary too."

"But I wanted a real grandpa," said Bea, hugging her bears.

"Are you going to marry us a daddy like he said?" Courtney demanded worriedly.

Tired as she was, Sam stared lovingly at each of her four darlings. Courtney couldn't trust the world, especially men, because of all that had happened to her.

Her precious, precious, little girls. Her rainbow brood. She had to protect them. All of them had lost their "real" parents. They were scarred, as she was. But they wanted to be a real family, as she did. Now that Tom was dead, how could she ever give them that?

Courtney's gaze was still troubled.

Are you going to marry us a daddy like he said?

Sam sank to her knees and took Courtney's dusky hand. "I won't marry anybody. Not unless you fall in love with him too, my sweet darling."

Courtney's mouth twisted. She looked away. Biting her lip, her big, dark eyes uncertain as she watched the cars go by. Sam was so tired, she couldn't think of anything reassuring to say, so she hugged her.

A daddy for my darlings, Sam thought. A husband for me. She'd been so lonely for so long. But who in the world would she ever find to take her and her four little girls?

Maybe that question got her thinking about Gabe again, Gabe who'd broken her heart, Gabe whom she'd told herself she hated. Or maybe it was just the familiar landmarks of her hometown that made her remember him all too clearly.

When Henry's luxury car glided past the inky gleam of Town Lake, Sam remembered the lazy summer afternoons Gabe and she had spent necking on towels above Barton Springs' crystal green waters after they'd gone swimming. Their lithe bodies had been wet and icy cold from the chilly, spring-fed water. Their kisses had been hot and eager and far more dangerous than a naive girl like her had been able to realize.

Well, from what Aunt Maura wrote, Gabe had had many women since her. Even though Sam was older and wiser and had no interest in him now, she wished with all her heart he didn't live next door to Aunt Maura.

Sam leaned back into her seat and closed her eyes. She didn't want to see anything else that would remind her of Gabe. Since she and Gabe had been all over this city together, she didn't open her eyes until Henry pulled up into Aunt Maura's drive. Until Bea dropped all her teddy bears and shrieked, "Mommy! Is that Pwince Charming's castle?"

Bea's open palms were eagerly plastered against

the window. She was staring in wonder at Gabe's huge house, which did indeed look like a castle.

Gabe—Prince Charming? Mr. Love-'em and Leave-'em? Mr. Super Jock?

Hardly.

"No," Sam said, her faint voice a little too fierce. "Girls, you stay away from that house, do you hear me? And stay away from the man who lives there."

"Why?" they demanded, thrilled as all little girls are of the forbidden, especially if it happens to be male.

"Is he mean?" Bea wanted to know.

Not exactly.

Miserably, Sam just shook her head. She couldn't answer. Her eyes felt hot, and there was something dry and hard in her throat.

Chapter 2

It was still dark when Gabe stepped outside in his running clothes. Next door Maura's house was black.

Let the games begin? Zafir up for grabs?

Gabe loped down his drive. It was Maura's fault his mother had gotten that wild idea.

Marriage? Granddaughters?

Not him! Gabe had felt lost growing up in his big family.

Samantha moving next door—to catch a husband?

Gabe stopped in the middle of the street and stared back at Maura's dark house for most of a minute. For no reason at all he remembered kissing Sam for the first time on Maura's porch. Sam had been wearing a bikini and a towel. She'd been wet and cold and hot all at the same time. They'd come home from swimming together because swimming at Barton Springs had been their special summer thing.

Swimming had evolved into necking on the lawn above the public pool, which had evolved into necking in private, which had evolved into ever more enthralling pastimes.

Samantha—next door. Hell, he still had baggage left over from her. He wanted to forget her.

Then why did he still think of her at the oddest times? Why couldn't he forget the anguish that had come into her green eyes when he'd told her he didn't want to marry her? The anguish that had come into his heart after she was gone?

Sam had been his first real love. Nobody had ever made him feel like that—not before, not since.

By the time he'd figured out how much she'd meant to him, she'd married Tom. He'd been stunned when he'd realized he couldn't forget her.

She was a widow now.

Don't fall for any of it, Langston. So what if Samantha was coming to town looking for a husband?

But some part of Gabe felt he had to win his mother's stupid bet or die. It was what he did in his family, how he earned his place. Just as Clu earned his by being there for Mom.

Gabe had been a jock in high school and in college, excelling in football and track—to please his father and the other football fanatics in his family.

He'd been both a star quarterback as well as a long-distance runner. Hell, he was still compulsive about jogging five miles a day.

Zafir? It was as if his dad were in the back of his mind, cheering from a bleacher again, egging him on. Dad had bragged about him constantly. God, how he still missed that.

And Samantha? Why had Maura thrown her name out like his old girlfriend was a prize too?

Maybe he would ask Maura later when Sam was getting in so he could invite her to lunch. They'd have a few laughs over old times and go on with their lives.

Not that Gabe Langston had time to worry about his mother or Sam this particular Tuesday morning after Mother's Day. He felt too edgy.

Why did everything happen at once? No sooner had he gotten home Sunday night, than Vicki had shown up on his doorstep in a black mini demanding to know why he hadn't invited her to his mom's on Mother's Day. Before he'd realized what she was up to, he'd said the wrong thing, and she'd broken up with him.

When he'd tried to call her Monday night, she hadn't answered. When his phone had rung, he'd had his apologies ready. But the disembodied voice at the other end had turned his blood to ice.

"What would you say if I told you your partner isn't good old Nelson George any more? That your software secrets—including Novadash—are up for grabs, buddy?"

After the caller hung up, Gabe had gone cold. He'd flicked the remote off and hunched forward, as still as death, staring at the black television.

Gabe had founded LXK right out of college and made a success of it. But there was a dark side to boom times. Everybody expected to get rich fast. Nelson had wanted to go public or to sell out to the big guys. Gabe had held on to power—at all costs.

Novadash was LXK's latest, hush hush, innovative Internet software. It was set to hit the market soon.

Gabe had tried to call Nelson and gotten his machine. Then he'd e-mailed him. Finally, he'd gotten Mark, his third in command, who had reassured him. Even so he'd been unable to sleep, so he'd put on his running clothes and gone out. He'd returned, too exhausted to move.

Nelson hadn't gotten back to him. Gabe had called Mark again, and Mark had reminded him that Nelson and he went back to UT.

Right. They'd fought over Sam back then. She'd chosen Gabe. Later, they'd fought over LXK. Gabe had won that one, too.

Samantha. Life had been so much simpler when they'd been young. What was she like now? To his surprise, he realized he really wanted to know.

Gabe hadn't slept much, and he didn't feel like jogging this morning. But he was a man of precise habits. When he raced out of his drive, it was still dark except for the lightning that crackled along the fringes of the horizon.

Out of the corner of his eye he saw a large shadowy object floating in the middle of his dark, opulent pool. Later, he'd see about that. He noted the empty spot in front of his house under the huge pecan tree where Vicki usually parked her yellow convertible. Its absence sharpened his feelings of loneliness.

But he didn't think about Vicki. Instead he wondered about Samantha as he jogged to the bottom of his hill straight into a driving wind. When would he see her?

His run took him past stacks of lumber piled high at the Coopers' mansion on the other side of Maura's. The old neighborhood was undergoing a facelift. Every morning when the residents drove to work, construction crews arrived by the truckload. Maybe because of all the strangers in the neighborhood, crime was on the rise. Gabe had had one break-in, but then he did own the biggest house of all. With its machicolated towers, turrets and false buttresses, the beige mansion had the look of a fairy-tale castle. Gabe hadn't cared much for the architecture.

He'd told the real estate agent, "It has to be big."

"I have a huge house with a wonderful yard. It'll be perfect for kids."

"I'm not married."

He'd bought the house because it dominated the park. He'd found the other older houses with their big porches and yards and spacious, sloping lawns nostalgic. With the influx of brash young millionaires to Austin—men in a hurry, men who didn't have time for long commutes, men like Gabe—Old Enfield Neighborhood was a choice place to live. The fact that Sam had grown up next door had nothing to do with his decision.

Samantha Martin. She'd been his first girl.

"And I'll be your last," she'd always sworn.

And here she was, moving next door to shop for a new husband.

And here he was, unable to get his mind off that fact.

Gabe Langston hadn't jogged even one of his usual five miles in Pease Park along the creek before gusts of wind began whipping the tall oak and pecan trees above him, sending paper cups and plastic grocery bags fluttering past him. When a branch cracked, and half a tree crashed into dry Shoal Creek right behind him, jarring the earth with a violent thud, he stopped and caught his breath.

All hell was breaking loose. Above the fringe of waving trees, he could see the turrets and towers of his house. That tree had been close. Way too close. It was time to pay attention. Time he got to the office and made sure that anonymous call really was bogus.

Reluctantly, Gabe turned back. Soon he was above the park and racing toward his house. Another minute had him underneath his portico, safe from the huge droplets spattering his street and lawn, safe from all the violent lightning bursts.

There was a lamp on in one of Maura's upstairs

windows, and her For Sale sign lay upended on the grass. Cardboard boxes were blowing from her yard onto his. Had Sam moved in while he was at work? Gabe was at his back door when his pool lights flashed on and off.

His body tensed. Thieves? At this hour? On such a wild morning?

No way. More likely something to do with the storm. But he decided to make sure. So, he went on the alert, swaggering toward his shadowy backyard as stealthily as a tough backstreet gang warrior.

When he heard a wrought iron chair leg scrape concrete, he leaned down and picked up a heavy stick. Maybe he lived in a tony neighborhood in a city now, but he'd grown up on a ranch. He was a Texan and a cowboy and a fighter to the marrow of his bones.

"Damn. Damn. Damn."

The familiar sexiness of that soft purr didn't register on Gabe as his callused grip tightened around wet rough bark. He coiled, readying himself to attack. The thief ran.

Only in the split second before he lunged, did he recognize her.

By then it was too late.

The last thing Samantha needed was to get caught in a skimpy, wet teddy sprawled face down on her towel in Gabe Langston's backyard. To avoid him, she'd stayed out of sight ever since she'd moved in.

Now here she was, on a secret mission right behind the very house where he lay asleep—she hoped.

A gust of wind blasted around Sam, whipping her waist-length red hair. She tucked a strand of the silken stuff behind her ear and stretched full length on her belly, extending her hand as far as she could toward Bea's beloved Pete. But the hot-pink, inflated dinosaur floated maddeningly just out of her reach in Gabe's big heart-shaped swimming pool.

"Oh dear...." She had to get the pool toy, get home...back to Bea, who was probably still wide-awake in her big bed full of stuffed animals as she waited anxiously for her mommy to rescue Pete.

"He wanted to swim...at the pwince's castle," Bea had sobbed out. "B-but then...when I let him, he swimmed away."

A chill had gone through Sam at the thought of Bea wandering over to Gabe's pool all alone in the confusion of their move. Anything could have happened.

Sensing Sam's fear, Bea's small voice had cracked and wobbled. "He swimmed away and wouldn't come back."

"Why didn't you tell me sooner?"

Bea's blue eyes had widened. "You was busy. Then Kim and Lee showed me their..."

"Their what?"

Bea clamped her hands over her lips. "Oops! I—I was scared." She'd begun to cry. Sam had hugged her close even as she'd worried what mischief Kim and Lee might be up to.

"It'll be all right."

But it wasn't. Here she was, trespassing in Gabe's backyard, waiting for Pete to stop bouncing up and down and drift closer.

The ching of a metal chair being pushed roughly aside behind her brought her to a sharp new terrifying reality. She was half-naked, and someone was stalking her from the shadows, someone who wanted her to know he was there, someone who savored her sudden fear because it added to his enjoyment.

In a panic, she got up and ran. He followed.

Gabe? But she was too scared to speak his name aloud as the brute's broad-shouldered frame materialized for a second and then vanished into the gloom.

It couldn't be Gabe. He didn't have a sneaky bone in his body.

A minute passed. She sensed the man on the other side of the hedge, looming closer. Then from the blackest part of the yard, he lunged.

Gabe. She had to call Gabe. He wasn't afraid of anything.

A scream formed and died in her throat as the man hurled himself on top of her. They rolled over and over together on the wet concrete until her head hit a terra-cotta pot so hard geraniums and mud splattered onto her face.

Then she seemed to fall, down, down with the brute on top of her. She struggled against him, but it was useless. His weight pressed into her, his breath hot and heavy and yet somehow familiar against her neck.

Her lashes fluttered. He had a dark tough face, a square jaw, longish, rumpled hair, and coal black eyes. The dangerous image wavered, refusing to come into focus. Vaguely she was aware of his muscular body beneath a wet T-shirt, of the heat of him, of her involuntary, nervous and yet somehow sexual reaction to him.

She felt herself blanch. "Don't...don't hurt me," she begged hoarsely, trying to crawl away from him. She slid down a stair. He fell after her.

"Samantha? What the hell—" The familiar voice was deep and more gravelly than she remembered.

Then she saw him, saw that square jaw, that rumpled dark hair, *really* saw him.

For a single instant, as if they were frozen, their astonished gazes were transfixed.

"Gabe?"

But it was too late for both of them. She lost her balance and tumbled downward, only vaguely aware of him falling too. Everything went black.

Slowly, several minutes later, she regained consciousness to raindrops spattering her face. The morning was still dark, but not so dark that she wasn't aware that her head lay on top Gabe's solid, warm chest, that her skimpy teddy was well above her thighs, that her long legs were intertwined with his.

Gabe had attacked her, pushed her down a short

flight of stairs. He must have thought she was a burglar. Somehow he'd hit his head too.

Blushing, she reacted instinctively, smoothing a black lock of hair from his brow. The dampness of his hair and its texture triggered old memories of those times they'd been wrapped in each other's arms after they'd gone swimming.

He looked so helpless, so vulnerable; she wanted to put her arms around him, to protect him. He was too handsome by far. So handsome, she remembered why she'd dreaded moving in next door to him even though she'd had to in order to help Maura.

Maybe he was a ruthless, world-famous millionaire, the kind of man she most distrusted—arrogant and self-serving, like her father. But in that single, heartstopping moment, he was still *her* Gabe—swarthy, hunky and all male. He was that same rugged boy she'd fallen in love with.

Nobody's shoulders stretched a T-shirt quite so tautly across a lean, shapely torso as *her* Gabe.

She sucked in a breath. Not her Gabe. Never again. She'd learned her lesson. Still, she couldn't leave him here.

"Gabe... We've got to get you inside. Out of the rain."

He mumbled something gruff and completely incoherent.

When she shook him, he groaned. "You nearly killed me!"

"You! You jumped me from out of the darkness! You threw me down these stairs!"

"Because you..." His eyes opened. "Sam! Dear God, it's really you! Maura said you'd come home to—" He broke off.

"Husband-hunt?" Sam felt her cheeks heat. "She and my father have the wrong idea about me—as usual!"

"Why the hell do you say that? You married fast the first time you set your mind on that goal!"

"You don't understand."

Gabe stared at her grimly. "You'll be a menace to every happy bachelor in this city." His lips thinned. "Except me. Forewarned is forearmed."

"Good morning to you, too."

"What the hell are you doing in my backyard?"

"Bea lost a toy in your pool."

"Bea?"

"My daughter. She loses things."

"And that gives you an excuse to come over—half-naked?" He grinned. "Then you have the gall to say you're not husband-hunting? What exactly are you looking for, baby? Maybe I can oblige."

His grin combined with his hot gaze had her aflutter with nerves. Suddenly, she realized she'd left her towel at the pool in her panic.

"You're the last man I'd choose."

"Is that so?" He couldn't seem to take his eyes off her face, and he was way too gorgeous when he grinned. All of a sudden, the way he kept looking at her made her feel beautiful and wanted...and not so lonely.

She remembered how much she'd loved him, how

deeply he'd hurt her when he'd dumped her just like her mother had, just like her father had. She'd sat in Aunt Maura's big bay window and cried and cried. No, she wasn't going to relive the past, which included Gabe and all her other failed relationships.

She had been over Gabe Langston for years. The less she had to do with him, the better.

"I'm glad you're here." His soft voice and hot eyes raked over her, made her feel steamy, made her too aware she was only wearing a transparent teddy.

"I—I should have gotten my robe, but it's in a box somewhere. So, I—I used a beach towel as a cover-up. And Bea was crying. I thought I'd sneak over here and get back in a flash. I got so scared when you—I jumped up so fast..."

"You always did have a maddening habit of not wearing enough clothes. I remember you had a bikini or two...."

Suddenly his insolent grin infuriated her, but she fought the instinct to shield her breasts from his gaze. "Don't start in on my clothes."

"The way you dress—you need a personal bodyguard."

His eyes went deeper and blacker.

"I said don't!" She felt her skin heat. They were slipping into their old relationship, into their spontaneous sexuality and old quarrels, way too easily.

How could she feel like this? About Gabe when she had already decided she was over him?

"Aunt Maura says you have a girlfriend in a yellow convertible!"

"Not anymore."

"Not that I care whether you do or don't."

"Oh, don't you?"

"No!" she flared.

"What if I said I wished you did?"

"You have quite a reputation with the ladies, Gabriel Langston."

Not that Sam wasn't enjoying just a little his gazing at her with admiration. And what if she flirted with him a minute or two longer? What if she left her towel where it was?

His mouth was gorgeous. He kept staring at her lips, and suddenly she couldn't quit staring at his, either.

What would it hurt if she led him on for a kiss or two and then dumped him just like he'd dumped her all those years ago? What if she let him think she was as guileless and unsuspecting as she'd been at nineteen when he'd seduced her and told her he wasn't ready for marriage?

Thus, when he took her silence for something other than what it was, when his arms slid around her, she didn't resist him or the almost painful current that bound her to him. Nor did she look away when he held her so close his dark face blurred. No, she let the tension thicken between them.

"We shouldn't," was all she said but with a flirtatious little gasp of sensual pleasure that belied her words as his mouth moved closer and their bodies melted wildly.

"I know, baby. But we will. Because we can't

stop ourselves now any more than we could back then.''

Their lips met, clung.

A kiss or two later—she lost count because of the sizzle—she thought he said, ''Baby, if you know what's good for you, you'll git and git fast.''

''Probably.'' But she laughed breathily, flirtily.

''There's gonna be trouble,'' he murmured.

''There always is when we get together.''

''I missed you, baby. It killed me when you married Tom so fast.''

''I sort of remember asking you first. You said no.'' Pain welled up in her heart, but when he ran his hands down her arms in a caressing gesture, she was mesmerized.

''But I couldn't forget you,'' he said.

''I ought to be fighting you...fighting this.''

''Me, too.'' But he laughed. His fingers stroked her hair, then her scalp, and his tentative and yet infinitely skilled touching swirled her back in time. He knew how she loved having her head rubbed.

Blunt, strong fingertips massaged the nape of her neck in ever-widening circles. Then those strong warm hands moved back into her hair and continued to tantalize.

She felt weak, out of control as he continued to caress all her most tender, vulnerable places, all the time whispering searing endearments against her earlobe. She arched her back like a purring cat needing to be stroked.

She could stop. She knew she could stop—anytime.

His skin was wet and cold from the rain even as his body burned underneath. She remembered Barton Springs, their long lazy summers when they'd made love passionately and deeply, when she'd believed he'd love her forever.

Oh, no, here we go again, whispered a voice deep in her heart.

Aloud she said, "Tell me we're older and wiser."

Chapter 3

"**O**lder and wiser, my..." Gabe muttered. Whatever he said next was smothered beneath her lips.

His fingers played over her body while she thought, *Just one more kiss. One more. That's all.* But each kiss and every touch made Sam needier for more.

She pushed free.

Who was she torturing? Him or her?

She was going to play with him and then dump him, right? Why was that getting harder and harder to remember?

She should never have let him put his hands in her hair. She was a fool to think she had any control over this situation.

Samantha was increasingly aware of how sexy

Gabe was and of how vulnerable she was to him. She was playing with fire, but like a child playing with matches, the game was too exciting to stop.

They were in the pool house, circling each other round and round in a wordless mating dance. She was fighting to get a grip on her emotions, fighting not to admire his lean, tall-but-not-too-tall, compact, wide-shouldered body. Fighting not to notice how his wet T-shirt clung to his shapely muscles. Fighting not to slide her palms softly underneath that wet cotton and stroke his warm, hard skin.

"I wish I was wearing high heels. You get too big for your breeches when I'm barefoot."

Yes, all the old battles and fun stuff were too easy to slip into.

His boyish laughter was spontaneous. His black gaze devoured her legs without a trace of resentment. "You saying I'm short, baby?"

She tossed her red head and laughed. "Maybe I'm just calling me tall," she teased.

He laughed. "That used to bother me—a lot—your conceit about your legs. But I agree with you—they're gorgeous."

"Maybe I was checking to see if you've matured."

"Satisfied?"

"Not yet." Her nerves raced wildly. Her heart thundered. "Not by a long shot."

The rain had stopped. He kept staring at her in her damp teddy. He could see through the thin silk, see her body. The air-conditioning was turned off, but that wasn't why the heat felt so intense.

It was Gabe. Just Gabe. His flame-dark eyes had her both fearful and excited, both alarmed and yet thrilled.

"I was sorry about Tom," he whispered on a raw, hoarse note that was so honest it shredded her.

She remembered the heat of that faraway jungle, the foolish recklessness of her youthful dreams, dreams that had been dashed long before the finality and terror of Tom's brief illness. She'd loved Tom. She had.

It was just that she wasn't ready to look back. "I—I can't talk about him."

"He died of a fever? He was a preacher?"

"A youth director. I said I still can't—"

"Sorry." Gabe came closer and brushed a warm finger against her lips. "I'm so sorry."

"There's too much to be sorry about for a simple word to suffice. So much more than you know. He was a wonderful man. A wonderful husband."

"Just what you wanted."

"Yes." She bit out the word. "But life gets the best of people. It got the best of us, of Tom and me. At least it got the best of me. He's gone and the girls and I have to go on."

"So, you've come home."

"You said I wanted to save the world because my mother ran away."

"I'm sorry about what I said. You used to be such an idealist. We used to fight about your dreams. But now I believe the world needs more people like you, people who inspire.''

"The world has too many eager young fools."

"No."

"Well, it doesn't matter any more."

"I'm glad you've come home." He kissed her mouth, gently at first and then with enough passion to send warmth and little spirals of sensual excitement fluttering through her that made her feel young and alive. That made her remember how she'd felt in his arms on long summer days.

She had to push him away. She had to run.

Instead, she wrapped her arms around his neck. Later she would tell him she'd been playing with him to get even because he'd wounded her so badly when they'd been kids. She'd tell him that she'd almost hated him through the years. But even as his warm tender kiss sharpened all those old hurts, she forgot about leading him on or wanting vengeance. His kiss awakened fierce, sensual needs. Suddenly what she needed from him was dangerously simple and profoundly complex.

Run.

Sam clung, kissing him back, savagely. Her kisses sparked a current, kept her on fire even when he stepped back and began to strip.

Run.

He tore off his shirt. Sam stood still and watched as he pulled it over his black head, taking it from him like a gift, her fingertips touching his. Then she flung it to the floor where it squished like a sodden rag.

She slid her teddy down her long legs and threw it on top of his shirt.

He drank in the sight of her, his gaze so implicitly sexual, her nipples grew huge.

Wow. He mouthed the word silently.

"Wow to you, too."

Then his shorts were gone and they were in each other's arms, murmuring one another's names in desperate shattered whispers.

"All these years I've thought of you," he said.

The years of hating him while loving Tom struck like a fresh blow. Yet her longing was too fierce to resist. Maybe later she would remember the hurt, which had been so cold and deliberately inflicted on his part. Maybe later his cruelty and the years of separation, and their separate lives and values would matter. Not now. Not when she was burning from the inside out just like she had when she'd been a kid. Nothing mattered but having him one more time.

"We're going to regret this," he whispered.

So, what else was new? She regretted ever meeting him. "Do you have a bed in here, Langston?"

"I thought you'd never ask."

More urgent kisses, each hungrier than the one before. Then he picked her up, carried her, and set her down gently.

She heard the squeak of bedsprings. A drawer opened. A plastic wrapper crinkled.

He cursed, fumbling. "They should use this stuff to make airplanes." Then he had the condom out and was deftly sheathing himself.

So, she wasn't the first woman he'd brought here. *But I want to be the last.*

She'd thought that as a foolish girl. Back then she'd thought love was so easy and natural. He'd taught her better.

He eased himself on top of her and when he began touching her and loving her, she soon lost track of space and time. Outside, it was really raining. Water gushed off the eaves in torrents.

She'd hated him, hated every line Aunt Maura had written about him and his women and his money. Then why did she long for him now, long for this? Why was the hate and the hurt all mixed up with this bittersweet longing that took her back to the idealistic dreams of her youth? Was it because he'd said he'd missed her? Was it because once Gabe's dangerous arms had been the one place where she'd always felt safe and whole and completely cherished?

"Wrap those long legs you're so conceited about around me," he ordered, "and don't ever let me go."

"You don't really mean that."

"What if I did?"

Sam obeyed. Then she lay beneath him, staring up into his blazing eyes until they both began to tremble in every fiber of their beings.

How could he make her shake and burn with just

those soul-dark eyes? It was as if he were making intense, pleasurable love to her, yet he wasn't doing anything yet.

Their gazes were still locked several minutes later when he entered her.

Two sharp thrusts, and he exploded. She cried out his name. He put his hands in her hair, and she burst into flames.

"Give me a minute and we'll do it again?" he whispered, shooting her that gorgeous grin that undid her. "Only slower. And sweeter. I missed you, baby. Damn, how I missed you. I didn't know how much till now."

"Older and wiser," mocked Gabe's voice in the back of her mind.

Then he kissed her, and the years fell away. She was a girl again. They were in love. And she believed he'd love her forever.

When Gabe stepped out of his house with his black umbrella, Maura was perched where she always was, in her front window, her binoculars aimed straight at him.

The rain had stopped, but dark clouds foretold the storms weren't over. Freshly showered, his rumpled black hair combed and a bit tidier than usual, he scowled at her as he made his way toward his pool. Using the hook end of his umbrella, he deftly snagged the inflatable pink dragon. Or was the thing a badly made frog?

Maura was still watching when he picked the

thing up and stalked across her wet lawn to her front door.

He wondered as he approached the house. Why hadn't she come straight back like she'd promised?

Gabe felt like a fool carrying the dripping pink toy by the tip of its ear up to Maura's front door. No sooner had he punched the doorbell, than lights blazed at every window. He heard shouts and then adult voices, saying, "quiet." Next he heard quick, scampering footsteps. The door cracked.

"Petey?" a small voice cried.

The door opened several more inches as if by magic. When no one greeted him, he pushed it a bit further.

With a little whispery sound of alarm, a golden sprite with waist-length yellow curls wearing a fluffy blue bathrobe jumped away from the door and hid behind the huge, thick-legged table that dominated Maura's foyer. The pretty child's huge blue eyes were glued to her pink dragon.

The scent of dusty roses sprinkled with orange peels and cloves wafted from a tarnished bowl that held potpourri. Maura was a collector. Her littered foyer smelled as it always had. Suddenly Gabe was twelve again.

It was Halloween, and Maura's porch overflowed with big orange pumpkins. His mother had brought him into town to trick-or-treat. When he'd tiptoed up to this grand old house, a little girl with bright red hair had opened the door for him. She'd run to hide behind this very same table.

Samantha had always said that's when she'd fallen in love with him.

"Is this your dragon?" Gabe whispered now to the little blond girl behind the table.

"Not a dwagon. Di-no-saur," she corrected, enunciating every syllable.

"Dinosaur," Gabe repeated gently. Then he set the thing down in the middle of the Persian rug, but she was too shy to come forward.

"Where's your mother?"

"Upstairs."

"Coming," Maura called, entering the room.

Oh, God.

With a gnarled hand Maura picked up the dinosaur and scooted it toward the little girl. "Here you go, Beatrice. Now don't you go over to Mr. Langston's pool again. Not without your mother! Not ever! Do you understand?"

Beatrice flung her arms around the pink toy that was bigger than she was and scurried off with it.

"You're going to have to fence that pool of yours," Maura said bossily, "now that Sam's here with her four little girls."

"It is fenced."

"Then how—"

"Where the hell is Sam? I'm in a hurry."

"As usual." Her shrewd black eyes studied him until heat crawled up his neck, staining his cheeks.

"I-need-to-talk-to-Sam." He enunciated every syllable just as Beatrice had when she'd used a big, unfamiliar word.

"Sam!" Maura craned her blue head toward the stairs. "A busy man needs to talk to you."

After a while Sam's voice floated down to him. "Get dressed, girls. Comb your hair. Guess what I've got in the kitchen—doughnuts?"

Sam didn't sound too organized up there. Several more minutes passed before Gabe heard footsteps on the landing. When he looked up, he froze. So did Sam, who had three squirming kids circling her.

So many little girls. He never dated women with kids, maybe because he'd always felt a little lost in his own family.

Then Sam's dark, expressive brows slanted, and she blushed. Kids or no kids, just the way this woman looked at him made his body go crazy. He remembered her long legs tight around his waist, how she'd used them as a lever, pulled him down. He got hot under the collar again.

Maura's gaze went from Sam to him.

The old lady knew.

Sam looked embarrassingly sexy in that snug white tank top that showed off her braless state. Tight, white short shorts and strappy high heels showcased her long legs.

"You'd better not leave the house in that outfit," he muttered so fiercely Maura's eyes brightened with more mischief.

"The upstairs AC doesn't work." Sam slapped her temple with the open palm of her hand. "What am I saying? I'm twenty-eight years old. Don't you dare tell me what to wear, Gabe Langston!"

As she sashayed toward him, hips undulating, his gaze drifted lazily down her legs, then back up again. His heart raced. Suddenly the foyer felt hotter than a sauna.

"Boy, do you need a bodyguard, baby."

At her frown, Gabe's gut clenched.

"Why didn't you come back over?" he persisted.

"Mommy? I'm hungry!"

"Who's that man, Mommy?"

The kids seemed to think he had no right to be here, and their possessive stares threw him off balance.

"This is Mr. Langston, girls, your next-door neighbor," said Maura. "Gabe, meet Courtney, Kim and Lee. That was Bea a while ago."

Courtney's dark inky hair was done in a million braids and yellow ribbons; her manner was reserved and a little distrustful. The twins' faces were all smiles.

What did you say to three little girls? He felt oddly vulnerable, outnumbered and scared, somehow sensing this first moment with Sam's little girls was of vital importance.

Gabe knelt, gave it his best shot. "Hello, girls. How old are you?"

"That's a dumb question," Courtney said, ignoring his smile, staring at the floor. "You don't care about me. You just want to be Samantha's next husband."

Sam gasped. "Courtney!"

The twins held up six fingers and then coyly hid

behind Sam. When Courtney stuck out her bottom lip and refused to look at him again, he stood up awkwardly. He couldn't talk to Sam with Courtney sulking, and Maura and Sam's girls hanging on his every word.

He gritted his teeth. "You said you were coming back."

"We had a crisis upstairs. My real life sort of took over." She looked distracted, harried, the way he did at the office.

"Mine too. I'm late."

"So, have a nice day."

"What's wrong?" he demanded, sensing a major rebuff and feeling hurt and way too vulnerable.

"Nothing."

She was pale and frozen, her tone offhand. Her kids watched him, rapt.

Carefully, he kept his voice subdued. "Can you come outside—so we can talk—in private? This will just take a minute."

Sam sighed and then wrapped herself tightly with trembling arms.

Courtney scowled. The twins tugged at her legs. "We're hungry, Mommy."

"Don't you know how to push stools against cabinets and get out your own bowls?" he growled.

Sam ignored his remark. "I know you are hungry, darlings. Run along to the kitchen, and I'll be there in just a sec." When they didn't budge, Sam didn't even try to make them mind. She said, "Aunt Maura, could you get Lou to watch them?"

Gabe gave a silent prayer of thanks for Lou, Maura's competent housekeeper.

Maura nodded, but her eyes were big and bright as she followed Sam and him to the door. No sooner had Maura shut the door than her blue head popped up at her big plate glass window beside four others. Everybody had binoculars.

Gabe gritted his teeth as he walked with Sam out to the big front lawn. "They're watching us."

"I don't have much time, Gabe."

His eyes met Sam's. "Why didn't you come back? I wanted to talk about what happened."

She stared at their fascinated audience. "Nothing happened, so there's nothing to talk about."

"Don't give me that."

"Hormones." She wouldn't look up at him. "Loneliness. Who knows? We got carried away. It can't mean anything."

"What do you mean...it can't...."

"I'd think a man with your reputation would be good at scenes like this."

Old hurts rushed back, slammed him hard. "If I've kept my relationships shallow, it's been to avoid entanglements with the likes of women like you. You wanted me to save the world. I knew I wanted to make money."

A white truck pulled up in the drive on the other side of Maura's house. Gabe jerked his head in time to see the burly blond repairman get out, ogle Sam and wave. She waved back.

"What about your reputation?" Gabe ground out.

"Do you have to flaunt yourself to every construction worker in Old Enfield?"

"*John* carried some heavy boxes for me yesterday. He's a talented musician and a composer. He has the cutest little boy."

"You could've asked me…to carry those boxes."

"Aunt Maura says you don't like to help." She paused. "I thought you wanted to talk about this morning?"

"We were hot. We were good."

"We were over years and years ago."

"I used to think so. I wanted to think so. Damn it, I've been determined to think so. But this morning changed everything."

"For you maybe."

Her soft, unsteady words hit him like bullets. His gut knotted when she continued in the same shaky vein.

"It's over. You refused to take our relationship seriously last time. You walked out, remember? Maybe it's my turn to return the favor."

He wanted to tear his eyes away from her, to race away in his sports car, to pretend he didn't care.

"So, this is—revenge."

"No," but her voice trembled. At least she looked pink and a little flustered.

"I dumped you, so now you're getting even?"

"Look, I'm trying to let us both off easy. Years ago we didn't work because we had completely different values. We haven't changed. I've got four kids. You don't like kids."

He glanced behind Sam, to the window where all her kids were lined up with binoculars trained on them. He glared at them. "Hell, I love kids."

"When was the last time you spent any time with a child?" She turned and waved at them.

"I—I...don't really know any."

"See!" When they waved back at her, he felt like his heart was being ripped out in front of a stadium of cheering spectators.

"I've really gotta look after them," Sam said, completely distracted. "Aunt Maura's house is far from being child-proofed. She's a collector, a compulsive shopper."

Gabe sighed and looked to the window once more. Four little girls. They were cute, even if they were watching him get gutted and savoring every minute of it. Real cute. He'd give 'em that. The twins began fighting over a pair of binoculars. But kids were trouble. More trouble than Maura, he'd bet. Because they were young, and they had energy.

"I've gotta go to work," he said, still in that quiet, flat tone. "It's going to be a tough day. If I can find an hour for lunch could I call you?"

"No."

"Maybe we could have lunch together instead? You could bring the kids. I could get to know them. We could do take-out, have a picnic."

"No."

His palms had begun to sweat. "Dinner then?"

"Gabe, do you ever listen—" She stood unmoving, yet she seemed as scared and nervous as he was.

"Dinner anytime? A phone call?"

She shook her head.

"Okay. Maybe you could come over again wearing almost nothing. We could hang out in the pool house and do it again and then pretend we didn't, and that it meant nothing. What do you say to nine or ten o'clock? That way we'll have all night."

His words struck her like blows. Or at least she went white until bright red spots of hurt and anger burned her cheeks.

"I'm sorry," he whispered. "I lost it."

But it was too late. She turned and would have run, but he grabbed her arm. "I don't give up easy, Sam."

"You're a busy man. I'll cling to the hope you'll get tired of wasting your time on me, a single mom. Aunt Maura says you have lots of women. You don't need me!"

"Aunt Maura doesn't know zip."

When Sam stared at his brown hand clamped on her pale arm, he shrugged and let her go. When she reached the door, Maura greeted her with the cordless telephone.

"It's Nelson George again, Sam." The old lady's bright gaze flashed almost gleefully at Gabe. "Two busy men after you," she said, before disappearing inside and returning to her perch at the window.

Gabe felt like someone had just pulled the plug and his life was over. "What's Nelson calling you for?"

Looking soft and guilty and a little lost, Sam put her hand over the mouthpiece.

So this was how it was going to be.... Gabe ached. "Is he about revenge too?"

"No. He's about starting over, about making more intelligent choices."

"That son of a bitch!" It was a cry from Gabe's heart. "Don't you dare take George's call!"

"But he's only returning mine."

"You slept with me, but you called him—"

"Last night...I mean...this morning...wasn't supposed to happen."

"But it did, damn you."

"Henry told me to call Nelson first thing. So, I did."

"Did Henry tell you to marry him too?"

"Henry does like Nelson."

Gabe's stomach knotted. After Sam's father had retired, Henry Martin had become a major investor in a lot of start-up dot.coms. Was he behind Nelson's betrayal, if betrayal there was? Was Sam part of Nelson's business plan?

What would you say if I told you your partner isn't good old Nelson George anymore?

"Nelson's an old friend," Sam said. "He has nothing to do with you."

"That's where you're wrong, baby."

Her tortured green gaze seemed riveted by him. "Goodbye, Gabe. I'm sorry it has to be this way. And...and stop calling me, baby."

"But you're my baby. You always were and you always will be!"

"No!"

When Sam ran inside in tears, Maura came to the door and waved several pairs of binoculars at him airily.

"Have a great day, Gabe!"

Chapter 4

As Gabe sped south on Mo-Pac, the bright red sun that lit the eastern horizon was burning a hole through his temple.

"You were right about George, Langston!"

Mark's voice began breaking up so badly in the static that Gabe flung his cell phone onto the passenger seat.

Bull's eye!

He rubbed the side of his head where it hurt. His dry eyes stung.

Nelson George had fired at him between the eyes at point-blank range.

The double-crossing bastard wasn't going to win. Gabe pulled into the lot of the gleaming black office building that crowned the gentle roll of cedar hills.

Doors swung closed behind him as he strode down the halls like a man on a murderous vendetta.

Nobody was going to tear down all that he'd built. Nobody else's name would adorn his twin black towers that dominated the southwest side of Austin. Just as surely as Gabe's huge beige castle crowned its green hill above Pease Park.

When Gabe slammed into his corner office, Nelson George spun around in Gabe's black leather swivel chair with the arrogance of a golden devil who thought he was calling the shots now.

"Got your messages," Nelson said with a smooth smile. "No need to get panicky."

Gabe felt haggard, exhausted. Even sitting down, Nelson looked tall and sleek, fresh and relaxed. Yet his air of nonchalance was a pose. He was as tense as a big cat before a sure kill.

Nelson wore a long-sleeved white shirt and jeans. His meticulously barbered hair was the color of rich butter; his eyes a dark, electric blue. He was tall and beautiful in a lethal sort of way. If the rumors were true, he'd led a lot of naive, idealistic women to their doom. *Women like Sam.*

"I'm offering you a deal," Nelson began silkily. "Give me a higher stake in LXK, and we'll be friends—like always." He shoved a raft of papers across the desk toward Gabe.

"Talk to my lawyer."

"You can't afford to sue me."

"Then I'll do it anyway."

"I have your top people and most of your clients. Novadash will hit the market. I'll clean up."

"Get out—"

"You're way too greedy, way too competitive, Gabe."

Gabe forced himself to sit down and pretend he was relaxed. Although it cost him, he leaned back in his chair, crossing his legs at the ankles. A nerve jumped in his jawline. When he finally managed a smile, it felt crooked. "Get out."

"I guess you're right. Look at us. We're like two tigers. One cat too many. If we stay together, we'll devour each other."

"One could hope."

Nelson laughed.

"Keep away from Sam."

"That's not negotiable. She and I have been in the works for a while."

"What's that supposed to mean?"

"I'm way ahead of you, buddy. Her old man told me she was lonely. Said she has four little girls, said she needs a smart husband. He asked me to look her up, so I wrote her and talked her into coming home."

"Leave her alone."

Nelson stood up, raised his long arms above his head and stretched, which made him seem taller. He stared down at Gabe. "You're too short for Sam."

Blood pumped in Gabe's temples. "You're after her money."

"Oh, and you don't care Sam's old man just happens to be one of the richest and most powerful men in Texas, and she's his only daughter?''

''She's got four kids.''

''As if you wouldn't pack them off even faster than I will to expensive boarding schools so she could focus on you.'' Nelson laughed derisively. ''Tell you what I'll do, buddy. I'll say hi to Sam when we have lunch on the lake today.''

''The lake?''

''My yacht.''

Nelson's sixty-foot yacht had bedrooms. Staterooms, he called them.

''The lake's beautiful, very romantic, this time of year,'' Nelson said.

For several suspended seconds Gabe thought of Nelson and Sam alone on that yacht. As if Nelson had read his mind, the handsome jerk shot him a superior, amused smile and was off.

On a spurt of anger Gabe summoned his staff to his office. Mark advised Gabe to take LXK public and give them, his key employees, a stake in the company.

''We work hard for you, Gabe.''

For once Gabe listened. ''I'll think about it.'' He paused. ''George will be vicious. This is war. Every client has to be called, their contracts reviewed, possibly renegotiated—fast.''

They divided their client list. Then everybody got on the phone. By the end of the day Gabe was exhausted as he sat flipping through his Rolodex. He picked up his calendar and jotted down two names beneath tomorrow's scheduled meetings. He was on his way out the door when Clu called.

"So, how is it, having Sam next door...husband-hunting? She came out to the ranch today. Mom says she's prettier than ever. From the outfit Mom described, I'd say sexier. Mom said she acted funny when Mom asked if she'd seen you."

Clu, his sensitive brother, the math whiz, had the buzz about Sam all the way from San Marcos.

"What do you really want?"

"If you marry her fast you could still win Mom's bet."

"What?"

"Mom's bet! Granddaughters. Sam's already got those four little girls."

"I don't give a damn about Mom's ridiculous wager or Sam's four daughters! Or Sam!" Gabe was so mad he nearly hung up.

"Better hurry," Clu said. "Guess who's getting married?"

Gabe held his breath and his temper. Only when he imagined Sam in a white veil holding on to Nelson beneath a heart-shaped stained glass window in some cutesy chapel, did he go apoplectic. Had Nelson proposed over lunch? With one sweep of his arm, he brushed computer manuals, diskettes, notebooks, his stapler, dozens of Post-it notes, envelopes and a soda can onto the floor.

"Rob! This weekend! He's in a big hurry for some reason."

Gabe let out an audible sigh of relief.

"Her name's Laura Abbott. So, if you could come out to the ranch this Saturday—"

"Sure."

Clu filled him in on the details. "Oh, and Samantha's coming too."

"What?"

"You remember how Sam loves weddings. Well, so, Mom invited her when she was out here."

Sam wouldn't give him the time of day, but she could find time to drive all the way out to visit his mom.

"Sam said she wouldn't miss Rob's wedding for the world. She even asked Mom if she could bring a date. Mom said sure—as long as she brought her little girls. I think Mom was hoping Sam would ask you. Has she?"

Gabe's temple began to throb.

"No," he replied in a smooth low tone that did not betray that he was breaking apart inside.

Carefully, calmly Gabe told his brother goodbye. He waited until Clu was off the line, then he slammed the phone down.

Chapter 5

Gabe drove home as if demons were chasing him, maybe because they were. He roared around the last corner and ripped past a long line of trucks in front of Maura's.

Incredible sex with Sam. Then she'd wanted nothing to do with him and everything to do with Nelson.

Theft. Betrayal. Expensive conversations with his lawyers. Desperate sales pitches to his most valued clients. And Sam on his mind every second, every minute, every hour while his clients played cagey. Not to mention, he still had his vicious headache.

What had Sam done on that yacht? Who the hell was she planning to take to Rob's wedding? Gabe imagined Sam in Nelson's arms on that yacht yet again, and his grip clenched the steering wheel. Had Nelson bedded her too? Gabe's foot fell heavier on the accelerator.

God, he needed a beer. He needed to swim laps. He needed a hard run. Most of all, he needed to forget Sam. Yet, most of all he wanted to taste her again.

Out of nowhere, a dusky-skinned cannonball clad in yellow came flying toward the road—headed right in his path.

He honked.

Courtney screamed and leapt away.

Gabe slammed on his brakes and was hurled hard into the steering wheel. A second later he had his seat belt off and was springing over the door.

"Courtney?"

Her long, gangly form, her skinny legs spread wide, lay sprawled face down on black asphalt.

When he heard footsteps, he spun around as Bea dashed up to him.

"Courtney?" Bea dropped three bears and knelt. She gently tugged on one of her sister's velvety braids. "Courtney!" she shrieked as her small hand brushed a loose pebble from her sister's cheek. When Courtney just lay there, making no sound, Bea turned imploring blue eyes on Gabe. "Is she dead?"

Courtney rolled over and blinked at Bea. "I'm fine." Then she saw Gabe and frowned.

Relief surged through him. Her yellow shorts were torn, and her knees were bloody from the spill she'd taken when he'd honked at her. But temper had to be a good sign.

"Are you okay?" he asked gently.

"Where's my new skateboard?"

"Mommy gave it to her for her birthday," Bea informed him. "And the ramp, too."

The skateboard was upside down, wheels whirring.

"Ramp?"

Even before Bea pointed to an obscenely tall spiral of wood, its spout at the end of Maura's drive, he saw it. The danger past, Gabe's anger got the best of him. If Sam weren't lunching on yachts and doing God only knew what else—

"What kind of mother would let a kid put a ramp in a driveway and aim it at the street?" he thundered. "It's completely hidden by those parked cars!"

"Twucks!" corrected Bea.

If he'd intended to make his voice forbidding, he'd succeeded. Even to him, he sounded harsh and crazed.

Courtney scrambled to her feet. "It's not her fault! It was your fault."

He glared at her. He didn't soften until she began to shake and a single big tear rolled down her smooth cheek.

"Honey—"

It was too late. A flood dribbled after the first. Courtney bit her lips. Then with an anguished little cry, she ran.

Bea frowned. "You made my big sister cry. Courtney doesn't ever cry." She forgot her bears and raced off too.

As he watched them flying across the green lawn, he glared defensively at the outraged crowd gathering around the circular flower beds that wrapped Maura's big front porch. They'd begun to stare at him like he was the monster who had put the ramp there.

Leggy and sexy as ever in those indecent short shorts of hers, Sam was talking to that burly fellow from next door. John, she'd called him. He was laughing down at her as she lifted his walkman and all the black wires that went with it over his broad, tanned neck. Half a dozen of his muscular buddies were putting in overtime in Maura's yard with spades, shovels, and hand clippers. No wonder— with Sam out there practically naked.

Not that a lot of work hadn't been done. Somebody had punched dozens of deep holes in the big circular beds. One big bozo was chopping weeds with a hoe.

Surrounded by boxes of petunias, Kim and Lee were jumping at each other in a mock sword fight with their spades.

When Courtney reached Sam, she bent her bright head to the little girl's. But as she listened, Sam's expression darkened. Then she redirected her gaze toward him.

He drew in a deep breath and pasted on a smile. Sam didn't smile back.

Damn. What was the use of going over there and telling his side, especially when he was still so angry? Better to grab the bears, put the Lotus away, and get a grip on his temper. So, he threw the bears inside and roared up his drive.

The last thing he expected when he finished in the garage was to find Sam, hands on her hips, looking sexy as hell, waiting to pounce.

"First you nearly kill Courtney. Then you yell at her."

Trembling with a mixture of rage and desire, he hit his garage door remote. "Blame the person that gave her a skateboard and then put the ramp at the end of Maura's drive!"

"Ramp at the end of the drive?" Sam's eyes widened when she noticed the ramp for the first time. "I specifically told Courtney she was only to use that ramp on the back patio."

"I'm sure it's hard to keep up with four kids when you're having so much fun flaunting those legs of yours at those muscle-bound…apes."

"If you mean John and his crew…"

"I mean every damn man in the universe!"

"I—I was listening to a song John wrote." She caught herself. "What am I doing? You have no right to tell me who I can or cannot speak to."

Gabe stared at her. "You slept with me this morning."

"Well, excuse me! My mistake!" She took a breath, looked over at the ramp again. "I can't believe Courtney set this ramp up out here." A shiver

went through her when she thought of how Courtney's defiance had made her daughter so vulnerable.
It wasn't like Courtney to ignore her, but none of
her daughters were acting the same since they'd
moved to this new place. Sam would have to have
a sit-down with Courtney later, to talk about this.

"Well, she disobeyed you then," Gabe said.
"The question is—what are you going to do about
it?"

"Gabe, she was nearly killed."

"Next time she will be. Kids need to mind."

"Don't tell me how to raise my kids. Besides, you
were driving too fast."

"All right, I'll slow down," he conceded, still
shaken. "But getting one driver to slow down won't
do much if you don't do your part."

"As if making kids do what you say is so easy.
My kids have problems, special problems. They
were all abandoned. Then Tom... You don't know
what they've been through."

"I can guess," he said in a gentler tone.

"We have to learn how to be a family. Courtney
has been in five foster homes. One of the fathers
used to beat her. Kim and Lee were three when I
got them out of an orphanage in China. They don't
think anybody really wants them. The twins make
Bea feel left out. She hasn't had it easy since she
came to live with me from Russia."

"Minding is important, even for a kid Courtney's
age."

"Who made you the expert?"

"I had a father."

"Well, my kids don't, okay? I'm all they've got now."

"From what I hear—not for long." He slid his gaze over her body. "Everybody knows you've come home to catch yourself a rich husband."

She was scarlet. "That's a joke. It started with Henry, but even if it were true, you wouldn't need to worry. You wouldn't make my list."

"Would Nelson?"

More hot blood rushed to her face. "Oh, I do hate you." But he heard tears behind her voice.

"How was lunch?"

She paled.

"Is Nelson on your list of eligible bachelors?"

She hissed air through her teeth. Then her voice rose. "Lunch was delightful."

"What else was delightful?"

"Nothing."

"Nothing?" Gabe gave her legs the once-over and then grinned just to madden her. "The same *nothing* that happened between us in my pool house? I hope you wore more than you've got on now to lunch on Nelson's yacht. You might have given him the wrong idea, baby. Or the right idea. Take your pick."

"Oh!" Her breath caught.

"He's after your money, Sam."

"Funny, he said the same thing about you."

"What else did that bastard say?"

"For starters, he's hurt you fired him just because he went to bat for the little guys."

"And you consoled that conniving liar?"

"What if I did...a little?"

He rasped a finger against a stray tendril of her hair, and she jumped.

"Did he take you to bed?

"No—you did! First thing! Just like always! If Aunt Maura's to be believed, I guess I'm just another notch on the Langston gun belt!" She took a breath. "Nelson was gallant and protective and extremely concerned about me when he heard we'd already run into each other. He was nice."

"And I'm not?"

"You took advantage of me this morning!"

"You didn't put up much of a fight. You did come over half-naked. Hell, you're doing the same thing now, woman. You tiptoe over here, in that skimpy outfit, all legs, knowing for damn sure after this morning that there's still something between us—"

"I'm not interested in you!"

"Well, let me tell you something. Life is based on scientific principles. It doesn't take a genius to get cause and effect. If you repeat the same causes, you get the same effects."

When she boldly met his hot, angry eyes, the powerful stirring of sexual arousal he felt made him even more furious. He forced his gaze from her face, lower, letting it linger on her breasts. But his careful insult backfired and made him hotter and angrier than ever.

"If you don't believe me," he snarled, "why don't you come in and have a drink?"

"No."

He hauled her against him. "What if I say yes to what you're offering? Maybe we don't need to go inside and make polite chitchat. Maybe what's between us is way more elemental. Why don't we skip the drink and cut to the pool house?"

When she gasped, he wound his hands in her hair at the nape of her neck. "Have I told you I like your hair long?" His masculine voice a husky caress.

She jammed her hands against his chest and squirmed to get loose. "I won't be one of your harem."

He lifted a heavy length of her fiery hair. His mouth sought the supersensitive spot beneath her ear.

"We'll go steady. There won't be anybody else."

"Don't."

He felt her blood pulsing against his lips.

"I want you and you want me. It's called biology. It's called sexual attraction." He continued to kiss her where she was most vulnerable. Only when she shuddered, did he stop.

"Sam, I was such a fool to throw what we had away."

"But you did it," she murmured, sighing helplessly. Then she caught herself. "That isn't the point. I'm a mother now. Men like you don't date single moms. Aunt Maura says…''

Almost angrily, he withdrew his lips from her throat. "To hell with Maura! I wish to hell I'd taken you up on your offer years ago."

She was silent.

"Do you hear me? I wish to hell I'd married you! I was wrong! I admit it! Does that make you happy?"

"No…." Her voice was little more than a whisper. "I—I don't believe you. Besides, it's too late."

"If you loved me so much, how could you marry Tom so fast? Did you just want a husband and kids? Would anybody do? Is that the same situation now? Well, if it is, choose me! I want you! Only you!"

"In your bed. Only in bed."

"That's a helluva start."

"Everything you say just makes this whole situation worse. I want to go home. Now."

She splayed her fingers and pushed harder against his chest, but he was a natural athlete. He'd stayed in shape. Not only that, he'd made love to her so many times, he knew all her weakness, where to touch her, where not to.

Maybe he wasn't playing fair, but he slid a brown hand into her hair again. Blunt, expert fingertips began to massage her scalp just the way she liked it. When she sighed, his lips brushed her brow, the edge of her hairline, her temple. He knew he was winning, when she stilled, when she lifted her lips seeking his, when her knees went boneless, and her fingers curled into his shoulders.

In no time he had her helplessly, intimately snugged between the garage door and his powerful body, had her shuddering from being stroked where she liked it, quivering too.

She moaned from somewhere deep inside herself. "I don't believe this. You wouldn't have married me! You just brought that up to get me in bed again!"

He was caught up in the physical. His long fingers caressed the nape of her neck, then her shoulders.

"Give it up, Sam," he whispered. "The past is over. You've lost this battle, the same as I have."

"I can't have an affair with you."

"But it feels too good to be in my arms, doesn't it?" He crushed his mouth to hers.

When she clamped her lips shut, he just nibbled the soft edges of her mouth and waited. When her breath caught on a sob, he brushed more hot kisses along her jawline.

"Sam…. Sam…."

His lips found her throat, and he licked the wild throb of her pulse beneath the pale skin there. Triumphant pleasure flared inside him when she went limp and began to whimper.

"Oh, Gabe…."

When his hands stole once more into her hair, she clung.

She sighed, trembling. "Play fair."

"Be honest."

"All right. My mother left. My father didn't want me. I loved you with all my heart. You took me to bed and then you left me too. Tom was there. I married him. We were happy.... We were!"

The way she said it, so forcefully, cut him deeply. "Were you? Was I so easy to replace?"

"Yes! Yes! And I've got four little girls now," she sobbed. "Four little girls who aren't easy. I don't care what you say you regret, this doesn't feel smart." Her wide, green eyes searched his handsome dark face. "I need a man who's committed to me, to marriage, and to my girls—forever. I don't want to make the same mistakes all over again."

"Oh, baby, believe me, neither do I."

"I don't see you as a father—"

"But do you see me as your lover?" He kissed her then, kissed her hard. When she opened her mouth and let his tongue inside, a jolt of electricity shot through him.

If he was on fire, so was she. Her hands were all over him.

Maybe that's why neither of them heard the light patter of tennis shoes on his drive.

"Mommy!"

"Gabe—"

Scarlet-cheeked, Sam wrenched free and stumbled backward. Shakily she tried to smooth her hair. "Bea, honey—" She knelt down and fought to focus on the little girl, whose face was full of curiosity.

Bea was staring at him with incendiary blue eyes.

"Mommy, Kim and Lee won't share their digger-things with me. They never ever play with me. I hate them."

Gabe's harsh breaths felt ripped from his lungs.

Completely absorbed in her daughter now, Sam put her arms around the little girl. "No, you just feel left out."

Left out. Gabe could tell Sam a thing or two about feeling left out. His blood blazed through his arteries. He was hard as a rock. He wanted Sam all for himself, but she had four little girls. She was a single mom. All he could ever be was one of the troop.

Had he meant what he'd said? Did he still mean it? He stared at Bea and felt unsure. He ran a brown hand through his rumpled, sable-black hair. When Samantha stood up, she was cooler.

So was he.

Defensively, Sam put her arms around Bea and held her close.

"The invitation's still open," he said, attempting a casual tone. "If you get a free moment, come over for a drink. We'll hang out in the pool house."

When she paled, he turned and stalked inside his cold empty house. But he left the door open just in case.

"Mommy!"

When Sam left with Bea instead, Gabe noisily slammed his door and grabbed a beer from the fridge. His housekeeper had cooked dinner, but he stored the neatly wrapped glass dishes in the fridge.

When he went into his den, his computer was on,

and his *Wall Street Journal* was laid out on his desk just the way he liked it. He sat down, but the black print blurred. He got up again and clicked the mouse of his computer. Then he paced. He felt out of sorts—incapable of concentrating.

Usually, Vicki came by around this time. Nights when he was alone, he surfed the Internet or read. Tonight he felt off balance, as if his carefully ordered, perfect bachelor life was sliding out from under him and the future was up for grabs. What did he really want? Fame? Money? The most beautiful women so other men would envy him? The old answers weren't working.

When Maura shouted outside, he dashed to his window. The old lady was bossing Sam, John and his men, and the four kids. Now that Maura wasn't pestering him or spying on him, Gabe felt lonely and left out.

Shafts of pure gold slanted through the glimmering pecan-laden branches and lit up his basketball hoop. That got him going.

Within minutes Gabe was in shorts and a T-shirt, on his way out the door. His phone rang. He paused just long enough to read Vicki's number on the caller ID. He slammed outside where he noisily began shooting baskets and dribbling the ball up and down his drive.

He missed quite a few shots because he couldn't really concentrate when Sam was next door with John and her kids. Not that they paid him any attention.

Finally, Bea tiptoed over carrying her big pink dinosaur and sat down to watch him.

Funny, how thrilled he was to have her there. His game improved. Then it fell off again as he began to wonder if Sam was ever going to notice her daughter's interest or his impressive shots.

When his basketball bounced crazily off the backboard toward his bed of day lilies, Bea screamed and rushed to get it.

"Throw it to me," he coaxed gently.

Bea dug his ball out of the lilies but set it down in front of her, her blue eyes alight. "You have to come see," she said softly, peeling back the thick leaves and slanting a cute, long-lashed glance his way.

"See what?"

She pulled another fat clump of tall green leaves to one side so he could see. Smiling impishly, she pointed.

He dropped to a crouch beside her. Next thing he knew, Sam was there too.

"Bea, I told you not to bother Mr. Langston."

"She's not bothering me—"

"Look—" Bea pointed at a nest of baby possums hidden in the dense green leaves. "Babies. I was afwaid he'd hurt them."

"Aren't they cute," exclaimed Sam.

"Indeed they are." Gabe wasn't staring at the possums. He was looking at Sam and her daughter.

"Where's their mommy and daddy?" Bea

breathed, her eyes sad and imploring as she looked at Gabe.

"They'll be back," Gabe reassured her.

Then Courtney came and stared in wonder at the little nest and at him.

Just as Sam's gaze rose tenderly to Gabe's, he caught a flash of yellow out of the corner of his eye. An all-too-familiar horn tooted jauntily.

Vicki slung a long curvaceous leg out of her yellow car. The brunette looked sexy in shorts that were even tighter and more revealing than Sam's.

Sam's sweet smile faded.

Funny, how he'd never minded Vicki dressing like that before. But Sam looked hurt and unsure as she lifted a significant eyebrow at him.

Vicki's shrewd, expertly painted eyes homed in on Sam, too.

"Missed you," she whispered, wedging herself between Sam and him.

He tensed; Sam flushed and backed away.

Vicki wrapped her arm around his waist. "New neighbors?"

"You should have called first," Gabe said.

"Lover, you should have answered."

"We'd better go," Sam whispered.

"I want to stay with the possums," Bea said, "till their daddy comes home."

"There's no need for y'all to go," Gabe said a little too heartily. Then he introduced everybody.

Both women stared at him as if he were crazy.

"Cute kids," Vicki said in an offhand tone.

"Nice meeting you, too, Vicki." Sam tried to smile, but her mouth quivered. "I said, come on! Girls!"

"Now, 'member, don't hit our baby possums with your ball, Gabe," Bea advised. "And tell me if you see their daddy—"

"Come on, girls."

Sam looked wounded, as wounded as she had looked all those years ago when he'd told her he wasn't ready for marriage.

"You don't need to go," he whispered.

"But we've got a lot to talk about, lover," Vicki said.

"Yes," he muttered in a fierce, dry undertone. "We certainly do."

When Vicki wrapped him more tightly than ever, Sam ran.

Desperately, Gabe called after them. "Hey, kid? Goldilocks!"

Bea turned.

"You forgot your three bears!"

Chapter 6

Sam hadn't been able to sleep last night because of Rob's wedding today. She needed to think, and she had to be alone to do it. When she let herself quietly out into the morning dark, she half expected one of the girls to dash after her. If they'd been clingy before the move, they never let her out of their sight unless they were asleep.

When Gabe's kitchen light came on, she stumbled over her long feet so clumsily, she had to grab the railing to catch herself.

But it wasn't her feet; it was a loose shoelace.

Gabe had said he wished he'd married her. Then he'd dropped her after Vicki had showed up. All week, Sam had tried to make sense of what he'd said and done, of what she'd felt.

Her heart racing, Sam knelt over her shoelace. Her eyes remained on his kitchen light and her hands shook so badly the string knotted.

Oh, God. What if she ran into him? She couldn't bear it if he shunned her. He'd avoided her and her girls ever since Vicki had dropped by. Doubtless, he'd gone back to his wild bachelor life with the sexy brunette.

Sam wished she could quit thinking about him, wished Aunt Maura would quit telling stories about Vicki and all the others. If only her father hadn't started that embarrassing rumor that had the whole city thinking she'd come home to catch a rich husband. Maybe then Nelson and Gabe wouldn't have gotten into this foolish contest, and maybe she wouldn't feel so uncertain.

But somehow her dad's joke, absurd as it was, was like a seed gone wild in the fertile soil of her imagination. It had started her thinking and dreaming as she had as a young girl. Maybe if Gabe hadn't taken her to bed last week and then said he wished he'd married her—

Well, it was all her dad's fault for getting her thinking she needed a husband and her girls needed a father.

Gabe Langston was an abominable choice.

Then why, oh, why, girl, did you let him wangle you into his bed the minute you got here? Not once, but twice?

Although she'd told Gabe their lovemaking had meant nothing, she'd had Gabe Langston on the brain ever since. But that was only because incredible sex with a man you were determined to dislike was upsetting. Especially when marriage to Tom had never...

The disloyal thought she refused to flesh out nibbled at her heart. She'd loved Tom completely! She had! He'd been dear and good.

But there was something about Gabe. Just knowing he was next door and that he thought he had some sort of claim on her again had her fluttering with excitement. She raced to the window every time she thought she heard a car in his drive.

The better to avoid him, she'd sworn to herself. That was why she was always peering over the hedge—to make sure he was nowhere about before she ventured out. Not that he'd been home much this past week.

She didn't care about him. Almost angrily she began her warm-ups. First she stretched. Then she hopped from one foot to the next.

His light next door went off. When a familiar, broad-shouldered figure loped down to the street, she gasped.

She'd set her alarm for the hour he jogged, but she told herself that that was the only possible hour in the day the girls would let her alone. It wasn't because...

The farther away he got, the fiercer her heart pounded.

Of course, he was in his running clothes just as she was. For some reason he seemed taller than usual and yet stark and lonely in the pool of yellow under the streetlight. He jogged off toward the park. He hadn't seen her. Soon he would be gone.

"Gabe!"

He stopped, turned around, and jogged back to her. She strained her eyes to see his expression. But the darkness almost swallowed him.

"Hi," he said, but his voice was flat.

Still, the single word sent a shock through her whole body.

"Haven't seen much of you lately," he said, still in that same cautious tone that betrayed no emotion.

As if it were she who hadn't been around.

"Well, you're up bright and early," he said, padding up the drive toward her.

Those knowing eyes of his lingered on her face.

"So are you."

"But it's my habit."

"Mine, too."

He laughed. "Since when?"

"I'm up, usually seeing about one of the girls. It's a rare night that everybody sleeps all night or sleeps in. Bea has nightmares and Courtney's afraid of the dark."

"And last night?"

"The girls were fine." She wasn't about to confess she'd had a restless night or that she'd dreamed about him and what he'd said about marriage and liking kids. And never ever would she admit that she'd gotten up at two o'clock in the morning and rushed to her window when his Lotus had zoomed up the drive, that she'd used Aunt Maura's binoculars to see if he'd brought Vicki home. That she'd hugged herself like a happy child when he'd come out of his garage alone.

His gaze swept her from neck to toe.

She was wearing a black jogging bra and a wispy pair of black jogging shorts. Whether it was her skimpy costume or her body that lit his fierce gaze, he soon had all her nerves jumping inside.

Vulnerable, wary of him and her tingling, raw feelings, she backed away a step or two. "If you say one word about the way I'm dressed, I'll—"

"Then can I say something about the way that bra looks shrink-wrapped...or the way you're... er...*not* dressed?"

"Gabriel, I'm warning—!"

"In that outfit, and at this hour...in Pease Park, you do need a bodyguard." His tone was laced with sardonic amusement. "Good thing I'm up and eager to apply for the job."

She went rigid.

"Admit it! You got up to see me!"

"Did not!"

He grinned, and she forgot Vicki and all her own reservations about him.

"Remember how we used to run together as kids?"

Her heart constricted. She wasn't about to admit she remembered every single thing they'd ever done together.

"You asking me to jog with you, Gabriel Langston?"

"And what if I am, neighbor?" He winked. "Just like old times."

The eager boyish glint in his eyes made her breathe more rapidly. "Hey! I'm glad you got up to see me!"

"Then catch me if you can." She sprinted off in front of him, smiling in spite of herself when she felt his heavy footsteps thudding easily on the pavement behind her.

They ran for a while without talking through the navy-black early-morning quiet. She felt his fathomless dark eyes on her the whole time. When her knees grew wobbly, he got cocky and spurted ahead.

"You're out of shape!" he yelled, a little breathlessly. Then, grinning back at her, he led her onto the path into the woods that ran down to the creek's edge. Once they were in the deepest, darkest part of the woods, he stopped so abruptly she almost fell into him.

She was gasping. Perspiration drenched her entire body.

"Austin's pretty humid," he said.

"Hot too," she said, still fighting for breath.

He held out a wide, brown hand, which she took to steady herself and held a little too long, not because even this brief and casual contact was indefinably pleasurable. But because it was early and she was feeling a little dizzy from the run.

His hand was warm, and the air smelled of cedar

and morning mist. Dear God, why did he have to be so handsome, even more handsome than when she'd loved him?

All of a sudden she realized what she was doing and yanked her hand away.

"Don't jog down here alone," he commanded, letting her fingers go, "especially not at this hour."

"I wasn't planning to. Not that I feel all that safe with you."

"I wonder why?" he said with a deadly softness.

"What happened with Vicki?"

"I finished that the night she came by."

"Then you haven't seen her again?"

"Jealous?" Under his disinterested tone, she heard some secret eagerness.

"Of course not! But...but you haven't been home."

"So, you missed me? I wondered if I quit pushing, if you'd—"

He shot her a long, hard look while she fiddled with her headband a little too self-consciously.

Finally, he said, "It's been crazy at LXK, and I thought maybe you needed more time."

"Why...why aren't you seeing her anymore? I mean, of course, that's your business."

"You know why."

"Not because of me, I hope—"

"Do you?" His voice was taut. "I wonder."

"Gabe—"

"I know you're sorry you slept with me. And

since it's made you unhappy, I wish we'd gotten off to a slower start, too."

"We're not starting...."

"Have it your way...for now," he began as if searching for words. "But I meant what I said before Vicki came over. And there's something else I have to know."

She tensed but tried to make her voice flippant. "Yes?"

"You asked Mom if you could bring a date to Rob's wedding today. Are you taking Nelson?"

She froze. Then she saw that his tanned face was ashen, his black eyes dark and desperate.

"What about Vicki?"

"How many times do I have to tell you she and I are through? So—what about Nelson?"

"Nelson's busy," she said, "with the start-up of his new company."

A pause, then his expression darkened. "Then...will you go with me?"

She tipped her head back. "And the girls?"

"Damn it, of course, the girls."

"And Aunt Maura?"

He nodded. "And Petey and all the teddy bears, too."

"It won't be a date."

His gaze roamed her shapely length as surely and tenderly as a caress, but he nodded.

Maybe he looked tough and arrogant to everybody else, but his intense black eyes devoured her face as if searching for something he wanted to find, desperately.

Tears stung her lashes. He didn't feel... She couldn't feel....

"This isn't a date! This isn't anything! Just two old friends going somewhere together!"

"Right." His voice was clipped, but his handsome face was filled with warmth and compassion.

"I know better than to ever fall for you again. You broke my heart."

"I broke mine, too."

"You, I mean a man like you, wouldn't really ever want to get married or ever have kids," she said.

"People change. Look at tough old Rob."

"Nothing is happening between us, Gabe Langston," she whispered in that small voice.

"You keep on saying that, baby. I hope to hell you're right." He drew a breath. "I'll be over at eight o'clock in the morning to help you get everybody ready?"

"Yes."

"Race you back to the house!"

"Only if you give me a head start."

"With those long legs? You've got to be kidding!"

"You said I was out of shape."

"The need to compete is a big motivator." He took off running.

Fool that she was, she tried to catch him.

Chapter 7

The best thing and the worst thing about the Langstons was they were all extroverts. No sooner had Gabe opened his mother's front door, than every Langston jammed into the tight rows of rented chairs, whirled and nodded "howdy."

"'Bout time you got here, boy!" Uncle Ed shouted.

Gabe wished the Langstons weren't such a nosy, in-your-face bunch. There was nothing his difficult family loved more—'cept maybe football, oh, and the women, being Texan gals, did go for big hair and had a weakness for jewelry—than butting into each other's business, especially each other's love lives.

Especially Gabe's, and most especially when Sam was back in the picture.

Gabe, who always felt like he got lost in the shuffle, dreaded these rowdy reunions as much as his mother enjoyed them.

It had been different back when he'd been a star quarterback. All of them had attended his games and cheered louder than anybody else in the stadium, screaming, "Way to go, Gabe!"

Back then, they'd made him feel like a hero.

Gabe wedged himself into the room. "Hi, people." Sam's soft sexy voice behind him lit his nerves and everybody else's too.

Eyebrows really shot up when they saw her, same as his had when he'd gotten a load of those teetering heels and that strapless gold sundress that hugged her slim curves tighter than a see-through wet T-shirt.

Uncle Ed let out a wolf whistle, and everybody laughed. Then the girls, who were still fighting over that slim copy of *Alice in Wonderland,* scrambled breathlessly inside after Maura.

"Way to go, Gabe!" Uncle Ed cheered.

"Sit down, Ed," his wife said.

No sooner had old Ed settled down, than Aunt Celeste struggled to her feet and let out one of her war whoops. "Sam and Gabe! Glory be! When did you two get back together?"

Sam blushed. "We're not together."

"Well, that's a trolling getup if I ever saw one, gal," whooped Aunt Celeste.

Emma said, "I invited her and her girls. Gabe was kind enough to bring them and Aunt Maura along."

The girls giggled shyly.

"Go! Go! Go, Gabe!" Uncle Ed roared, using another one of the family's old football yells.

"Now that brings back good old glory days," somebody said.

Gabe's expression darkened. "Sorry we're so late. You all just get back to doing what you were doing."

"It's my fault," Sam said. "It's a battle getting six women dressed and in the car. We wouldn't be here yet if Gabe hadn't helped."

"I vomited on my new dress," Bea explained shyly.

"Gabe mopped up the mess," volunteered Kim.

"With Bea's dress and my favorite towel." Lee pinched her nose to indicate how bad that had smelled. "Yuck."

"That's why I'm in my favowite overwalls," Bea said, snapping a peach-colored suspender. "I lost my shoe and Gabe got his head stuck under the couch."

Everybody laughed when the suspender popped. Everybody except Gabe, who was beginning to feel as impatient as he had when it had taken Sam and the girls so long to get dressed.

"Never mind, darlings," gushed his mother, who looked happier than he'd seen her since Dad's death. "We reserved seats for you all right up here in front."

Where everybody could stare holes in his and Sam's backs.

When Bea grabbed the book away from Kim and tried to dash past the twins, she knocked a wedding gift off a side table.

An audible gasp of alarm went through the crowd.

"My *Alice in Wonderland!*" cried Kim, scooping it off the floor and running.

Bea was in tears, so Gabe rushed to the rescue. He lifted her gently so she could replace the package. Eyeing the crowd through her long damp lashes, she laid her head on his shoulder. Then her shyness caught up to her, and she tucked her face against his throat and hid as he carried her the rest of the way.

Mom stared at him and then at Sam with that oddly tender expression on her face she usually reserved for Clu. By the time Gabe found their seats, an indefinable sense of gloom was swamping him.

But hell, even if you had to go to a wedding and get your family in an uproar because you'd brought your old girlfriend, this particular morning was flawless. The sky was blue and the fields sweet and colorful with Texas wildflowers.

Not even two weeks since Mother's Day, and Mom had the house as festive as he remembered it on holidays when Dad had still been alive. Every table was ablaze with candles and roses and yellow-centered daisies.

Gabe had barely gotten his bunch settled before the whispers started.

"Rob'll win Emma's bet for sure."

"Don't count Gabe out yet. Not when Sam's already got those four girls, and he's so good with them.''

"Sam's a fast one. With her looks and the way she packages them, she'll catch Gabe easy. She's a change from what he's used to.''

"If you ask me, that's what always gets 'em.''

Well, nobody's asking you, Margie Lou Langston, Gabe wanted to turn around and holler. But he held his tongue, if not his temper.

So, as Margie Lou kept on with her prattling, Gabe's collar got stiffer and scratchier and his dark, handsome face grew more mulish. Finally, he turned around and glowered so hard Margie Lou shut up. But that only made Hank Vetters wink at him.

Gabe turned back around and slumped in his seat, staring glumly at the table stacked with gifts. Then Hank snickered to Gus Lee about the engineering of Sam's strapless dress and that got Gabe so furious he had to count and then recount every single fussy little tulle bow and white rose that climbed Mom's banister.

Why the hell couldn't Sam ever dress the way she was supposed to?

"No need to be so nervous,'' Sam whispered.

"Who's nervous?'' he growled, crossing his legs and then recrossing them.

"Well, you're awfully fidgety.''

"You know how my family gets to me.''

"Because you let them. They're darlings. I love them all.''

"Weddings get to me. That postage-stamp dress of yours gets to me, too. And your perfume—"

"I'm sorry if you don't like…"

As if that were it! Hell, his eyes heated every time they drifted from her lovely face down that tight gold bodice that left nothing to his imagination.

"I like it. Okay? I'd like to peel it off you in my pool house later."

She flushed. Suddenly he was acutely conscious of every other eye in the vicinity glued to her.

"This isn't a date," she reminded him.

Sam's sexy dress and his pesty brother had gotten this wedding thing off to a bad start. No sooner had Gabe helped Sam out of Sam's SUV, than Clu had started in on Gabe to turn this wedding business into a real horse race and propose to Sam—today.

Their cousin, Gus Lee, had whistled at Sam and socked Gabe in the arm. "Never knowed you to come in second, hellion. What would your daddy say about Rob beating you to the altar?" He eyed Sam and Gabe together. "Hell, cuz, I never realized you were so short before either."

"He's not short, I'm tall," Sam had blurted.

Gabe had bristled. "You wouldn't be so tall, if you didn't wear those damned heels!"

"Hey! Hey!" Josh Wilson had interrupted. "I hear the bride is pregnant."

"That's my sister-in-law you're talking about! Hell no, she is not pregnant!" Gabe had flared. "And don't you be broadcasting lies to ruin her reputation!"

"You ought to ask Sam to marry you—today. That'd be a lot more fun to broadcast," Clu had countered. "The way she dresses, she won't be single long."

Gabe fumed as he remembered the conversation. If everybody, especially Clu and his mother would stop staring at Sam and her little girls and acting so silly, maybe Gabe could concentrate on the sacred ceremony. After all, Rob was getting married. Not him.

But the wedding jarred him, got him thinking. He wanted Sam, wanted her in his bed. Reality check. She had kids—four to be exact. Getting them dressed and then playing baby-sitter in her back seat on the hour-long drive from Austin had made the morning seem endless.

The girls had been all over him, vying with each other for his attention, squabbling and hitting each other with teddy bears even when he'd read to them. He'd realized that when her girls' shyness toward him really thawed, her ready-made family was going to be work. Every single one of her daughters had spent their babyhood without parents. Then they'd been adopted and lost Tom. They were a needy bunch. Whoever married Sam would have to be a world-class daddy.

Like his own dad had been.

God, being here made Gabe miss him.

The bridal march began, and Sam got so excited she clutched his hand and laid it on her glittering thigh. A hush went through the living room as Laura descended the wide stairs in a cream-colored suit.

Not that Gabe even saw Laura. All he registered

was Sam's rapt face and the electrifying warmth of her leg under that thin gold fabric.

If he married Sam, he could touch her in bed any time he wanted to. Hell, he could lie beside her wrapped all night in her arms—every night. If they could keep four clingy girls out of their bedroom—

Marriage? To a mother of four! What was he thinking of? He wasn't thinking.

It was Clu who had said to make this a horse race, to propose today.

Hell, she'd hardly talked to him since that morning in the pool house, and he had no idea how serious she was about Nelson. No sane man went to bed with his old girlfriend and then asked her to marry him a week later just because she'd married so fast before.

But suddenly, instead of Laura, Gabe imagined Sam floating down those stairs, Sam wearing gauzy white, Sam blushing shyly every time she looked at him the same as Laura did any time Rob was near.

He forced himself to remember it wouldn't ever be just Sam and himself. His Sam would be preceded by four little flower girls.

As if her thoughts were running along the same path, Sam's fingers tightened on his.

"You were great in the back seat with the girls," she whispered. "I was awestruck."

"Was that a test?"

"I didn't know you could read like that! All those different voices. So much emotion. You really had them going."

"I had myself going. I never read *Alice in Wonderland* before. Especially not to little savages who practically tore the pages out of the book while I was reading."

"Don't bwides 'spose to wear veils and white princess dresses?" Bea piped from the other side of Sam in a voice loud enough for everybody in the whole room to hear.

"Shhh," whispered Sam.

As Pastor Bryan went through the vows, Rob put his arm around Laura's waist and bent his dark head close to hers.

So, when had Rob become such a toucher? His brother couldn't seem to keep his hands off his bride, which made Gabe slide his hand a little lower along Sam's leg.

"Stop it," Sam whispered.

At her obvious discomfiture, Gabe grinned and put his lips near her ear. "It's been days since you hit on me at my pool."

At his long level look, she turned pink. "I want to forget that."

He clenched her fingers. "And I want to do it again." Teasingly, he brushed her leg with his callused thumb. "Why don't you come over for a swim later this afternoon."

"With the girls?"

"Another time. I thought we'd skinny-dip."

"Behave. This is a wedding."

"People don't get married because they want to behave."

"It helps if they're in love," Sam said softly, shivering a little as his long brown fingers stroked her thigh.

"No. They get married because they want to see each other naked."

With a muffled moan and a wounded look, she pushed his hand away and refolded her hands in a tense little knot. "I'll bet you've done that lots and lots of times without getting married."

Gabe's gaze roamed her long shapely legs. He imagined her naked, her legs circling his waist, and got so hot he could barely stay in his chair.

Ever since she'd moved home, his perfect bachelor life had soured into something bleak and shallow. Into something lonely. His whole future, his business, LXK, beating Nelson, every imaginable success felt empty—without her.

When the ceremony was over, Mom was looking at him and Sam and the girls with that same maddeningly dreamy expression on her face she'd had when she'd proposed her stupid wager—as if he and Sam, and the girls, were already a done deal. Clu was staring at him and grinning sappily, mouthing the words, "horse race."

Marriage? Propose today?

A guy didn't have a chance when this family started in on him.

Somehow he had to talk Sam into leaving first thing.

Before the cake.

Before...before this crazy bunch really got to him and he did something really, really crazy.

Chapter 8

Sam wanted to bolt. Weddings usually made her feel as if she were a princess in a fairy tale. Not today.

Not that she hadn't always loved this loud, boisterous family who welcomed her so heartily. But something about being here with Gabe, and everybody believing that their relationship might end in a tender ceremony like Laura and Rob's, shredded her.

Nobody could stop talking about Emma's cute wager and how fast Rob had rushed to the altar. Then there were the rumors that she, Sam, was shopping for husband number two. And every time Gabe explained they weren't a couple, ridiculous old hurts attacked her and made her feel vulnerable, lost and abandoned.

Gabe had this big wonderful family and all she

had was Henry, who hadn't been there for her, and Aunt Maura.

Gabe was exciting, far more exciting than Tom, but that was why Gabe was so wrong. Still, he made her long for what couldn't be. Yet Gabe's hot lingering gazes coupled with Emma's wistful glances and everybody's excessive interest had Sam trembling with nerves.

As soon as the ceremony was over, she decided the best thing to do was separate from Gabe and Emma and mingle with safer people. Gabe let her. But separation only made her miss him, made her more aware of his compelling magnetism that kept her attention fixed on him no matter where he was.

An hour passed. Pretending to ignore him, she chattered brightly, to everybody else. And yet never ever did she lose sight of Gabe who'd spent most of his time with Clu.

All too soon it was time to throw the bouquet. When a dozen girls jumped for the bundle of white roses and missed, she jumped back with a mixture of horror and unfeigned delight when flowing satin ribbons landed on top of her pointed gold toes.

"Yes!" She knelt. Then her eyes, soft and dark, lifted to Gabe's.

He was still drinking champagne with Clu and his cousins. When she smiled at him over the roses, his dark, flushed face stilled.

"Go, Gabe! Go!" roared Uncle Ed.

Everybody except Gabe laughed. He drained the

last of the champagne in his flute and went rigid.
Then Clu said something that made Gabe scowl
darkly. Was it a trick or did he really seem a lonely
figure standing beside his brother, amidst his family?
In the next instant the music started, and Gabe's
broad-shouldered frame was hurtling toward her,
through cousins and friends, as if he were a quarterback again scrambling for a ball.

He caught her arm and led her into a corner.
"Don't you know better than to bend over in that
dress?"

Her confused gaze sought his furious black eyes.
"I'm sorry. I—I didn't think—"

"Everybody's watching you, watching us, wondering about us. It's driving me crazy."

"Me, too."

"Let's dance."

"But my girls…"

"Clu said he'd entertain them…if I'd…" He
broke off lamely.

"But—"

"Baby, he's a teacher. He's great with kids. He's
going to show them the ranch and let them get acquainted with Zafir."

"The prize?" she whispered in a small lost voice.

He stared at her. "So, you know about that, too?"

"Do you have to win?"

"Is that what you think?"

"You always have to win. Everybody's saying if
you marry me and my girls, you'll win that wager.

They think it's a shoo-in 'cause I'm your old girl-friend, and I'm shopping for a new husband."

"We know differently, don't we?" he whispered, furious. His heavy hand tightened around her waist. "We know about Nelson George. He made your list while…"

"Don't—"

"I don't want to talk about him any more than you do." Gabe pulled her closer, dancing behind a cluster of potted plants, apart from the curious throng.

"Sam," he said on a violent shudder.

"What?"

"Marry me?" His low voice was raw.

She lifted her head. "Because of a wager, because of some joke?"

He stared at her. "No! Just marry me. I don't know why. All I know is that I don't want anybody else to touch you, and I can't lose you again."

"Is this…because of Novadash?"

He stood stock-still, but went on holding her so tightly it was hard for her to breathe. "I don't care about that."

"You're bound to. I know what Nelson did to you. I know he wouldn't have done it if my father—"

"I don't care about that." He sucked in a breath. "This has to do with us. Only us. I want you. Marriage is the only way."

She was struggling to understand. "My father would invest heavily in Nelson's company if…if he and I…"

"This isn't about money."

She bit her lip. "But if you and I marry, Daddy,

I—I mean Henry, would back you, wouldn't he? You're rich and powerful...like him. Henry respects you."

"You've always always held my success against me."

"Money and power are so important to you, the same way they are to him. Tell me—I have to know—is that why you'd marry me?"

His arms dropped to his sides. She couldn't bear the dark hurt on his face. Still, she persisted.

"Is winning on every level all you can ever be about? I want a man who would put me and my girls first."

"And you think I can't?"

"I don't know. Maybe I don't want to know."

"I love you, you little fool."

"You're furious and desperate because they've been teasing you till you're half-crazy... And you're a little...drunk...and a little shaken because your brother beat you to the altar."

"That's not why I asked you to marry me!"

Somehow this less than loverly proposal moved her more than if he'd gotten down on a bended knee. She clung to him there tightly, because she was afraid.

When the song finished, she pushed him away. "I have to see about the girls."

"You didn't answer my question."

"Marriage? I—I can't afford any more mistakes."

When she ran from the room, she thought she heard someone yell, "Go, Gabe, go!" But she was crying too hard to be sure.

* * *

Gabe raced outside after her.

Damn it, he loved her. He'd always loved her. That's why he'd made such a mess of his life. That's why he'd had to win—he'd had to prove he hadn't cared that she'd married so fast on the rebound. The women had been a shield to cover the profound pain of that loss. His money, the big house—they were shields, too.

He stopped on the porch. He needed time to swallow his pride, time to figure out what to do next.

From the front porch, Gabe watched Sam with Zafir and her daughters in the front pasture. The great horse's white head was lowered as docilely as a lamb's, and four small hands were stroking his velvet nose.

"Is he mean? Will he bite?" Bea wanted to know, jerking her hand back a little when Zafir snorted and she got a glimpse of his big teeth.

"Not Zafir," Clu said as Gabe loped up to them.

Sam paled when he approached. Then she looked away, but the girls beamed up at him. His family, especially Mom, had been courting them. All of them, even Courtney, were much friendlier after the hour-long ride from Austin to the ranch in Sam's SUV.

Maybe that was the key—the girls. If he couldn't win Sam, maybe he should woo the girls.

Gabe went up to Bea and brushed Zafir's head, too. "Do you want to ride him?"

"Do you think it's safe for them to?" Sam whispered.

"There's a risk to everything," Gabe replied pointedly.

Sam froze.

"Trust me," he murmured. "I won't let anything happen to them."

Zafir jerked his head back. The girls jumped away, staring fearfully from the big horse and then to Sam and him.

"Could we shwink him like in *Alice in Wonderland*, when Alice takes the magic potion?" Bea wanted to know.

"No, but I'd lead him by the reins," Gabe said. "I wouldn't let any of you fall. If you try this, you'll have more courage next time."

"Promise you'll stay?"

He held up his hand. "Scout's honor."

"You weren't a Scout," Sam scolded.

"Shhh."

Soon all four girls sat on Zafir's back—Courtney, Bea, and then the twins. Gabe led the Arabian around the ring while Sam walked silently beside him. It wasn't long before Sam was humming and the girls were singing along to Zafir.

"I don't want them trusting you," Sam said quietly to Gabe as the girls continued their song.

"So, you want them to stay dependent on just you? Do you want Bea crying every time she loses something? Or the twins so close they can't let anybody else in? Is this an ego trip...for a girl with abandonment issues?"

"Gabe! I—I just don't want them hurt."

"I asked you to marry me. I'd be good to them, good for them, too."

"Don't make me repeat myself."

"You're afraid, aren't you? That's what this is all about."

"Among other things."

"What if I won your girls? What if they wanted me for their daddy? Would you have me then?"

"You! Don't you dare! Don't dare use my girls...." Sam whispered loudly.

"I'll do any damn thing I please, Samantha Martin."

"Gabe. You're forgetting about Tom."

"No. But you are. That's why you're so scared. Tom was a mistake, wasn't he? Just like my bachelor's life was a mistake." He lowered his voice even more as the girls sang merrily on. "That's why you hopped in bed so fast with me."

"I hate you."

"No. You slept with me and you're going to marry me. You're going to get naked with me every night. Because you want it as bad as I do."

She blushed.

"You were right about me after all, Sam. This is about winning. I have to win. Only Zafir isn't the real prize. Not as far as I'm concerned. You are!"

Chapter 9

Gabe clenched the phone tighter. Why wouldn't Sam answer?

He knew why. He would have given her more time, but there was an important computer banquet coming up. Nelson might ask her first.

On the fifth ring, Maura's wordy message came on again. By the time her machine beeped, damn if he hadn't popped every knuckle.

At the electronic silence his heart plummeted to his stomach. While Maura's tape whirred, his throat got tight and dry. Finally, he managed to speak. "Why the hell don't you ever answer your phone?"

He clamped a brown hand over the mouthpiece. No, that was all wrong. Rapidly he thumped the eraser end of his pencil against his desk. "There's an important benefit dinner Friday. I've got two tickets. Five hundred dollars apiece." His controlled voice sounded terrible now, dull and flat. "Sam, I'd like to take you."

He tapped his pencil so hard it broke. More whirring blank tape.

God, he'd been a fool to mention money. With Sam that was always a mistake. How in the hell could he repair the damage?

No way to. He slammed the phone down, and just sat there, waiting, staring blankly at the wall.

She didn't call back.

How did you woo a woman and her little girls when they were never home, when Sam wouldn't answer her phone or return his calls?

Not that Gabe didn't have plenty to distract him. Work was war. Nelson launched Novadash. Gabe sued. The press got into it. In a biased television interview, Nelson charged that Gabe was the worst CEO in the industry, that he abused his employees, neither respecting nor listening to them. What if Sam believed him? What if she saw Nelson as an idealist?

The lying jerk ended the interview by cheerfully announcing he'd soon have something personal to share.

Had Sam said she'd marry him? Gabe felt tired and worried.

At least Mark and his top people stuck by him. In appreciation, Gabe relented and gave them a piece of the company.

Nights when he got home late, Gabe stared at Maura's black windows, missing Sam and her girls even more than he'd missed her years ago when she'd married Tom. He even missed Maura and her binoculars.

He wanted to stomp over there and see what they were all up to. He wanted to scream to the rooftops that he loved Sam, that he'd always loved her. And he didn't care who heard him.

Instead he unwrapped solitary suppers and ate them alone. He climbed the stairs to his bed, too tense and exhausted to sleep only to be in the dark going crazy wondering about Sam and Nelson.

Finally, Gabe got so desperate, he stormed to Maura's front door one morning and asked the girls over to swim later.

Courtney was very fidgety, hopping from one foot to the other. "Mommy too?"

With a head full of braids she'd looked like a thin, little waif—a hyperactive waif. The kid never quit moving.

He'd nodded, and she'd smiled in that nervous quick way that made him feel she didn't quite trust him. Then he'd asked for Maura to see if she was still having problems with her porch light. He couldn't bring himself to ask about her pigeon problem.

Maura was all smiles. "So, Rob's wedding scared the pants off Sam too?" When that blow got no reaction, she belted him harder. "You'd better get in gear or Nelson will beat you to the punch."

"You through?"

"Not quite." No, she was just getting started. "Sam's a fast marrier, you know."

He gritted his teeth, took a deep, calming breath. "What do her kids eat for supper? I thought I'd plan a picnic by the pool."

"You are serious." She nodded her blue head in approval. "Hot dogs and marshmallows and colas. Anything greasy and sugary that gives an old lady like me indigestion. But if you ask me, too, I'll get Lou to shop. I'll tell her to throw in a T-bone for you."

"Make it a big one. And...and invite Sam, why don't you?"

A dubious expression played across her crafty face.

On impulse, Gabe had brought a spare computer home and loaded it with games. He set it up in the pool house, so if the girls got tired of swimming, they'd have something to do—at his house.

When Maura and Lou and the girls trooped over that afternoon without Sam, he tried not to act disappointed.

"Why is Mommy mad 'cause you're being nice to us?" Courtney wanted to know.

"I'm sorry she feels that way, but we're neighbors. We should get to know each other anyway."

"She said you asked her to marry her. Then she threw Bea's bears at the toy box and shut them in the dark."

His gut tightened. He didn't know what to say.

"If we like you, she will."

They stared at each other until Courtney threw her towel down and raced for the pool.

To get his mind off Sam, Gabe focused on the kids. Like his dad, he couldn't think sports without thinking competition. Any good coach could take a mismatched group and turn them into a team. Soon he had the three younger girls racing their hearts out. He got a stopwatch and timed Courtney, who was plenty fast, encouraging her to beat her own records.

When Bea proved to be a natural, beating the twins soundly again and again, everybody was impressed.

"It's because she has big feet," said Maura. "They're as big as flippers."

Everybody but Bea laughed.

"Don't cloud up, Bea. You're my champion." Gabe bragged so excitedly Bea puffed out her chest and began to glow again.

"We can run faster than Bea," Kim shouted.

"We'll have that race later," Gabe countered. "How about some basketball?"

Maura was sitting very still, watching him. "Sam isn't going to like your getting them to compete."

"She should have come over."

Bea eyed Maura's house wistfully. "Then she would've seen me win."

"I saw you," Gabe said, and was rewarded when Bea shyly threw her arms around his brown legs. "Yuck. You is hairy."

The junk food and the picnic were a hit too. After

supper everybody went into the pool house and watched the girls play computer games. Courtney was a natural.

"Sam doesn't like computer games for the girls," Maura volunteered.

Gabe was having too much fun fighting the girls for his turn on the computer to worry.

Then Sam called. "Why aren't the girls home?"

"Because we're having fun. Not that we don't miss you, too," Gabe said softly. "Why don't you come over?"

"It's past their bedtime," she whispered.

"You sound a little desperate. Tell you what—I'll help you get them into bed. Then you come over, and you can put me to bed."

"Don't do this, Gabe."

"Ditto," he purred.

She hung up.

He courted her girls for five straight days but that only made Sam dig in. By the end of the week his pool and outdoor furniture were littered with all the toys Bea forgot to take home.

On Wednesday, two days shy of the computer benefit, Gabe was standing on Maura's porch in his running shorts, flipping her light switch on and off to make sure the fixture worked before he put it back together.

He grabbed the brass pieces and his screwdriver and climbed the ladder. Just as he'd fitted the fixture to the ceiling and was about to screw it up there, the door opened, and a naked woman with long red hair stepped out of it.

Sam was Venus come to life in her big pink shell.

"Good God!"

He jumped back and spun around so fast he nearly fell. Screws spewed everywhere. The light fixture crashed onto the porch planking and shattered. Maura cried from inside the house, "What was that, Gabe?"

"Nothing," Sam cried, closing the door and staring up at him. "Well, you sure fixed that."

"You aren't naked."

"Does your mind reside in the gutter?"

He blinked. She was wearing a tight knit sheath the color of molten flesh that had gotten his male imagination going. The peach-colored fabric had a tantalizing open-weave pattern right where her nipples were. For a second longer he gaped at her in the golden sunlight.

"It's just that you look good," he finally said. "I've missed you."

"Don't," she whispered. "And quit being so chummy with the girls. I know you're just doing it, just fixing this light too—to get to me."

"I seem to be making a mess of everything." He stepped down a rung. "But I want you. That's for sure. I've been trying to call you. I left a message about the charity thing...."

"I've got a date that night."

"Nelson?"

She notched up her chin. "What if I did?"

"Break it."

"Just leave me and my girls alone. You've completely thrown them out of their routine. They don't want to do anything except..."

"Play with me?" He grinned. "Why don't you come over and play too?"

"This can't go any further."

"Wanna bet?" He jumped off the ladder and crunched through shards of broken glass to get to her.

"We're moving, Gabe."

"Where?"

"Not so far that we can't see about Maura. But far enough so..."

"So, the girls can't see so much of me."

"We need our own place."

"Move in with me."

"I gave you my answer.

"Not your final answer."

"Nelson's right. You don't listen—"

"Nelson...." On a burst of white-hot fury, Gabe closed the distance between them. He gripped her arms, yanking her against him. "Are you going to do something stupid and break both our hearts again?"

Before she could answer, he crushed his mouth to hers. The fire that had threatened to consume him all week devoured her, too. An instant later, her heart was pounding as fiercely as his. Even though she fought, she melted against him, too.

He let her go. He hadn't meant to kiss her, and

he knew it was the worst possible move he could have made. But at least he'd been honest.

She fell back against the side of the house. "You...you beast!"

"I love you. I love you."

"You just want to get me in bed!"

"That too."

She retreated toward the door, wiping her mouth with the back of her hand. "Stay away from me, Gabe! And stay away from my girls!"

"The house is a great value," the real estate agent, who'd driven Sam and the girls over, was saying. "It was a rental. It needs a little fixing up."

Sam corrected her. "A lot!"

"But you have the cash. If you don't make an offer, it'll move. I just got the listing. This is a hot market."

"We don't want to move here, Mommy!" Bea cried, her words echoing as she raced about, her hard-soled shoes clomping from room to room in the empty house as the twins chased after her. "Gabe said he wanted to marry us! He said we could all move into his castle and be his pwetty pwincesses!"

That snake.

Almost wistfully, Sam eyed the uneven, water-damaged oak floors, the broken windowpanes, and the chipped tiled wall in the bathroom. Then she thought of Gabe's wonderful house.

"Gabe's house has six bedrooms," said the twins.

The twins were holding hands with Bea. Each of the three had a teddy bear. Since when had the twins decided to include Bea? Since when had Bea decided to share her bears?

"I don't like the cars and trains!" said Courtney.

The two bedroom, fixer-upper stood on a hill directly over Mo-Pac, which was a hideously busy freeway that seemed to get busier by the day. A railroad ran down the median. Every time a train went by, the little house rattled.

"When we paint it and put our own things in it, it will be gorgeous, girls," Sam attempted in a feeble voice.

They stared at her as if she'd lost her mind. Then they stomped outside together. "We like it at Gabe's." Then incredibly, she heard them all shout, "Gabe! Gabe!"

"Hi there, Goldilocks and company!"

"Is that Gabe Langston?" The agent fluffed her hair and deserted Sam too.

By the time Sam made it outside, the agent was hanging all over Gabe, smiling at everything he said. Apparently she'd sold him his big house.

"Want a ride?" he said to Sam. "You're right on my route home from work."

"Yes," the girls screamed, playing easy to get. "Yes!"

It would have been churlish to say no. So Sam said, "There's not room enough for all of us in the sports car."

"You go then, Mommy," her girls all whispered and then giggled.

The clever little females.

"Linda, could you drive the girls home?" Gabe asked.

Linda.

"I'd be glad to, Gabe."

"Then it's settled," he said with that cheerful, arrogant confidence that was so endearing. No, that was so maddening! "Girls, when we get home, how about a swim?"

"Yes!" they all screamed. "Yes!"

"Mommy, will you watch me?" Bea implored. "Please! Please!"

"Goldilocks is quite a champion." Gabe grinned at that, a smug male grin.

Sam fought to ignore Gabe, so she smiled at Bea. It felt good that Bea wanted her to watch her. Of late, the girls had been far less clingy, and although Sam knew it was good for them to be independent, she missed being so all-important in their lives. The twins had even taken him up to their room to let him in on some secret they still wouldn't show her.

"Yes, darling, I'll come watch you."

"So, it's settled," Gabe repeated. "You're finally coming over."

Settled? Before she could argue, Gabe had her door open, and they were roaring away as fast as the wind under the tall pecan trees.

He angled his black head toward her. "The computer benefit's tomorrow night. I still haven't asked anybody else.''

''I told you, I have a date.''

His mouth thinned. He speeded up. ''If you change your mind, call me. I won't ask anyone else.''

The raw note in his voice almost made her admit she had a rare date with her father. Mary was out of town, and Henry had said he had two tickets to an important affair. She'd said yes to Friday because she'd known Gabe might ask her again and that she was tempted to weaken. Now she wished...

When she went over to his house to watch Bea, Gabe was so good with the girls, she felt left out. But he'd made a real effort with them. Surely no man did that if...

Sam began to wish she was going out with Gabe and not her father. The conflict in her heart worsened later that night when her daughters piled into her bed on top of her.

''What is it, my darlings?''

''We want to marry Gabe, Mommy. He asked us too, you know.'' They held out eight little hands. Each girl had a great big bubblegum machine ring. They wiggled their fingers, delighting in the garish sparkle. ''We said yes! We're engaged.''

''Mine's 'sposed to be a diamond.'' Calm for once, Courtney stared at her prized bauble. ''I never had a diamond before.''

''Gabe's got a pretty ring for you, too,'' Bea said.

"In a little black box," Courtney couldn't resist adding.

What was happening to them? To her? Oh, what in the world was happening?

The next morning when Sam shopped for groceries, there was a sexy little lamé halter with matching capri pants in the exclusive boutique in the same shopping center. Sam couldn't resist trying it on, any more than she could resist buying it as she thought of how Gabe had looked at her when she'd stepped out onto the porch and said he thought she was naked. The hunger in his black eyes had lit her entire being.

That's when she knew she was going to break her date with her father and call Gabe and say she'd go. But when she called him, his secretary said he was out and not expected back. He wasn't home either, so she left a message, promising she'd go with him.

We want to marry Gabe, Mommy.

She couldn't stop thinking about the ring he had for her in the little black box. Why? Because she wanted to marry him too. Because she loved him. Because she'd always loved him. Even when he'd abandoned her. Even when she'd felt so horrendously bereft after he'd jilted her, and she'd rushed into marriage with Tom too fast just because he was there.

On an impulse she called Gabe again. At the bleak sound of the tone, she said three little words.

Those three precious words told the deepest truth in her heart.

Then shyly she hung up and hugged herself as expectantly as a kid waiting for Christmas. She sat beside the phone for a long time, waiting for him to call.

He didn't.

And as the seconds ticked into minutes and then into hours, she realized she'd bared her soul to a machine—for nothing.

Chapter 10

Heads turned when Gabe strode into the ballroom late. People were already seated and started on their salads, but he knew where his table was—right in front, where it always was.

Sly glances and raised eyebrows increased his tension as he moved through the competitive throng. Then he saw Sam—beside Nelson.

Gabe felt like he'd been punched in the gut. He sucked in a breath. At his hard stare, her face took on a flushed look of utter vulnerability.

Damn her. Did she have to come half-naked? She wore a gold lamé halter and skintight pants and gold heels. Every other woman in the room had on a business suit. The invitation had called for business attire. A woman shopping for a rich husband wasn't above using every cheap trick in the book.

Nelson looked big and handsome. An aura of cruel confident victory leant a heady charisma to the triumphant smile he shot Gabe. Nelson had Nova-dash, and he had Sam. Tonight he was savoring those successes immensely, just as Gabe's enemies were gloating too.

Pretending to ignore Sam, Gabe sat down and greeted everybody at his table in his most casual voice. He read the program. All the speeches had to do with innovative Internet software. Because of Sam, the meal, the polite, predictable conversation and the lengthy speeches were unendurable. Gabe stiffened as speaker after speaker shot Gabe nervous glances before jokingly hailing Nelson as their man of the year.

They were roasting Gabe alive, and like cannibals around a campfire, everybody was enjoying the meal immensely. When the last pompous windbag invited Nelson to the podium, Gabe bolted.

Gasps spread through the room. Then a hush fell over the crowd as Nelson arose with pantherlike grace and bent his golden head to Sam's, kissing her lightly on the forehead. The crowd erupted in applause when Nelson seized the microphone.

Gabe left the room. Nelson had won. He deserved Sam. She deserved a winner. Not a loser, like him.

But as Gabe emerged from the building, a woman came running out after him. When Sam called his name, he didn't turn.

Sam didn't matter anymore. He sprinted even faster to his car. He got in, slammed the door and did a wild U-turn, big radials biting deeply into asphalt and spinning black gravel as he raced back to her, then gunned the motor like a furious kid when he pulled abreast of her.

Her head drooped, and her eyes were bright with pain. "Gabe?" Why did her voice sound so strange and broken?

"What'd you come out here for? To gloat? Like everybody else? Go back inside—to Nelson. You deserve each other. I see that now. He's going to be very rich with your daddy's—excuse me, baby—Henry's money behind him. So buy him, enjoy him, marry him—husband-hunter."

Gabe savaged a long, deep breath. "You were right about me, baby. The last thing I need is marriage to you and kids!"

He stomped down hard on the accelerator and flew out of the parking lot.

He knew better than to look back. But he couldn't take his eyes off the desolate figure in his rearview mirror that grew smaller and dimmer as it crumpled to its knees on the pavement.

"We want to go see Gabe!" Four mutinous faces stared at Sam who'd been crying her eyes out for hours in bed.

How could she tell them about tonight? About how Gabe thought she'd deliberately gone out with Nelson? About what Gabe had said to her in the parking lot?

If she'd felt as bereft as a girl when he'd told her

he couldn't marry her years ago, this was worse. Now she knew she couldn't run away from this kind of despair in any other man's arms.

She wanted Gabe. Only Gabe. She'd always loved him, even when she'd been married to Tom. She just hadn't let herself see it.

Her daughters squealed when they heard a car rip up Gabe's drive, and dashed to the window. Slowly, like someone in a trance, Sam glided after them.

The girls produced binoculars and watched him come out of the garage.

When his kitchen light came on, Bea turned to her. "I forgot Petey again...."

"No."

Bea began to cry, so Sam took her in her arms.

"I'll go get Petey," Courtney offered.

"Darling, it's dark. You know you're afraid of the dark."

"Then we'll go with her," the twins offered.

They all, every single one of the little traitors, wanted to abandon her for Gabe.

"No.... No...." Sam took them all in her arms. It was all she could do not to cry again too.

She couldn't ever remember not loving Gabe Langston. That was the truth. But what could she do about it?

"Why is everybody crying?" croaked a querulous voice from the door.

"Aunt Maura!"

The blue-haired figure floated across the big bedroom as spryly as a girl. "Gabe up to anything in-teresting?"

"We want to marry Gabe," Courtney said. "But Mommy won't let us. He gave us rings!"

"Girls," Maura said, grinning slowly as she held up her own garish bubblegum ring so that it flashed wickedly, "why don't you run along and let me talk some sense into Mommy. And...and leave all my binoculars here. I've been looking for them every-where."

When they were gone, Maura took Sam in her arms as she had when Sam had been a lonely, aban-doned, little girl.

"Oh, Aunt Maura. I love him so much."

"There. There. Everything will work out."

"But how?"

"He loves you. That's how."

"You don't know what he said tonight."

"I know how much he loves you and how much you love him. Love makes a way where there is no way. Do you remember how I thought he was too old for you way back when? How he had to court me first to get me on his side?"

"That's all in the past."

"He's been so good to the girls and to me lately. You know... Oh, Sam, I have a little confession." Maura was rubbing Sam's head as she spoke to soothe her and give her hope.

"A confession?"

"Emma isn't the only parent who wants her child

happily married. Henry and I have been trying to get you and Gabe back together.''

"What?"

"I deliberately wrote Oleta and you complaining even more than I usually do, so you'd take pity on me and come home. Henry did his part by getting Nelson interested in you to make Gabe jealous.''

"He didn't!"

"Gabe's so competitive. We thought... But Henry never believed Nelson would go so far. He told me about Novadash...about everything tonight.''

"I can't believe..."

"Well, at least you and Gabe are back together,'' Maura said unabashedly.

"No."

"I just got off the phone with Henry. He had a long talk with Gabe tonight. Henry confessed everything. He's very sorry Nelson thought he'd back him financially and then betray Gabe. Then Gabe confessed too. He told Henry he didn't care about Novadash, that he could always make more money, that he loved you.''

"You've got to be wrong."

"Apparently he's been listening to some message you left on his machine—over and over, the way Bea likes to listen to *Alice in Wonderland*.''

"How do you know all this?"

"Because I'm a lonely, gossipy old lady with a very long nose and four sets of excellent binoculars.''

"Have you tapped Gabe's phone?''

"What a good idea!"

"You are incorrigible."

Maura beamed with pride.

"But I love you, Aunt Maura. I do love you."

"Don't tell me! Go over there and throw rocks at Gabe's window...so I can watch...and then tell him. Show him! Why don't you invite him into his pool house again?"

"Aunt Maura!"

When Sam's alarm went off the next morning it was still dark. Quickly she pulled on a skimpy scrap of spandex cut low over her breasts and curving high above her shapely hipbones. Then she crept down the stairs, let herself out, and scampered across the lawn to Gabe's house at the exact minute he usually got home from his run. There, at the end of his drive in the early morning quiet punctuated by the coos of morning doves, the stir of leaves overhead, and the trickle of dew from the eaves, she waited beside his garage.

Her heart leapt when she saw a lone, broad-shouldered figure jogging up the street. Then she flashed his backyard lights on and off. When he shouted to her, she rushed to his inky pool and tugged her suit off.

He caught up within seconds. "What are you doing here?"

She dove, and when she emerged, she gasped. "You invited me to swim...again and again. You did say you wanted to get naked for the rest of our lives."

He picked up her swimsuit. "You're not wearing much."

"Only your pool." She arced her hand across the water's surface and sent black diamonds spiraling into the air.

Laughing when she splashed him, he began to strip. "You'll be sorry."

She swam in circles until he dove in and joined her. "I didn't have a date with Nelson."

"I got your messages a little late. Then your father called and told me."

"Why didn't you call me?"

"It was late. Besides, it's your move."

"Always the sportsman."

"No. I was giving you time. This isn't a game. I love you."

"And I love you."

"I know. I got that message too. I listened to it...er...several times."

"Aunt Maura told me."

"How did she know?"

"That old rascal knows everything."

He nodded. "I could've told you that."

"One more thing?"

"Anything."

"What are the twins hiding in their room?"

"Pigeons. There's a mama pigeon and some squabs out on their windowsill. They've made a helluva mess, and the twins don't want Maura to know."

Sam laughed. "They do trust you, and I'm glad."

She sighed. "I think I came home to Austin…to find you. Then I got scared and lost my nerve."

"So did I." He took a quick breath. Then he suddenly pulled her to the shallow end where he began kissing her, a little too roughly as he sometimes did, but for a very long time.

She tasted chlorine and him. The combination was delicious. Her heart beat wildly. Every doubt was erased.

"What do you say," he began huskily, "that we adjourn to the pool house?" His hands were smoothing her wet hair.

She drew a deep breath and stared into his eyes. "I thought you'd never ask."

Inside the pool house, he saw her put down the bag she'd picked up off a pool chair along the way.

"What do you have?"

She laughed. "Maura's binoculars. Every single pair. She's quite the spy, you know."

"A meddling old busybody…just like my mother. Can you believe they were all in this together?"

"I didn't think my father cared enough to meddle."

"You were wrong about him. He loves you, Sam."

They talked for a while. He told her how much he'd always liked her father and for the first time he made her see that she had resented her father's marriage so much that she'd probably acted as awkwardly around his new wife as Mary had around her. None of those dynamics were really her father's fault. Changes occurred in families. Changes people weren't ready for. She'd felt abandoned and left out, but not because Henry hadn't wanted her.

Then the time for talking about the past came to an end. Gabe carried her to bed and kissed her again. When his kisses got hotter and their bodies steamier, and he rolled over to fumble in his drawer, she pulled him back, folding her hand over his.

"You don't need that tonight."

"What are you saying?"

"You asked me to marry you. I'm saying yes. I want to have your baby, a little baby boy with inky black hair. A sort of…short boy…who's way too cocky."

"A clone? Maybe we should try a test tube."

"No. This is more fun."

He laughed. "What if we have a tall redheaded girl?"

"I love little girls."

"So do I. Oh, so do I. And I especially like girls who aren't so little."

She took the hint and wrapped her long legs around his waist and hugged him tighter.

"But most of all, I love you," he said, massaging her scalp so that she arced and almost purred for him. "You're my baby."

"You're my baby, too. So, baby, when do I get *my* ring?"

"That was supposed to be a secret." He grinned. "Later. After…"

He slung a leg across her thigh. His hands were already working their magic in her hair as he began to nibble her earlobe.

"I told you'd I'd be your last girl."

"And the mother of all my children." He held her close. "I was such a fool."

"Well, you'll just have to make up for lost time, won't you? Every time we do this, you'll have to see if you can beat your record."

"I'm game."

When he made love to her, tenderly and gently with his whole heart thrown into the poetry their bodies made, when he was deep inside her, when his arms held her tightly, finally, she felt that at last she'd come home, that at last she was where she truly belonged. That at last and forever she was safe. And so were her four little darlings.

She had a lover and husband, and they had a daddy. He wasn't going to abandon them. Ever.

"You're my baby," he whispered.

"You're ours too."

They slept. A long time later, he got up and returned with a small black velvet box. Then he slipped a sparkling diamond onto her finger.

She held it up. "Oh, my, it's huge. You do have a thing about size."

"You started it. You and your conceit about your long legs." They both laughed. Then he hugged her and they made love again lying afterward in each other's arms, just as they would every night for the rest of their lives.

Dear Reader,

Being asked to write a Mother's Day story really brought home to me how different our society has become since I was having my babies in the late 1950s and early 1960s. So much more is expected of women, it seems. Or perhaps we expect more of ourselves these days—getting a good education, establishing a career and trying to find time for a home and family.

I've discovered that men are having the same problems—establishing a career is made even more difficult if they wish to have a part in having a home, being there for a wife and helping to rear a family.

My story is about how two people who are quite successful in their chosen careers deal with the dilemma of working out a way to have it all— including love.

I hope you enjoy their story.

Sincerely,

Annette Broadrick

I'M GOING TO BE A...WHAT?!
Annette Broadrick

To Jennifer Nauss...

Like Laura in my story, I hope that you can find it all.... You certainly deserve to.

Chapter 1

A Monday in May

Laura Abbott strode into her office in the Travis County, Texas, administration building at eight o'clock Monday morning, a full hour before she usually arrived. She wasn't surprised to see that her secretary, Sebastian, was already at his desk, handling any calls that signaled some sort of crisis in the various departments for which she was responsible as county manager.

As soon as he saw her, Sebastian rolled his eyes while smoothly responding to whomever was on the phone.

Sebastian could be counted on to field the calls and handle them without her unless the call was from a politician. She recognized his look, which meant that she was going to have to deal with something right now.

Oh, great. It was going to be one of *those* days. Just what she needed.

Laura rubbed her stomach, wishing she hadn't bolted down her coffee and cereal this morning. It didn't seem to matter what she did or didn't do, what she ate or didn't eat. Her stomach bothered her lately.

She was probably getting an ulcer.

It didn't help that she was sleeping poorly, waking up in the middle of the night wondering what new crisis was going to develop because of something that slipped through the cracks, or thinking about something that went wrong that she would be chastised over in public.

Stress. She knew that was what was causing her physical distress. She just didn't know what to do about it, which was why she had a three o'clock doctor's appointment this afternoon. She needed some medical advice on her situation.

The appointment was one of the reasons she'd come in early in hopes of attacking the pile of work on her desk before she was called away to handle some problem or other.

Laura dumped her purse in her bottom drawer, then sank into her chair and looked at the day's schedule. Her nine o'clock appointment was a meeting with the department head of emergency services. They needed to discuss the ongoing budget problems for a county that was growing at an unprecedented rate. Emergency services needed more equipment and more personnel at a time when the budget continued to shrink.

How was she expected to provide the necessary services for emergencies if she couldn't fund the request for new ambulances, additional aero-medical equipment and trained personnel?

The fact was, she couldn't. So she and Dan Parker, the head of the department, were meeting to see what they could put together in the form of a budget request that would force the politicians to take another look at the situation. There was a public outcry at the increasing ambulance response time that could only be alleviated by facing the significant problems caused by the increased population.

Sebastian cleared his throat, causing Laura to look up. He stood in her doorway with a small smile on his face.

"I've already taken a call from *Austin American-Statesman* and Fox7 News about the impending vote to issue jail improvement bonds," he said. "Judge Hernandez has been calling to have you pull together some talking points on the subject because he's been getting the same calls. He wants to know why it's so much money and the consequences of a no or split vote."

Laura leaned back in her chair and stared at him. "Did he happen to read this morning's paper about the jail escape last night? Doesn't he realize that if we don't make improvements we can damn well count on—'' She paused, took a deep breath, exhaled, then quietly said, ''I'll call him back,'' before accepting the pink message slip. ''Is that it?''

''Another call from the budget office.''

''I'll have my proposal over there by noon.''

''There's a problem with one of the staff. She's threatening to file a lawsuit if someone doesn't deal with her complaint—someone besides the department head, of course—I told her you'd speak to her personally.''

''Okay. Find a time for it. What else?''

''We have to finish preparing the weekly report for Commissioners Court tomorrow.''

''I think we have most of it. Remember I have a three o'clock meeting away from the office. I'm not sure how long it will last.''

Sebastian studied her for a moment and said, ''You know, Laura, you're turning an interesting color of green. You feel all right?''

''I feel lousy, but what else is new?''

''You need a vacation.''

She laughed without amusement. ''Tell me about it. Maybe next year. Too much to do in an election year.''

''I'll get Judge Hernandez on the line for you,'' he said, going back to his desk.

She grabbed her phone on the first ring.

''Good morning, sir. Yes, I know the media is doing a story. Yes, you have that information, but we'll get another copy to you. By the way, you need to know that the sheriff is going to say that we owe the taxpayers a safe community, and in his opinion, it's not safe without these improvements. The escape last night makes his point for him. Yes, I know he could have come and talked to you before all this media attention, but he didn't, so I would suggest you say you didn't have all the information you needed to make an informed appeal to the voters and that the vote has been rescheduled. If there is something the sheriff wants to add to the situation you'd be happy to hear it.''

She hung up the phone and shook her head. After glancing at her watch, she gathered up her file on emergency services and headed for the conference room.

By the time she left the office that afternoon at a quarter to three, Laura was limp with fatigue. She felt more like seventy than thirty-five. She hoped the doctor could give her something to help her sleep, settle her stomach, relieve her of her headaches and boost her energy.

She realized that she didn't need a doctor—she needed a magician.

The receptionist at the doctor's medical clinic gave her a blank smile as Laura signed in at the window. Laura glanced around the sitting room. Two other women were there. She hoped they weren't waiting to see Dr. Samuels, her gynecologist and the only doctor she really ever went to for any sort of medical exams. Apparently the good doctor was running late. She supposed it was only natural to expect an ob-gyn to be at the mercy of babies with the kind of impeccable timing guaranteed to disrupt a doctor's schedule.

She settled into a chair with a recent copy of *People* magazine and allowed her thoughts to drift as she absently skimmed the photos on display.

Thinking of babies insisting on entering the world on their own timetable caused Laura to reflect on her own life, plans and goals. She couldn't remember the exact time in her life when she first realized that she would never become a mother. She had chosen to get her undergraduate degree in political science, then went on to study public affairs in graduate school. Her first job was with the Department of Commerce in Washington. Somehow, the years had slipped by without her noticing.

She had dated during those years, but had never seriously considered the few marriage proposals she'd been offered. The one man she fell in love with had made it clear early in their relationship that he had no intention of getting married. Even if he had, she'd always known he wouldn't consider her as marriage material.

She just wasn't the docile, malleable type of female that most men expected to have for a spouse. There were times in her life when she sincerely wished that she wasn't so opinionated, so quick to disagree, so ready to get involved in a really spirited debate. However, she also knew that her personality was much too ingrained to be changed for a man, even a man she loved.

Accepting a job at the White House had more

than made up for her lack of a long-term relationship. As head of the research department for the drug administrator's office, Laura had held a classified position in a secure building, feeling as though she was taking an active part in the war against drugs.

After three years, another administration had moved into the White House and Laura had returned to Texas, luckily finding her current job within a few weeks of her return.

She'd enjoyed her present position with Travis County until recently, when it seemed that she didn't have enough energy to keep going and she began to feel overwhelmed by the problems and pressures.

She closed the *People* magazine and opened a *Family Circle*. The photos of children and pages of recipes and articles on marriage she found there seemed to be from another world, one which she had never inhabited. Her life path had been set in the political arena. Most of the time she was more than content. If only she could get to feeling better, she was certain that her love of her job would rapidly return.

"Ms. Abbott?" a woman in slacks and a white jacket said from the doorway leading to the doctor's examining rooms. She had the clipboard with the list of names Laura had signed when she came in.

Laura tossed the magazine aside and stood. After following the nurse to one of the rooms, she submitted to blood pressure and temperature checks, had her weight duly noted, then was told the doctor would be in shortly.

Laura was surprised to discover the nurse had been telling the truth when Dr. Krysteen Samuels walked into the room a few minutes later.

"Hello, Laura, I was surprised to see your name on my list of patients today. Your annual physical was only six months ago. What's going on with you?"

Laura had known Krysteen for several years. They'd met while attending the University of Texas there in Austin. When Laura had moved back to Texas and needed to find a physician for her periodic checkups, she'd been delighted to discover that Krysteen had fulfilled her college dream of becoming a doctor.

"Probably nothing that a do-nothing vacation wouldn't mend. The problem is, I don't see how I can schedule a vacation with all that's going on at my office these days." She smiled at the petite, dark-headed woman in front of her. "I'm hoping you can suggest something I can take—vitamins, hormones—something that will boost my energy."

"In that case, I'll need to take some blood and a urine sample to make certain you haven't picked up a low-grade infection that's pulling you down. You might as well get into that glamorous little paper gown we have for you and I'll be back in a few minutes."

More than an hour later, Laura had to admit that Krysteen was definitely thorough with her exam.

When she was through, Krysteen told Laura to dress and then come into her office. Laura had been unable to read much from Krysteen's expression during the question-and-answer period or the actual exam.

After dressing, she slipped into her low-heeled shoes and went down the hallway to the last door, which was open. Krysteen sat behind her desk, making notations on a file. She glanced up when she heard Laura.

"Have a seat. I'll be with you in a minute."

Laura glanced at her watch. It was already four-thirty. She had to return to the office before going home to make certain that everything was ready for tomorrow, when all she wanted to do was to curl up and go to sleep.

She hoped Krysteen was going to be able to help with her low energy problem.

"You've lost weight since last fall," Krysteen said without looking up.

"Maybe five pounds or so."

"Were you trying to lose?"

Laura laughed. "Not really. As long as my clothes fit, I don't pay much attention to my weight."

"Or anything else, it appears."

"What do you mean?"

"You haven't had a period in three months, Laura," she said, raising her head and meeting her gaze. "Didn't that concern you?"

Laura shrugged. "Not really. You know I've

never been all that regular. I figured I might be going into early menopause. Or I might be premenopausal. Stress sometimes affects my regularity, as well.''

"Well, I have a much simpler explanation for you." She paused, her dark eyes grave. "You're pregnant."

Laura continued to sit there...waiting for the punch line. Krysteen was joking, of course. She had to be joking, for heaven's sake. There was no way possible that she could be pregnant. No way in—

"Pregnant?" she repeated as though her hearing was none too reliable.

Krysteen sat back in her chair, watching her intently. "That's what I said."

"You're not kidding."

"Believe me, Laura, I don't kid about something this serious."

"But I— There must be some mistake. I never thought I could *get* pregnant because of the problems I had as a teenager. The doctor told me the scarring on my tubes would likely prevent a pregnancy."

Krysteen glanced down at Laura's ringless hands clasped on the desk before her. "I take that to mean this isn't something you planned."

Laura's gaze also fell on her clasped hands. "Uh, no. I can't believe that— I mean, after all this time to have something like this happen...I can't seem to take it in."

"Well, this certainly explains all your symptoms. You haven't had morning sickness, I take it?"

Laura shook her head slowly. "Not really. I've been so nauseated at times it would have been a relief to actually throw up. I just thought I had the flu or something."

"It's definitely something. From my calculations, your due date is around the middle of October."

Laura groaned. "Right before the elections."

Krysteen laughed. "Honey, you're going to have a lot more to deal with this year than the elections."

Laura's mind was racing with a dozen different thoughts at once, none of them particularly helpful at the moment. "I must have gotten pregnant in February."

"That's about right."

"This is just unbelievable."

Krysteen glanced at her watch and straightened in her chair. "I've written a couple of prescriptions for you—vitamins and something to help with the nausea, if necessary. If you're thinking about not going through with the pregnancy, I need to remind you that you're at least twelve weeks along. I can't in good conscience—"

Laura held up her hand. "I've always believed in a woman's right to choose what took place with her body, but I would never terminate a pregnancy, Krysteen. That's not an option as far as I'm concerned."

Krysteen smiled. "All right. Then I'll need to see you in a month. You're going to need to slow down, get more rest, and in general, start to treat yourself better. This has obviously been a shock to you. Go home and relax for a few hours, get a good night's sleep. You'll get used to the idea soon enough.''

Laura numbly took the prescriptions. She made some response, but she couldn't remember what. She walked down the hallway, dazed by this wholly unexpected information, and requested another appointment in a month.

She forced herself to concentrate on traffic as she drove back to the office. By the time she arrived, everyone was gone, thank goodness. The blessed quiet was a balm to her soul at the moment.

Sebastian had left her a stack of phone messages with notes on how he had handled some of them. She went over the papers waiting for her approval and signature, then with great care, as though she'd only recently learned how to ambulate, she left the office and drove home.

Laura owned a small home in the western hills of Austin. She'd used the inheritance she'd received when her mother passed away to buy the place. Her father had died while serving in the military when Laura was a child. She'd been raised by her mother, grateful that she'd shared a wonderful relationship with her only relative.

Losing her mother had been very difficult, not only because they had been so close, but also because she had no other relatives. If only her mother were here now. She felt so alone at a time when she desperately needed to talk to someone. There were no sisters or brothers to call with this stunning news, no cousins or aunts and uncles who might be willing to sit down with her and look at her options. She'd never known either set of grandparents.

Her profession had become her life, in part to replace the void that a lack of family made in her life. She had friends, of course. However, the fact that each of them was as busy as she meant that they didn't actually get together often enough to establish the kind of closeness she needed now.

Laura pulled into the attached garage and went into the kitchen, where the two stray cats she'd adopted not long after she moved into the house greeted her.

Vagabond, an orange and white tomcat with a belligerent attitude, had showed up on her doorstep within weeks after she'd moved in. He'd been battered and starved and she couldn't resist feeding him. Even now, he made certain she paid attention to him as soon as she walked into the house.

Shadow, a dark gray tabby, had arrived a couple of years later, looking extremely thin and hungry. Now plump and sassy, she sat beside her nearly empty food bowl with a pained expression on her face as though she'd been left to starve once again, despite the fact that she hadn't missed a meal since she'd joined Laura's household.

Laura had known as soon as she'd paid to have each cat neutered that she was a sucker for waifs and kept her fingers crossed that no other homeless animal made its way to her door.

"Hi guys," she muttered, closing the door to the garage and leaning weakly against it. "Boy, do I have some news for you!"

Neither one looked particularly impressed by her announcement. She poured fresh food into their bowls, replenished their water supply and went to her bedroom. She sank down on the side of the bed and stared into the mirror above her vanity dresser.

The same woman who'd last peered at her in the mirror just that morning stared back at her. She was surprised that there was no obvious change in her appearance. At the very least, she would have expected her shoulder-length, light brown hair to have turned a shocking white in the past hour or so.

She looked pale, her gray-green eyes the only color in her face.

Laura placed her hand on her stomach and wondered what her baby would look like.

And for the first time since she'd been given the news, Laura finally allowed herself to think about her baby's father.

Chapter 2

Robert Whitfield Langston had been a Big Man on Campus at the University of Texas when Laura had been a freshman. A star quarterback and all-round athlete, Rob Langston had caused many a feminine heart to flutter whenever he appeared.

The young Laura had been shy around men. She'd been more comfortable keeping up her grades than she had improving her social life.

But she had certainly noticed Rob. He'd been outgoing and gave amusing interviews on television after the Longhorn football games. Although she seldom went to the games, she always watched to see if the reporters would seek him out. His grin made her knees weak and she immediately recognized the sound of his mellow baritone voice whenever she heard it.

Although it was his senior year, Rob happened to be in one of Laura's classes the last semester of her freshman year. In a large lecture class there was no reason to think he even knew she was there. She used to make sure she was already seated in one of the corners before he came in. She didn't want to give him any reason to think she wanted to sit beside him or converse with him.

Laura was content to notice him from afar.

Once Rob graduated, Laura heard nothing more about him. By the middle of her junior year she was seeing a classmate and studying hard to keep her grade average up.

So it was a shock, years later, to spot Rob Langston as part of the White House detail of the Secret Service while she worked in the official White House war-on-drugs office. It was an even greater shock when he walked over to her and said, "Didn't you used to go to the University of Texas?"

Laura felt as though one of her movie idols had suddenly stepped off the silver screen and singled her out.

She was standing with a co-worker at the time, ready to go to lunch. Forcing herself to take a calming breath before replying, Laura smiled and simply said, "Yes."

"Laura Abbott, isn't it? We had a couple of classes together, as I recall."

She wanted to correct him about the number, but was afraid she'd give away how aware of him she'd been back then.

"And you're Rob Langston," she replied.

He grinned. "Wow, I didn't think you'd remember me. I recall that you made the best grades in class. So what are you doing here these days?"

"The same thing as you, it appears, working for the government. How long have you been with the Secret Service?"

"About six years." He glanced at his watch. "I've got to go but I'd like to visit with you some more. Would it be too presumptuous to ask for your home phone number?"

Presumptuous, no. Shocking, yes.

However, she managed to give it to him with what she hoped was dignity before going off to lunch with Fran Siebell.

"My gosh, who was that guy!" Fran asked once they were at the restaurant. "He looked as though he was ready to devour you for lunch!"

Laura grinned at the exaggeration, although he *had* appeared to be pleased to see her. "An old schoolmate."

"So I gathered. He made it clear he was definitely interested in renewing an old friendship."

"There was no friendship. We were classmates. That's all."

"He obviously wants to change that," Fran said. "Lucky you."

Rather than argue with her, Laura changed the subject. As it turned out, Fran had been right. Rob made it clear when he called her that night that he wanted to get to know her better. He teased her with the idea that they were two Texans wandering lost in the maze of Washington politics and needed to bolster the other by keeping up some hallowed Texas traditions while away from their homeland.

His teasing had reminded her of how drawn she'd always been to his lighthearted personality. That, together with the new maturity she could see in him, made him a lethal threat to her already vulnerable heart.

In the following months Laura had to keep pinching herself to be certain she wasn't dreaming. She was actually dating Big Man on Campus Rob Langston...who seemed to enjoy her company, laughed at her pathetic jokes, and made her feel she was everything he could possibly want in his life.

Until the day he informed her that he was being reassigned to an overseas office to work undercover.

He'd never promised her a future; he'd never told her he wanted her to be a permanent part of his life. Instead, he told her how much he would miss her and how he wanted to stay in touch.

Right.

And she was Miss Piggy.

He didn't break her heart, of course. She spent months reminding herself of that fact. She was happy with the way her career was going. She had everything she could possibly want in her life.

The news of her mother's illness came not long before the change of administration in Washington. So Laura had returned to Austin and had slowly put Rob Langston out of her mind.

Until three months ago.

She'd been in Washington for a national conference of county managers. After a full day of meetings, she'd returned to her room, exhausted. When the phone rang she contemplated ignoring it, but the thought made her feel guilty and she answered.

"Hello."

"Hello, Laura."

Her breath caught. Here was a voice from her past, one she hadn't expected to hear.

"Rob?"

He chuckled, the husky sound that had always made her blood race. "I wasn't sure you'd remember me."

"How did you find me? Where are you? I thought you were working overseas."

"Well, I—uh—saw in the paper that county managers were meeting this week. I heard that was what you were doing these days and thought I'd take a chance on your attendance. Of course, if you'd married, I wouldn't have known your last name, so when I discovered you were registered under Abbott I was encouraged to think that you might be available for dinner tonight."

"Tonight? Oh, Rob, I don't think so. I've put in quite a day, not to mention what I had to do at work to clear my schedule enough to come." She was trembling and surprised that her voice sounded so calm.

"Oh. Well, it was a thought," he said slowly, his disappointment obvious.

Her refusal had been a knee-jerk reaction. She knew what kind of effect this man had on her; knew it would only stir up feelings that she had fought long and hard to bury.

"You asked about my assignment," he said after a moment of silence. "I came back to Washington about six months ago. I found out you'd left the city. In my spare time, I did a little checking to find out where you were. Quite frankly, I'm impressed with your newest job. You're doing well these days."

"It's hectic but I've enjoyed it."

"What made you go back to Texas?"

There were so many answers to that, some that would make her much too vulnerable to this man.

"My mother was diagnosed with cancer about the time of the change in administration, so it was an easy choice for me to return home to be with her."

"I'm sorry to hear about that. How is she doing?"

Her throat clogged for a moment. "I lost her a year ago."

"Oh, Laura, that's really tough. I lost my dad about three years ago now."

"Was it cancer?"

"No, it was his heart. None of us had any warning. He and Mom had been out on the ranch when he started complaining of chest pains. She managed to get him to the hospital, and they notified me as well as my two brothers. Unfortunately, I didn't make it home in time to see him. By the time word reached me, it was too late. I flew home for the funeral."

"It's tough, losing a parent."

He sighed. "Yeah. It certainly makes you stop and think about your priorities. I kept thinking about why I hadn't spent more time with him during his last few years. I guess I felt I had all the time in the world to make my mark in my profession before taking time out to visit. You were lucky to have some kind of warning."

"Yes. She did really well for a few years and we were hopeful that the medication she was on would keep her in remission. I've never been sorry I was there for her."

She would never have expected to have this kind of a conversation with the Rob she remembered. He sounded different, more subdued. Laura knew that she was being a coward by avoiding him.

On impulse, she said, "We finish up Friday afternoon but I'm not flying home until Saturday morning. If you happen to be available that evening, I'd be happy to meet you for dinner."

"That's great!" he replied. She could hear the smile in his voice. "I'll pick you up at the hotel around seven. I'm looking forward to seeing you again, Laura. I've really missed our friendship, you know? I tried to call you when I found out about my dad, but you'd already left D.C. and I had no idea where you had gone. That's when I realized how sorry I was that I'd neglected to keep in touch with you. It was my loss."

"Then I'll see you Friday evening, Rob. I'm looking forward to it."

* * *

They had gone out that night. Their hours of conversing and catching up had flown by. She'd ended up spending the night at his apartment, then catching a cab early the next morning to the hotel where she'd quickly gathered her belongings and checked out.

Now she was faced with the task of contacting Rob to tell him that their night together, the first night they'd ever spent together, had had unexpected repercussions.

Chapter 3

The phone rang three times before R. W. Langston grabbed it after he let himself into his condominium.

"Langston," he barked into the phone.

"Hello, Robbie."

There was only one person in the world who could call him that and live to draw another breath.

"Hello, Mom," he replied, removing his jacket and tossing it over the back of the kitchen chair. "What's up?"

"I hope I'm not disturbing you."

"Nope. Just got off work."

"Oh? I thought you had the late shift."

"I was assigned a new detail this week, so I'll be on days until further notice."

His mother sighed. "I know it must be exciting

for you to be a Secret Service agent, but I worry about you. It's such a dangerous business.''

Not that again, he thought, sitting down at the kitchen bar. "Mom, after all these years, you should be adjusted to the fact that I work for the Treasury Department," he said patiently. "Actually, my job is very boring," he added, conveniently ignoring his undercover work overseas. "The problem is, you've watched too many movies about my job. Believe me, it's nothing like the movies.''

"Well, I wanted to call to thank you for the beautiful bouquet of roses. They arrived Saturday afternoon.''

"You're welcome. I hope you had a good Mother's Day yesterday.''

She sighed. "Well, of course it was quite nice. Clu and Gabe spent the day here at the ranch with me. I really missed having you here.''

He stifled his sigh. Of course his two brothers had been there with her. Clu lived with her, for Pete's sake, and Gabe was barely thirty-five miles away in Austin.

"I wish you could have been here," she added, wistfully.

"I know, Mom. I'm sorry I missed it. I've already explained that I couldn't get the time off.''

"Everything is just so different now. I know I should be used to being without your dad. I'm sorry to keep bringing it up.''

Rob massaged his brow, feeling the headache that he'd had since he woke up that morning pick up its beat. He knew how hard being without her mate was for his mother, even after three years. She and his dad had been so close. His loss had been devastating to the whole family.

Robert Langston had been much too young to die.

Rob, being the oldest, continued to struggle with the pain of not being there when his father had needed him. Even though his dad had encouraged him to follow his dream of going into law enforcement and had been proud of his acceptance into the Treasury Department, Rob had known that his father had hoped he would want to stay in Texas and work the ranch.

Rob's guilt continued to eat at him.

"I know, Mom," he said into the phone. "We all miss him."

"I told your brothers yesterday—and I want you to know—that I made a new will a few months ago. I've split everything equally between the three of you."

"Mom, you don't need to be concerned about all of that. You've got years ahead of you and—"

"That's what we thought about your father, Robbie. Now look where we are."

"At least he left his affairs in order, Mom. You don't have to worry about the future. He provided for you."

"Yes, but now I have to see that the three of you get your share once I'm gone." She paused as though waiting for him to comment, but he could think of nothing else to say. "I do have a problem, though," she finally added.

"What's that?" he asked, running his hand through his thick hair. He was beat. He wished this conversation could have been postponed a couple of hours so he would have had enough time to eat something, maybe drink a couple of beers and relax.

"You know how your dad always loved Zafir, ever since he brought him to the ranch."

Another pain shot through his chest. He knew quite well what that horse had meant to his dad. His father had rescued the white Arabian from wedding carriage duty on the streets of Houston several years before he died. The horse was a particular favorite of all the family members.

"I know," he managed to say gruffly.

"Well, it's obvious that I can't divide a horse three ways."

Her frustrated tone made him smile. "He has a home on the ranch. If Clu's going to keep the ranch, then it only makes sense to—"

"I'm not sure Clu wants the ranch."

"Well, I certainly can't do anything with it, not from here, and Gabe's got enough on his plate without dealing with anything else."

"In other words, nobody wants anything that I have to leave you, is that it?"

"No! Of course not. It's just that you're worrying about something that isn't a problem. Clu is there with you, looking after you and—"

"Clu has his own job and his own life. I doubt

that he'll want to settle here permanently. Frankly, I'm not sure why he's stayed on here. I've tried to tell him that I'm fine on my own.''

But she wasn't. He, Gabe and Clu had discussed the matter. Their parents had married early in life and had been constant companions. All three of them knew she was lost without him. Clu had agreed to stay for as long as necessary, but it was true. He had his own life to live and their mother didn't seem to be adjusting very well to her loss.

Rob wondered if Clu was getting restless with the arrangement. He'd need to call and discuss it with him some time when Mom wasn't within earshot.

His mother continued. ''Besides, what I want has nothing to do with the land and other property your father left me. All I've ever wanted, as you very well know, are granddaughters. I told you boys all the time you were growing up that since I didn't have any daughters, the very least you could do for me is to provide me with granddaughters.''

Her teasing tone made him smile. ''As a matter of fact, Mom, I do believe you may have mentioned that a time or two—thousand.''

''So what I told your brothers yesterday was that I'm tired of waiting,'' she said, sounding more serious. ''All of you are in your thirties now. In fact, Robbie, you're staring at forty in a couple of years. You've had plenty of time to pick a mate and settle down.''

He suddenly thought of Laura. ''You're right, Mom. You always are. The problem is, no woman will have me. It's probably all your fault. You spoiled me for any other woman."

"Hogwash."

"The truth is, I don't have a job that is conducive to putting down roots, Mom. We've discussed that." He lightened his tone. "Besides, what makes you think any of us would produce girls, anyway?"

His mother laughed. "Well, you know the old saying—if at first you don't succeed..."

"I'm afraid I can't help you with this one. Talk to Clu and Gabe. I'm sure they could help you out."

She sighed. "I guess that lets you out of the competition, then."

"What competition?" he asked suspiciously.

"I told Gabe and Clu yesterday that the first one of you boys who gives me a granddaughter can have the horse. Zafir will be perfect to take a little girl for a ride in the buggy around the ranch."

"You can't be serious."

"I'm extremely serious."

He laughed. "Well, tell them both I wish them good luck."

"So when do you expect to come see us?"

"I don't know, Mom. I'll look at my schedule and see what I can work out."

"I miss you, Robbie."

"I miss you, too, Mom. You take care now. I love you," he said, hanging up.

He wondered what Gabe and Clu thought about this latest harebrained idea their mother had come up with. She'd been harping about wanting grandchildren since he turned thirty, eight years ago now. He couldn't help but wonder if his mother honestly thought that any of them would decide to produce a child in order to inherit a horse?

He was afraid his mother was losing it.

He went into his bedroom and changed into sweatpants, then scrounged around his kitchen for something to eat. After making himself a sandwich, Rob opened a bottle of beer and headed for the couch in front of the television.

He didn't know why he was letting his mother's phone call bother him. Bless her heart, she wasn't asking for much, really. She just wanted to see the family continuing. She wanted her legacy to be passed on and none of them were being cooperative.

Rob had only met one woman that he could ever have considered sharing his future.

Laura Abbott.

He still remembered how she'd looked as a young girl at college. She had a quiet serenity about her that immediately drew him to her. Of course she probably didn't even remember him back then, although she had recalled his name when they met years later.

There was something about her eyes, her smile, the way she walked, the way she had of glancing at him as though she wasn't certain what he might say next. She'd always had an air of self-sufficiency about her, with a hint of mystery thrown in.

He'd found himself being careful around her, as though she were an unbroken colt that needed tender handling and a lot of patience. The problem had been that both of them had demanding jobs and their schedules seldom meshed.

It had taken real effort to be able to see her once or twice a week. And then he'd gotten reassigned and that blew any attempt he might have made to push the relationship to a more intimate level.

Until three months ago.

Man, oh man, he'd really blown it then. He'd spent months tracing her movements after she left Washington. Then, when he finally found out where she lived and worked, he didn't have the guts to call her and chat. He'd made sure to find out that she was single and not seriously dating anyone. In fact, he'd picked up the phone a half-dozen times but couldn't finish the number sequence before he chickened out.

Until three months ago.

He'd gathered his courage and called her while she was in Washington, then got turned down for dinner. That should have been that. But somehow, as they continued to talk, she finally agreed to see him on her last night in town.

And he'd blown it big time. He'd come on too strong. He'd pushed her to talk about how she felt about him, and whether she thought there was a chance for them to work on a relationship.

She'd turned him down, pointing out their different lifestyles, pointing out how long-distance relationships never worked. How she was content with her life.

However, he certainly had managed to make one point clear—to both of them.

She found him physically attractive. When he'd brought her back to the condo for a nightcap before returning her to the hotel, he'd had no intention of seducing her. He wasn't a masochist, after all. If the woman wasn't interested in him, there was no reason to torture himself with new memories of her.

Intimate memories...of kissing her until he thought he was going to explode; of having her respond to him in a way she never had before; of caressing her, of seeing her come apart in his arms.

Her responsiveness was his undoing. They'd gone into the bedroom, stripped off their clothes, and spent hours exploring each other, loving each other, until he thought he might expire of the pleasure.

They'd fallen asleep, both of them exhausted. He'd had some idea of opening up the possibility of a future with her once again the next morning.

But when he awoke, she was gone.

For the first several weeks after she'd been there, he'd call her, but would only get her answering machine. If she was there, she refused to answer. And she wouldn't return any of his calls.

Finally, he had given up. She'd made her views of marriage in general and him in particular quite plain. It must have been his ego that thought he could convince her of a future relationship by sharing the hottest lovemaking he'd ever experienced with anyone.

Laura Abbott.

The one who got away.

The only woman he could ever love.

The phone rang, jarring him out of his morose mood.

Who would be calling him at this time of night? He reached over and grabbed the receiver.

"Langston," he muttered.

"Rob?" Laura replied, her voice sounding odd. "We need to talk."

Chapter 4

Friday evening

Laura paced before Gate 16 at the new Austin-Bergstrom International Airport, wondering how in less than a week her life had suddenly gone from a calm, orderly routine from which she drew comfort in its predictability to being totally out of her control.

Absently she rubbed her abdomen, acutely aware of the tiny being that was even now taking over her life. In the past four days she had done her best to go on with her established routine.

She'd gone to work each day and dealt with the usual crises that were part of the job. When Sebastian asked how she was feeling, she lied and told

him she was much better. She'd had a long meeting
with Judge Hernandez on Wednesday and had come
away feeling that they had managed to deal with
some potentially flammable issues without resorting
to name-calling or body blows.

Although she had always admired the man's in-
telligence and ability to quickly grasp the nature of
most situations, she had often been repelled by his
brusque, less-than-cordial manner with her and others. He did not suffer fools for more than a few
minutes before ripping their theories and attitudes to
shreds. There had been times when she'd had to go
toe to toe verbally with him to convince him that
what she proposed should at least be considered.

He'd listened to her this week, asking incisive
questions and suggesting ways to incorporate her
points in a touchy political situation. The exchange
had made her feel he considered her to be an important part of the problem-solving process for the
county.

By this morning she felt as though she'd faced
some major professional hurdles and safely sailed
across them. However, it had only taken one phone
call that afternoon to jar her out of her comfortable
space of denial about her personal situation.

Sebastian had signaled her on the intercom. When
she picked up, he said, ''Rob Langston on line
two.''

She was amazed how a few short words could
send her into an emotional tailspin. She reached for
the phone as though it might explode if jostled.

"This is Laura," she managed to say, a suddenly dry mouth causing her to swallow hard and reach for her glass of water.

"Sorry to bother you at work," he said briskly, "but I only have a few minutes before we start boarding."

"Boarding?" she repeated, wondering what he was talking about.

"My flight arrives in Austin a little before eight. I was hoping you'd be able to pick me up. If you can't, then I'll rent a car."

"You're coming to Austin? Today?"

She heard a short sigh before he repeated, "Can you pick me up?"

"Oh! Well, of course, if you really think that—"

"Good," he said, cutting her off. "I'll see you soon."

She was left holding the phone to her ear.

This was not what she had planned. Not at all. When she'd called him Monday night, she had made it clear that she in no way wanted him to feel that she expected anything of him. However, her own sense of integrity had mandated that she inform him of the unexpected news she'd received as soon as possible.

She had braced herself for various reactions he might have to the news. He could emphatically deny that he could be the man responsible. He could demand that she get another opinion—or two, maybe three.

He had done none of those things. He had listened

as she carefully explained why it had taken three months for her to discover that she was pregnant. His only question during that part of the conversation concerned her health.

Then she carefully followed the list of particulars she'd jotted down before the phone call, hitting each point that she wanted to make—that she was healthy, that she could support herself without financial help, that if he wished to be kept informed, she would notify him when the baby was born.

After she finally ran out of steam, she waited for his response. And waited. Finally, he replied in a quiet voice, "I appreciate your letting me know, Laura. I can certainly understand how the news could catch you unprepared. We'll deal with all of this just fine. Don't worry about anything, okay?"

Since she'd just finished giving the most impassioned speech in her entire career clearly stating how she would not need his help in any of this, she was a little disconcerted with his admonishment not to worry. Hadn't she just told him she had everything under control?

They'd hung up a short time later and Laura had gone to bed at the end of that momentous Monday feeling that she could efficiently face the coming months with equanimity. She would read up on pregnancies and newborns and integrate the knowledge into her life. There was no reason to think that a baby would make that big a difference, really.

She'd sat staring at her phone for several minutes after he'd hung up. Obviously Rob had not come to the same conclusion after his assessment of the situation. Why else would he be coming to Austin at this particular time? If he was coming back for a family visit, why call her?

She was pulled out of her introspection by the sight of the large silver plane pulling up to the jetway.

Her heart started pounding. He was here. Oh, dear. She wasn't ready to face him. Ever, but especially not now.

She stopped pacing, stopped twisting the ring she wore, a gift from her mother when she'd graduated from college, and waited.

Laura spotted him while he was still in the jetway, his tall figure a head above most of the people disembarking. She always forgot just how good-looking he was—a defense mechanism she put in place, no doubt, once she was away from him. This time the idea suddenly hit her that her baby could very well look like this man. And probably would.

She could feel her cheeks grow hot just as he saw her standing there. The blush was in no way precipitated by his sudden grin and wave when he recognized her, she assured herself.

Laura held out her hand, prepared to greet him with her usual reserve, but he didn't seem to notice when he reached her because he dropped his carry-on bag and threw his arms around her, hugging her close to him.

"You look wonderful, Laura! Impending motherhood definitely agrees with you," he announced to everyone within listening distance. Then, to utterly compound her embarrassment, he kissed her in full view of all the inhabitants currently in the airport.

As usual, his kiss turned her knees to jelly, which was the only reason she clutched his shoulders in a death grip.

When he finally pulled away slightly, she was breathless and flustered beyond belief. "You're absolutely glowing, do you know that?" he asked, grabbing his bag once again and draping his arm over her shoulder. Only then did he take in the area around them. "So this is the new airport. What an improvement over the old one. So, where's the luggage claim area?"

Laura knew that she was going to have to get a grip on her reactions to him or sound like a blithering idiot at a time when she wanted to maintain her dignity at all costs. So she limited her response to, "Downstairs," and nodded in the direction of the escalators.

He didn't remove his arm from her shoulders. Instead, he matched his stride to hers as he continued to look around the airport, taking in the food stands that represented some of the most popular restaurants in Austin.

"This is really something. I'm impressed."

When they reached the escalators he allowed her to step ahead of him on the moving stairs, resting his hand in the small of her back as though he had a real need to keep some physical contact between them.

Once at the baggage carousel Laura racked her brain for something to say other than the inane comments about his flight and if he'd eaten, if he was tired or where he wanted to be dropped off. Instead, she concentrated on the need to breathe. She had the most annoying habit of holding her breath whenever Rob was anywhere in the vicinity.

A very annoying habit. No wonder she always seemed to feel lightheaded around him.

Eventually, he removed two large pieces of luggage, attached his carry-on to the handle of one of them, then said, "Lead the way, honey. Where did you park?"

Honey. He'd called her honey. She almost smiled at how natural it sounded rolling off his lips. "I'm just across the street in the garage. It isn't far."

When he saw her two-seater convertible he burst out laughing. "This is yours? I would never have guessed."

She wasn't sure why he laughed. Was he making fun of her? "It has much more luggage space than you'd guess." She popped open the trunk and watched as he efficiently stowed his bags. "And there's quite a lot of leg space as well," she added when they both slid into the contoured leather seats. "What sort of car did you think I'd drive?"

He grinned. "Oh, I don't know. Something conservative, perhaps. This is the kind of car *I'd* like to own if I wasn't afraid of leaving it parked in a garage for long stretches.'' He patted the dash. ''She's a beauty.''

Feeling inordinately pleased by his comments, Laura backed out of the parking space and headed toward the exit.

''I hope you don't mind stopping somewhere for something to eat before we head to your place, do you? I skipped a couple of meals today but even with that, couldn't force myself to eat the airline offerings.''

Her foot probably came down on the brake a little harder than necessary as she slowed at the toll both. He was planning to go to her place?

Oh, my.

''Do you have a preference of food?'' she asked.

''Not at all. Surprise me.''

''Then I'll take you to my favorite—Marie Callender's. The pies there are absolutely sinful and totally irresistible.''

He laughed. ''That's the most enthusiasm I've heard from you in a while.''

She blushed. ''I should have known something was different when my appetite picked up this spring,'' she ruefully explained.

Later, Laura waited until they were seated in a cozy booth and had given their order to the attentive waiter before she said, ''I apologize if I sound a bit dense, Rob, but I don't understand why you're here.''

He had settled back into the comfortable bench seat looking utterly relaxed, but at her words he slowly straightened and leaned forward, his gaze never leaving hers.

He studied her as though he intended to produce a drawing of her—or describe her to a sketch artist—before he responded.

His explanation took her breath away.

Again.

"Like you, I have spent this week thinking about the baby and how it will impact on our lives. I've never seen myself as having a family, being a father or a husband, but the fact is, I'm now going to be a father, ready or not." She started to speak and he held up his hand. "Please. Let me get all of this out and then we can discuss it, okay?"

She was reminded of how quietly he had listened to her on the phone earlier in the week. She certainly owed him the same respect.

She nodded her acquiescence.

"After giving the matter considerable thought, I put in for an emergency family leave, which was granted, as you can see. We owe it to ourselves and the baby to sit down together and discuss the matter and to decide what we need to do in the best interests of the baby."

He paused as though expecting her to argue, but she couldn't. What he was saying made a great deal of sense. She prided herself on being reasonable as well as logical. Her training came into practical use, even though what they were discussing was an emotionally volatile situation.

She could handle this. She would just take it one step at a time.

Their food arrived and they ate in silence. Because her job meant hours of conversation every day, Laura appreciated her evenings where she had no reason to talk with anyone—unless it was Vagabond and Shadow.

Now she waited, trying to think through some of the options and decisions she'd made this week about the baby. Since none of them had included Rob, she was at a loss to think what he might have in mind.

It wasn't as though she was a thoughtless teenager who had suddenly found herself in a family way. She certainly didn't expect him to rescue her from the situation. So if that was what he had in mind, she would have to disabuse him of the notion.

However, he'd said something that had caught her off guard. They needed to consider what was best for the child. Didn't he think she would make her decisions with that in mind?

Rob waited until they were enjoying pie and coffee before he said, "I was hoping you'd let me stay at your place tonight and go with me to the ranch tomorrow. Mom knows I'm coming, but not why."

"I'm not certain that I understand that, myself."

He nodded. "You're right. I'm getting ahead of myself." He shook his head and chuckled. "I can't remember a time when I was as nervous as I am at this moment."

"About what?" she asked, bewildered by his manner.

"Our conversation. You made it quite clear when you called that you didn't expect anything from me with regard to the baby...."

She nodded.

"So what I'm trying to do is to get you to look at the situation from an entirely different perspective."

His intent gaze was making her even more nervous than she already was. "All right," she said slowly. "And what perspective might that be?"

"That we get married as soon as possible."

Chapter 5

A strong bout of lightheadedness swept over Laura before she remembered to breathe. She took several slow, deep breaths without saying a word. All she could do was stare at him with a sense of panic.

From the expression on his face, Rob didn't appear to be encouraged by her silence.

He reached over and placed his warm palm over her icy fingers. When she didn't pull away he cupped her hand between his and gently massaged it.

"I guess my suggestion comes as a shock to you."

She continued to stare at him wordlessly.

He cleared his throat. "I truly believe this is the sensible thing to do and I believe that, once you get used to the idea, you'll agree it's the best thing we can offer our child—my name and my protection."

The warmth of his hands seemed to slowly seep through her body. She couldn't understand why she felt as though she were on the verge of bursting into sobs. What in the world was wrong with her? The doctor had mentioned that her hormones were all working overtime. Was that why she suddenly felt so vulnerable? Or was it being with Rob, hearing him suggest they marry, that had caused this reaction?

After another long silence, he said, "I'll be here a month. I thought if we got married right away, that would give us a few weeks to get to know each other better. Of course if you have a roommate, that might make things a little awkward...." He paused, his endearing lopsided smile flashing for a moment.

"I have two roommates, actually," she said, "both felines."

"Ah," he said, "well, hopefully they'll tolerate me. Where do you live?"

"I have a small home west of Austin."

"If you agree to the marriage, I'm sure you can see that the sooner it's done, the better. I thought we might talk to Mom tomorrow and see if we could have the wedding at the ranch, give us a little privacy that way, and have our families there."

She shook her head. "I have no family."

"Oh. Well, those are things we need to know about each other, don't you think? We're going to be in each other's lives from now on. I want to give our child the most stable start to its life that's possible. Having two parents is a good first step.''

"I don't see how this can possibly work, Rob," she said after another long pause. "You have your life in Washington. Mine is here in Texas. I don't think I can just give up my career in order to—''

"That's not what I'm asking you to do. Not at all. Mom has been trying to get me to move back to Texas for years. Maybe now is the time I can look into that. As I said, we can take it one step at a time. We have six months before the baby arrives. That should give us plenty of time to decide what we need to do about our careers.''

She looked down at his large, tanned hands that had finally coaxed some warmth into hers. "I never considered the possibility of marriage.''

"Yes. I had already figured that out, which is why I decided I needed to come here and discuss it with you in person. It's much too important a decision to make over the phone. To be frank, I needed to be here, to touch you, to reassure you that I know we can make this work. I'm aware that you're prepared to do it on your own. I'm just saying that there's no reason for you to face this situation alone. From everything I know—and I'll admit it isn't much—as you progress in your pregnancy you're going to need more rest, somebody to be there for you, to give you a back rub, maybe, or massage your feet.''

She felt as though she was drowning in his gaze.

He made it all sound so reasonable.

He was right. She had only been looking at the situation from her perspective. He was going to be as much a parent as she was. Just as she had felt it necessary to notify him immediately after she learned about the baby, she now knew that his perspective—as well as the welfare of their child— must be considered.

He glanced at his watch. "Look, you don't have to make a decision right now. Maybe a good night's rest will help you get used to the idea. I'm hoping you'll let me stay at your place tonight, or is that too presumptuous of me?"

She didn't know what she thought.

About anything.

What Laura realized with sudden clarity was that her life was no longer her own. She had to give up thinking that she had the right to make any and all decisions that pertained to her.

It was that thought that scared her spitless.

"I don't mind if you stay with me. The thing is, I would rather not—I mean, if it's all right with you, I'd prefer..." She stopped, feeling a little foolish about requesting that he stay in the guest bedroom, particularly after the last night they'd spent together. It was a little late for her to become so decorous.

He squeezed her hand slightly. "I understand. It was out of character for both of us to behave the way we did. I probably owe you an apology for losing control like that, but I can't in all honesty tell you that I'm sorry for making love to you, Laura. It was an unforgettable night. What I *am* sorry about is that it has put you in this position."

"It wasn't your fault," she replied. "You used protection. There was no reason to believe that I— that anything could..." She ran out of words once again. Oh, this was just great. She'd never before had as much trouble articulating her thoughts as she was having tonight.

"One step at a time, remember? We've accepted the situation as it is. No one is trying to attach blame here. We're responsible adults. We'll continue to be responsible. It's my hope that after you give it some more thought, maybe sleep on it, the idea of marriage won't seem such a terrible life sentence to you."

He said the last with a grin and a lilt to his voice that made her smile. Rob Langston really was a good man. A considerate man. He would probably make an excellent parent...much better than she probably would.

She couldn't think of anything that made more sense than to follow his suggestion. But he was right. She wanted to sleep on the idea first.

It was almost eleven when they reached her home. Laura was exhausted.

Rob retrieved his luggage and followed her into the house where they were greeted by two really irritated cats. She had not followed their routine and they were letting her know about it with a great deal of vocal animation.

"Let me show you the other bedroom," she said

over her shoulder, leading him out of the kitchen and into the hall. "Then I'll take care of my critical cats."

"They certainly look healthy enough. Neither one look as if missing a meal would hurt them."

"It isn't that. They're used to curling up with me in the evenings while I either read or watch television. I've upset their routine by coming home so late."

Rob laughed.

She opened the door to the bedroom and stepped aside. "There's a bathroom through there," she said, nodding to a door across the room. "I believe it has everything you need. What time would you like to get up in the morning?"

"No particular time. Why don't you sleep in if you can?"

"Fine. I'll see you tomorrow."

She turned and walked away, hoping he didn't see how she was trembling, hoping he couldn't feel the tension she was experiencing as they both stood in the small room with a bed as its prominent feature.

How was she going to make any of this work?

She knew nothing about being a wife. She knew very little about men in general or Rob in particular.

All she knew was that the safe little world she had created for herself had disappeared. She now stood on the edge of the abyss of an unknowable future. Tomorrow she would be stepping off into the void with no idea where she might land.

* * *

Rob quickly showered, then crawled into bed. By the time he'd come out of the bathroom, he could hear no sound in the house, so Laura must have placated her fussy felines and gone to bed. He'd felt guilty keeping her up late when she looked ready to collapse. The smudges beneath her eyes told him that she hadn't been getting enough rest and it was early days into her pregnancy.

He stretched out on his back with his hands behind his head and stared at the ceiling, reviewing their first meeting.

At least she hadn't immediately dismissed his suggestion. That had been one of his many fears about this negotiation.

He certainly couldn't call it a courtship.

He smiled at the thought. During the few months they had dated four years ago he'd quickly realized that if he had given her any hint about his burgeoning attraction to her she would have run as far and as fast as possible. He wasn't certain why she was so insistent that marriage and a career couldn't mix, but he had accepted the fact that she was really sold on that line of reasoning.

So he'd gone along with her back then. Agreed with her. Convinced her that they could enjoy each other's company without complicating the relationship. Meanwhile he had continued to hope that eventually she would see that they could make a great life together if she'd only let him get closer to her.

It hadn't worked out then, thanks to his reassignment, but he was now being given a second chance and he intended to take full advantage of the situation.

Some way, somehow in the next few weeks he was going to find a way to convince Ms. Laura Abbott that this pregnancy was the greatest gift either of them had ever received...a chance to become a family and plan their future together.

But first, he had to find out the reason behind her resistance to the idea. Maybe he had too good an opinion of himself, but he didn't think she had anything against him personally. That night they had made love had given him the necessary encouragement to actively pursue her, which was why he'd been puzzled and—all right, he'd admit it—hurt by the fact she wouldn't return his calls.

His last thought before falling asleep was how grateful he was that she had called him about the pregnancy.

Shadow woke Laura the next morning by patiently patting Laura's nose with her soft paw. When Laura finally opened her eyes, Shadow greeted her with a quiet meow. Laura closed her eyes and stretched, wondering if she had time to roll over and go back to sleep. It was Saturday, after all. No reason to jump out of bed.

When she looked at the time, she was surprised to see that it was almost ten o'clock. Shadow rarely let her sleep that long before becoming her furry alarm clock. Laura scratched Shadow behind her ear, her eyes drifting shut.

That's when she recognized a hint of coffee and the delicious aroma of frying bacon wafting through her room. She sat up, pushing her hair out of her face with a sense of panic. What in the world—!

Rob.

Rob Langston had arrived last night and was there at the house.

How could she have forgotten something as momentous as that?

Laura tossed back the covers and sat up, her feet sliding to the floor. How could she have forgotten? She must have been much more tired than she realized to have lost that particular memory during the night.

How long had he been up? Probably hours while she'd slept through a large part of the morning. Oh dear. What a way to start their relationship.

She hurried into her bathroom and quickly showered, thinking about his presence there and what it meant. She knew that the honorable thing to do would be to marry him. She was lucky to have a man in her life who *wanted* to accept responsibility and was willing to make a commitment to her and their child.

What was wrong with her, anyway? She should have quickly agreed to his plan last night before he changed his mind!

The problem was that agreeing to marry him and actually being married to him seemed—in her mind, at least—poles apart.

She had seen what the loss of her father had done

to her mother. Her mother had suffered tremendously and had never been the same after she'd lost her husband. Watching her mother's anguish from her seven-year-old viewpoint had made an indelible impression on Laura.

It taught her not to rely on anyone but herself because otherwise there would be more pain than she would ever want to face if she were to lose a loved one. Her mother's suffering later and eventual death confirmed and validated that belief.

A baby changed everything. A baby would make her vulnerable whether she liked it or not. To add a husband to the mix was asking for heartache, particularly since he wasn't in love with her.

She'd tried to convince herself that she wasn't in love with him, either, but she knew better. She would never have made love to him if she hadn't loved him deeply. Other women her age had affairs and thought nothing of it. Wasn't it ironic that the very first time she allowed herself physical intimacy, she would get pregnant?

Not that she intended to ever let Rob know that he'd been the first man she'd been with. Because of the pelvic infection she'd battled at sixteen and the many examinations that she'd gone through, technically she'd no longer been a virgin.

She'd never had any desire to experiment with sex and had never given the matter much thought all those years. The problem had been her loss of control with Rob. She hadn't had the experience necessary to know when to pull back once her emotions had taken over. Instead, she had been eager to pursue what was happening and to find the elusive completion that clawed at her.

He'd been so gentle with her and so very loving...and considerate...and very passionate.

And now he wanted to marry her.

What more could she possibly want? She'd been a coward not to immediately agree with him.

She found a pair of elastic-waist pants and a sleeveless blouse to wear. She'd recently noticed that she grew uncomfortable when there was anything tight-fitting around her waist. That should have been a signal to her that her body was changing, but she'd been blissfully unaware.

By the time she walked into the kitchen, Laura was dressed for the day, including a light application of makeup and her hair pulled away from her face.

She found Rob sitting at the small kitchen table reading the paper and drinking coffee. He wore a pair of faded jeans that hugged his frame in an almost indecent manner, and a blue shirt that brought out the deep blue of his eyes.

And he was barefoot.

He looked completely at home, sitting there in her kitchen, with the ruffled curtains at the window framing him without detracting in any way from his masculinity. Vagabond and Shadow watched him from their perch on the window ledge.

"Good morning," he said with a smile. "Hope you slept well."

She went over and poured herself a cup of coffee.

"Embarrassingly well. I'm sorry I didn't hear you get up."

"I'm not. I did my best to be as quiet as possible. I'm pleased that you were able to catch up on your sleep." He nodded toward the counter. "I have bacon ready. I thought I might make us some eggs and toast to go with it once you were up."

"You don't have to do that, Rob. I can—"

"Please. I'd like to take care of you. I hope you'll indulge me."

She felt uncomfortable with his offer, but decided she had to learn to relax with him, so she nodded and settled back into her chair.

"How do you feel about going out to the ranch after we eat? I didn't tell Mom when I'd be arriving, but let her think it would be some time today."

"Well, I—uh, I suppose I could go if you want me to," she managed to say before ducking her head for another sip of coffee.

"And—did you give my proposal any more thought?" he finally asked, his back to her.

She looked up but couldn't see his face. However, his shoulders looked tense and she realized that he was actually worried about her turning him down. Well, she could disabuse him of that notion right now.

"I agree with you. I think that marriage is a necessary step. I want you to know how much I appreciate that you are looking out for the baby's interests."

He turned and faced her and she saw him struggle

with a grin, then give up and laugh. "Believe me, marrying you isn't going to be a hardship," he finally said. "Oh, Laura, you're something else. Mom is going to love you!" He turned back to the stove, which gave her a brief moment of privacy.

Laura knew she was blushing—at the fact that he laughed at her as well as at the warm look in his eyes. Either he was quite an actor or he really *was* attracted to her.

Her friends had told her often enough over the years that men enjoyed sex for its own sake and that it didn't necessarily mean anything when a man made love to you. So she was trying not to seem naive to him, but somehow she'd still managed to amuse him.

She smiled weakly at him when he returned to the table with two plates piled high with food. Her stomach rumbled and she said, "I guess I was hungrier than I thought. This looks delicious."

"We'll get you fattened up in no time," he said, sitting across from her.

Feeling lighter than she had in months, Laura grinned and said, "I don't think we'll have to worry about that," and they both laughed.

Maybe this would work out all right, she thought. As long as she didn't place any expectations on Rob. The thought of having him around for the next few weeks was less daunting today.

She could adjust. She was certain of it.

Laura felt the tension ease from her neck and shoulders while she made short work of Rob's delicious breakfast.

Chapter 6

Laura insisted that Rob drive them in her car out to the ranch since he knew the way. She used the time to enjoy the scenery and prepare herself for the next step—meeting Rob's family.

Her routine had already been shattered beyond repair. Saturdays were busy doing weekly chores such as cleaning, grocery shopping and washing clothes. None of that mattered today.

Rob was now officially a part of her life. Therefore, meeting his mother and brothers was the logical next step. So why did she wish she were still in bed with the pillow over her head? She should be relaxing and enjoying herself.

She rarely had the chance to just "be." Now was her chance.

"Don't be nervous," Rob said as though he'd been reading her mind. "Mom's going to love you."

"How could you possibly know that, Rob?" she replied with a hint of irritation. "For all you know I'll remind her of a lifelong enemy, or someone she was jealous of when she was in school."

"Wow! Where did *that* come from?" he asked, laughing. "Has anyone ever mentioned to you that you have a vivid imagination?" He took her hand. "It will be fine. I promise."

"It's going to be a shock and you know it. She's never heard of me and now you're presenting me as your fiancée. She's going to have a thousand questions."

"Maybe, but you won't hear any of them. She will be polite and gracious."

"Will your brothers be there?"

"Clu may be since he currently lives there with her. Mom didn't say. Gabe lives in Austin. I don't have any idea what his schedule might be. But you'll meet them soon enough. If not today, then at the wedding."

She covered her face with her hands. She didn't know whether she wanted to laugh, cry or scream. Did all men make things sound so simple?

When they finally reached the ranch, she was pleasantly surprised to see that it wasn't a show place. Instead, it was a working ranch with outbuildings that included barns and storage sheds.

They drove up to the house. A woman stepped onto the porch from the house and stood waiting for them. She was an attractive woman, tall with sandy hair. She wore jeans as though they were a part of her...and she was smiling.

As soon as Rob turned off the engine and opened the door, she bounded off the porch and ran straight into his arms. Laura stepped out of the car and watched as mother and son hugged, laughed, kissed, hugged again. Their obvious joy at seeing each other again caused a lump to form in Laura's throat.

She missed her own mother so much; never more so than now when she needed her wise counsel and understanding.

Rob turned his mother toward Laura when she walked around the car and joined the Langstons. "Mom, I'd like you to meet Laura Abbott," he said, grinning.

Laura could see where Rob got his clear and direct gaze. With a wide smile, Emma Langston quickly assessed the woman who had arrived unannounced with her son and held out her hand. "Welcome to our home, Ms. Abbott. Let's get inside before we all melt in this heat. It's hard to believe it's only May. I think we're breaking all kinds of weather records this week."

Emma led the way into the house. Rob took Laura's hand and gave it a quick squeeze of reassurance.

They stepped inside and Laura discovered they were in a large country-style kitchen with plenty of counterspace and a large round table.

"You have a beautiful place here," Laura said,

looking around the room. It felt like a well-used and well-loved gathering place for a family.

"Why, thank you. I've always enjoyed it." If she noticed that Rob and Laura were holding hands, she ignored it. Instead, she said, "Are you from Washington, too, Ms. Abbott?"

"Please...call me Laura," she replied, then glanced at Rob.

He immediately filled in for her. "Laura lives in Austin, Mom. She and I went to college together, although she's three years younger than me. We met again years later when we both worked in Washington. And the reason that we are here is to let you know that Laura accepted my proposal last night. Since she has no family, we're hoping you'll help us plan a very small wedding."

"A wedding!" Emma Langston's shock was obvious, but she appeared to be delighted with the news...almost disbelieving. "What in the world are you talking about! Why, it was just a few days ago that you convinced me you had no intention of ever getting married!"

"Shhh, Mom, or you'll scare her off," Rob said with a wink. "At the time you and I talked, I never thought I'd convince Laura to marry me. And since I knew there would never be anyone else for me, I figured I'd stay single for the rest of my days."

Nice save, Laura thought, watching Rob wrap his mother around his little finger. If Laura didn't know better, she'd believe his story, as well.

Emma looked at Laura. "You were playing hard

to get, just to break my young-un's heart?'' she asked, her eyes betraying her amusement.

"Not exactly." Once again she looked at Rob for guidance. She hadn't had to tell him that she didn't want everyone to know right away that she was pregnant. It would become obvious soon enough. He seemed to understand her feelings instinctively. For now, she wanted to meet his family without their wondering why the sudden marriage.

Not that they probably wouldn't guess.

"I only have a few weeks leave before I have to go back to D.C.," Rob was saying. "And Laura has a high-powered job in Austin, so we'll have a modern, long-distance relationship for a while. That means that I want to marry her immediately. If not sooner. I want to be able to spend as much of my leave with her as possible." He smiled at Laura with just the right touch of yearning.

Emma shook her head. "You were always in a rush, Robbie, even when you were a child. Never had the patience to wait for anything."

Laura noticed that he actually flinched at the name "Robbie." Now that was interesting to know. He obviously didn't like it, but didn't rebuke his mother for using it.

"Mom, you have no idea how patient I am. I have waited for this woman for years and years. Now that I finally got her to say yes, I don't intend to waste any more time."

"Well, let's sit down so we can talk about your plans. Have y'all eaten?"

Laura held her stomach helplessly and Rob laughed. "We're fine, Mom. I should have warned Laura that you're always offering food to everybody."

"Nothing wrong with that," Emma retorted. "I love to work in the kitchen. Whether it's cooking, roasting or baking, I enjoy it." She went to the refrigerator and pulled out a large pitcher of iced tea. Without asking she filled three glasses with ice and tea before waving them to sit at the table. "How about you, Laura? Do you like to cook?"

"When my mother was alive, I cooked for the two of us on a regular basis, but it's difficult to cook for one. I have no idea how to prepare meals for large gatherings."

Emma looked first at Rob, then at Laura before asking, "How large a wedding are you planning?"

Laura answered, feeling like a coward for allowing Rob to answer his mother's perfectly normal questions. "We'd like something small and informal. I've never been interested in planning a large, intricate affair." The fact that she never had given wedding planning any thought at all didn't need to be mentioned.

"We were thinking about next Saturday," Rob added. "We'll have our license by then."

"Next week! How do you expect to—" Emma paused, then nodded. "We can do that. Clu and Gabe will come, of course. I might invite a few of my friends and of course anyone you would like, Laura." She got up from the table. "I'd better contact Pastor Bryan to see if he can officiate. I'll be right back.''

As soon as she left the room, Rob said, "At least I warned you, didn't I? Mom can jump in and take over any project before you know what hit you.''

Laura smiled. "I'm relieved, actually. If she's willing to plan it, then I'll do what I can to follow directions and show up when I'm needed.''

"As much as I'd like to spend this week at your place, I know Mom would have a fit. I have my luggage in the trunk. I'll get it now while she's on the phone.''

Laura realized that she was disappointed he wouldn't be coming home with her. That was certainly a warning not to allow herself to become accustomed to his presence. She would have to keep a strong vigilance on her emotions. No doubt her highly emotional state was due to the pregnancy. Everything was heightened for her these days—her fears, her reactions and her frustrations.

A few minutes later she heard Rob return behind her and turned her head just as he leaned down to her. He kissed her with a leisurely thoroughness that caught her off guard. When he finally raised his head, she heard his mother walk back into the room and say, "I hope you're planning to stay the night, Laura. We have so much to do between now and next weekend. Oh, and Pastor Bryan said if we could make the wedding around ten o'clock he would be available, but otherwise, next Saturday afternoon and evening are already scheduled.''

Rob sat down next to Laura and took her hand in his. "Morning's fine, don't you think?" he asked.

Laura was still trying to get air to her lungs. Neither Rob nor Emma seemed to think anything of the kiss just now. Perhaps it was normal for an engaged couple, but Laura still felt like a fraud.

He'd probably heard his mother returning and wanted to make her think this was a love match. He'd definitely been giving off those kinds of comments since they arrived.

"Yes, morning will work," she managed to say. "I can't stay overnight, though. I'm sorry. I need to get back to my cats."

"Oh, that's too bad. Clu won't get home until after eight tonight. I forgot where he said he was going to be today. Gabe tries to visit when he can on Sundays so I thought I'd call him and give him our news." She laughed. "I can't remember when I've been so excited."

At the moment, all Laura wanted to do was to lie down for a few moments. She felt overwhelmed with the sudden changes in her life. It was probably the pregnancy that had her feeling so sleepy and drained.

Rob must have noticed something, because he said, "Laura, why don't you stretch out for a nap. I know you've had a busy week and are exhausted." He glanced at his mom. "Is that all right with you?"

That's when Laura knew that Rob's mom figured out she was pregnant. Her lightning gaze shot from Rob to Laura and back, but that was the only sign she gave that she might find it strange for a young, healthy woman to need to rest.

"Certainly," Emma said. "We have a very nice guest room. Let me show you where it is."

Rob stopped Laura from immediately following his mother by holding on to her hand. "It's all right, Laura," he said in a low voice. "Please believe me."

She was numb with fatigue and an overabundance of nerves that had drained her of energy. "Thank you for suggesting I lie down. I *am* feeling a little weary," she said. She tugged her hand away from him and followed Mrs. Langston out of the room.

One week later Laura stared at her image in the mirror of that same bedroom. The past week had been a blur. There had been times during the day while she was busy handling her job when she had to remind herself that she was actually getting married this week.

The thought kept her awake nights but there was nothing to be done except continue on as best as she could. Each evening Rob met her as soon as she returned home. She'd given him a key to her place and he'd begun to set up a routine for them.

He would have a light meal waiting for her. He would insist she relax and get comfortable, prop her feet so her ankles wouldn't swell and in general he played the besotted fiancé with a great deal of imagination.

She didn't remember Rob being such a toucher.

He rubbed her shoulders whenever he walked up behind her, stroked her cheek or hand and looked at her in a way that caused her blood to race. And each night he left her before the hour drew late, to return to his mother's ranch.

Tonight he was moving in with her, at least until his leave was up.

Tonight she intended to invite him into her bed.

Part of the reason was practical. The other bedroom needed to be converted into the baby's room. They had talked about what needed to be done closer to delivery, such as removing the present furniture and buying baby equipment. However, she could see no point in delaying the renovations since he was going to be home during the day with very little to do.

Which meant he would need a place to sleep.

He would be her husband in another hour. There was no reason not to allow him into her bed, except for her fears of getting too attached to him. Sleeping beside him, making love to him, would strengthen the bond that was already being formed between them.

She looked into the worried gray-green eyes in the mirror and tried to reassure herself that all of this was necessary for the baby.

In the almost two weeks since she'd found out she was pregnant, her body had begun to reveal the changes it was making to accommodate the new being. There was a hardness to her abdomen so that even when she was lying down, the slight roundness was there. Her breasts had enlarged, forcing her to buy a larger size bra, and they were more tender than usual. It wouldn't be long until she would have to buy maternity clothes.

There was a soft tap on the door.

"Come in," she said, turning away from the mirror and facing the door.

The door opened and Emma slipped through into the room. "Ah, Laura, you look absolutely gorgeous."

Laura had decided not to be married in a traditional gown, given the circumstances. She had chosen a cream-colored suit with matching heels.

"Thank you."

"Pastor Bryan just arrived, so if you're ready...?" Emma let her voice trail off in a question.

Laura forced herself to smile. "Of course." She picked up the small bouquet of flowers that Rob had gotten for her, straightened her shoulders and nodded. "Is Rob nervous?" she couldn't help but ask.

Emma smiled. "On the contrary. He's giving his brothers a bad time because they haven't taken the leap into matrimony before now. They're all terribly competitive, you know, each in his own way. The truth is, I've never seen Rob so happy, at least not since we lost his father. Bless you for that."

Emma opened the door and waved Laura through.

When Laura walked into the living room, there appeared to be a sea of faces, but she quickly separated the family members and various friends from Rob and the pastor.

Rob grinned and walked over to her, giving her a hug. "You look like a million bucks, as well as calm, cool and very collected. But then you always do seem to have everything under control."

She smiled back, her lips quivering slightly. "You already know better, though."

He took her hand and led her to where the pastor waited, near the fireplace that was now filled with freshly cut flowers.

She greeted the pastor, she was almost certain, but then everything seemed to run together into a blur. She must have made all the right responses, because the next clear words she heard were, "You may kiss the bride."

Rob took his time kissing her until the others began to chuckle, clap and make comments. When he finally drew away, he said, "Welcome into my heart, Mrs. Langston."

Chapter 7

Rob couldn't remember a day when he felt so much relief as he did today. She was now his wife. All week he'd been afraid that she might come up with a reason why it would be better for them not to marry. It was only when the ceremony was completed that he felt he could draw a deep breath.

Since then, he'd spent most of the day watching his new bride become acquainted with his brothers and various friends of the Langston family.

She was such a contradiction. On the one hand, Laura was the consummate public official—warm, friendly, charismatic with everyone, regardless of how well she might or might not know them. And yet...

With him she seemed to become more reserved

and spent their time together with little to say. The public side of her was well established but he was beginning to realize that she wasn't used to showing anyone her private side—that part of her guided by her emotions.

He'd been surprised when Laura had invited only a handful of people to the wedding, mostly those she knew from her job. He hadn't realized what a small circle of friends she had. Another indication that she didn't open up to too many people.

At least he'd known her well enough to know that the only way he could convince her to marry him was to appeal to the logical, rational and reasonable side of her. So far, so good. At least now they were officially a couple.

The next step was to convince her that nothing could make him happier than to establish a home and family with her.

Because he loved her.

A fact that he knew had to be presented to her in just the right way at just the right moment.

He glanced over at her and smiled even though she wasn't aware of him at the moment. She looked adorable with her hair pulled up into a topknot with curling strands framing her face. She stood talking to his mother and one of the guests she'd invited, Judge Arthur Hernandez, who seemed quite taken with Emma. Rob's smile turned into a grin. Maybe that's what his mother needed, someone to take her mind off the fact that she was alone.

After all, it had been three years since his dad had

died. She was still a vibrant, attractive woman who needed more on her mind than when she was going to have grandchildren.

He appreciated the fact that she had not questioned him about possible reasons for this hurry-up marriage. However, he had to admit that she had a certain glow about her as though at least one of her wishes had come true. He thought they'd wait another few weeks, then tell the family. That is, if Laura had no objections.

One of the things he was going to have to learn now was that there was someone in his life with whom he needed to consult before making decisions. Observing Laura made him better understand why he'd been drawn to her all those years ago.

She knew her own mind. She expressed herself well. She was strong and capable and—

Rob paused, realizing that Laura was very much like his mother in personality, except for her shyness in expressing her feelings. He hoped that hanging around him would help loosen her up a bit.

He walked over to where the three stood talking in front of the large picture window. He slipped his arm around Laura's waist and kissed her cheek. "Are you ready to go?" he asked quietly into her ear.

She looked at him with a startled expression. "Go?"

"I know you have to be at work Monday morning, but I did have a quick honeymoon planned if you're interested."

She turned an interesting shade of pink. "Oh! I didn't realize. I didn't pack anything for an overnight...and the cats won't—"

"I put out enough food for them for a couple of days and managed to gather a few of your belongings together in a bag which happens to be in the trunk of the car."

Emma patted her hand. "I'm sure you know Rob well enough to know that he's tenacious about getting what he wants. You might as well go along with him and save your energy."

He grinned. "Mom's got a good point. Look how long I've pursued you—years and years. And I finally got you."

He watched with amusement as she almost rolled her eyes before she remembered that others were watching her, but he could see from her expression that he was going to have to explain that one to her.

Well, why not on his wedding night? There were worse things to tell your bride than that you've loved her for years.

The trick would be to get her to believe him.

Laura set her glass of ginger ale down. Since it was the same color as the champagne that everyone else was sipping, he knew that she felt that she'd carried off her secret for a while.

He, on the other hand, wanted to shout the news to everyone. He was going to be a daddy. He couldn't believe how pleased he was with the idea, given the fact that he'd been shocked when she first gave him the news. He'd found it ironic that his mother had called earlier that evening to berate him for not carrying on the family line. Now, in about six months he would present her with a grandchild.

How was that for familial duty, Ma?

He took Laura's hand and they spoke to each and every person there, thanking them for coming, planning more get-togethers at a later date. Several people asked him if he planned to continue to work in Washington or relocate. Since he didn't have any answers, he'd just smiled and said all of it would be worked out in time.

When they finally got to the car, he noticed that Laura was looking a little pale.

"Was all of this too much for you?" he asked as they drove away from the ranch.

She shook her head. "Not really. I just realize how strange all of this must seem to everyone. I mean, we work cross-country from each other. We both have demanding jobs. They must wonder why—"

"It really doesn't matter what they think," he said, taking her hand and placing it on his thigh, then dropping his hand lightly over it. "You worry too much, you know that? Let's don't jump so far ahead. This is our wedding day. Let's just think about today and what I have planned for the weekend."

"Which is?"

"I rented a wonderful little place not far from Bandera. There's a year-round creek nearby. I thought we would enjoy getting away from everything for the night and come home tomorrow afternoon.''

Laura didn't answer right away, which certainly caused him to believe she wasn't overly enthusiastic about the idea.

"Vagabond and Shadow will be fine, I promise."

"It isn't that," she said slowly.

"And the place has two bedrooms. Please don't think I'm trying to place you in an uncomfortable position."

She glanced at him, her expression registering surprise. "I wouldn't think that."

"Well, thanks to me you're going to be a mother. I can certainly understand why you might not trust my judgment in other matters."

She lightly stroked his thigh, causing his whole body to go into full alert. "We've already discussed this," she said. "I'm not holding you responsible for what happened. We're both adults. We both knew the potential consequences."

"I don't want you to feel as though you have to give up your career."

She sighed. "I've been thinking about that these past couple of weeks. Whether we like it or not, a baby is going to change everything. It isn't some doll that we can set aside when we get tired of playing with it. It's difficult to know what to do."

"Don't make any hasty decisions. I'm sure we could work out something where everyone's best interests are taken into account."

"I can't ask you to give up your present assignment, either."

"As I said, let's put all that aside for now and just enjoy the day. We picked a beautiful one, don't you think? That front that moved through here last night certainly cooled everything off to a reasonable temperature."

He knew he was grasping at straws, trying to get her mind off their situation by discussing the weather. Somehow, someway, he needed to get her to turn off her mind and just feel. If he could ever find out some of those feelings, he would be a long way to understanding her better.

Laura stepped out of the car and looked around at the pastoral surroundings. Rob had rented a cottage built to look like a log cabin. Once on the front porch she could see the river that meandered through the rock formations as well as the rolling hills surrounding the place. The cottage was secluded. There were no other buildings within sight.

"This is beautiful, Rob. How did you know about it?" She wrapped her arm around one of the posts that braced the roof over the porch and took in the panorama laid out before them like a giant painting.

He placed their bags inside the door before joining her. "Actually, I know the owners. They've been trying to get me to come out here for several years, but I never seemed to have the time. They were delighted when I called."

She glanced around at him. She couldn't believe

how nervous she was now that they had actually arrived. She was acting like some kind of virginal twit wondering if she was going to be ravished by this stranger she was married to.

She knew she was being absurd but her clear inner voice of reason was being drowned out by her ridiculous emotions. Chronic mood swings seemed to have taken over her existence in the past several weeks.

Nobody had warned her that pregnancy could play havoc with your sanity.

"You must be tired, " he said quietly. "Why don't you lie down for a while? I need to go over to the main office and let them know we're here."

She should feel relieved that he was giving her some space after the stressful day of pretending to be the blushing bride thrilled with the new state of matrimony. Instead, she was feeling abandoned.

Insanity was definitely taking over.

She smiled at him. "Thank you. I believe I will." She continued to smile as she walked inside and looked around, allowing the smile to disappear once she heard the car door slam and knew she was alone.

The cottage did have two bedrooms, she noticed, but the second room had bunk beds. Somehow she didn't see Rob being very comfortable in either one of them.

The master bedroom was as large as the sitting room, with a nice sized bathroom opening off the bedroom. She wandered in, glanced at herself in the mirror, and groaned. She was the same color as her suit. No. Actually, the suit had a creamy look while she was definitely on the green side.

Not exactly a blushing bride. Poor Rob. He had been so wonderful today, treating her as though she were the most precious gift he'd ever received. She'd done her best to keep up her end of the charade, but it had been difficult.

She was a fraud. She didn't know the first thing about being a bride, a wife, or a mother. She'd been counting on the next six months to help her learn a little about babies and what to do with them. She'd allowed Emma to take over the entire bride's planning for the wedding.

And now she needed to be a wife.

She walked back into the bedroom and sat down on the edge of the bed. Even if she hadn't already made up her mind that she was going to be a real wife to Rob, this cottage would have convinced her that he'd made enough sacrifices.

Not that she necessarily thought he was eager to make love to her again. His gentle affection had been very soothing to her and his consideration of her emotional and physical well being had stripped her of the walls she'd placed around her heart.

How could she not love the man?

The thought scared her to death.

She removed her suit, her heels and hose, then stretched out on the bed in her slip. She would rest for just a few minutes, until Rob returned. Then she would tell him some of what she was feeling.

* * *

Rob felt like an idiot when he returned to the cottage almost an hour later. Here he was on his wedding day getting distracted and visiting with the owners of the cottage for much too long. He did get some necessary information from them while he was there, including the name of a nice restaurant where he and Laura could have dinner.

When he stepped up on the porch he heard nothing from inside. Easing the screen door open, Rob entered the sitting room. From there he saw that Laura was asleep on the bed.

Their luggage was still where he'd left it. He took his bag to the second bedroom, then paused with dismay in the doorway.

Bunk beds?

His friends hadn't mentioned them. But then, why should they? This was his wedding night, after all. He set down his bag and wearily rubbed the back of his neck. Well, it couldn't be helped.

He returned to the main room, glanced at his watch, then decided that if they wanted to go into town and eat before nightfall, they needed to leave soon. He wasn't particularly eager to find his way back to this secluded cabin after dark.

Rob walked into the bedroom, his heart picking up its beat. Laura's hair had come loose and lay in scattered curls across her pillow. She looked so pale. He was concerned about her and felt helpless to make things any better.

There was no reason to waste energy thinking

about all the "if only" scenarios. If only he'd told her months ago—years ago—how he felt about her, he wouldn't be in the position now of trying to convince her that he truly loved her.

He could tell that she didn't believe any of his comments to his family and friends about his love for her. No doubt she was convinced it was all an act. Although he prided himself on being able to handle himself in most situations, he wasn't that good of an actor.

He sat down beside her and lightly brushed a curl off her forehead. The thin slip she wore lovingly clung to her soft curves, revealing the top of her breasts. He had to fight the urge to stroke his hand down her face, her neck and along the satiny skin of her breasts.

However, he wasn't superhuman, after all. He could no longer resist kissing his bride awake.

Chapter 8

Laura had been dreaming about Rob and his kiss made her sigh with pleasure. She slipped her arms around his neck and returned his kiss, as she slowly became aware of her surroundings.

She drew back from him and opened her eyes. He stared at her with a heated gaze and she could feel herself blushing.

"It's good to see some color in your cheeks," he said dryly.

"I didn't mean to fall asleep. I was just going to rest my eyes for a few minutes."

"You don't have to explain or apologize to me, honey. I know what a strain all of this has been for you."

"You, too," she replied quietly.

He grinned. "Oh, I don't know. I've enjoyed being home, visiting with family, catching up with friends, not to mention acquiring a beautiful bride."

"You don't have to say things like that, Rob. There's no one around to hear you, now."

"I'm sharing my thoughts and feelings with you. I never say anything I don't mean."

Her smile was wry. "Except around your family."

He arched an eyebrow. "On the contrary, I'm especially careful to be truthful to my family. You'll find out that all of us are rather outspoken. We say what we think...and we mean what we say."

He continued to lean over her as though he enjoyed their closeness. Her breasts pressed against his chest.

His remarks were startling. She thought back to the things he'd said to his mother last weekend, and other comments he'd made today.

She stared up at him, bemused.

"Yes, ma'am. You're finally beginning to understand, aren't you?"

"Understand what?" she managed to get out, sounding breathless.

"From the time we started seeing each other back in D.C., I knew that I wanted you to become a permanent part of my life, but you were so skittish I didn't dare come on too strong for fear of spooking you. I kept thinking that if I went slow enough you would know how very special you are to me."

"I'm finding this a little hard to believe, Rob.

You were so casual with me. I considered you a friend and I thought that was how you saw me as well.''

"We *are* friends," he said, nodding in agreement. "I hoped to get you used to having me in your life on a regular basis before suggesting we make it more. I never planned to make love to you last winter when you were in Washington, but once it happened, I thought that we would move into the next phase of our relationship." He brushed his lips against hers as though unable to resist touching her. "Only you wouldn't return my calls after that, so I knew that I'd really blown it, big time."

She didn't want to talk about this. She really didn't. She felt trapped when all she wanted to do was to run, like she had run early that morning when she had awakened in his bed and fully faced what she had done.

The problem was that she knew that Rob deserved an explanation. Look what he had done since he'd found out about their baby. He'd taken action. He'd done the honorable thing. And he'd done all of it with good humor.

"It wasn't you," she finally murmured, closing her eyes. "Not at all. I was embarrassed to talk to you."

He straightened. "Embarrassed! About what?"

Given the extra room, she sat up and away from him. "I thought it was obvious that I'm not very experienced. Never before had I allowed myself to get into that kind of situation—I'd never gone to a man's apartment, much less—'' Her voice broke and she stopped speaking.

He stroked her shoulder and she quivered.

"I thought you were wonderful that night, Laura," he whispered. "You were warm...and vibrant...and so very alive. You glowed. I thought that it was because we were together again after all those years apart. I thought that you were feeling what I was feeling, that you wanted me as much as I wanted you..."

She slowly turned her head so that her gaze met his. "That's the way I felt," she replied. "You have always had such an impact on me. I've had a crush on you since the first time I saw you on campus." She squeezed her eyes shut, unable to believe that she'd actually told him such an intimate secret. "When we dated I thought you were just feeling sorry for me because my job had become my life. I didn't really have a social life at all."

He chuckled. "Oh, honey, I'm afraid I'm not that altruistic. I know I used that line about us being two Texans away from home, hoping that you'd take pity on me. I certainly wasn't asking you out to make you feel better."

She could tell that he was staring at her profile but she couldn't meet his gaze.

"You really had a crush on me back in college?"

She nodded, still staring at the print on the wall.

He placed his hands on her shoulders and gently turned her so that she was facing him. "How about now?"

She blinked in surprise. "Now?"

"Mmm-hmm. How do you feel about me now?"

She could feel a quiver starting deep inside of her. "You're a very gentle and kind man," she began to say when he gave her a tiny shake.

"Nonsense. I'm neither gentle nor kind. Except with you, of course. That should tell you something."

She forced herself to look him in the eyes. "You told your mom that I was the only woman you'd ever wanted to marry." She hated that her voice shook.

He nodded, very solemnly. "I meant it."

"But only because I'm pregnant with your baby."

"No. The baby is an unexpected bonus. I'll admit that I never really thought I would get married because you had made it quite clear to me that you had no intention of ever marrying anyone. I thought you were warning me away from ever harboring ideas in that direction. But when you told me you were pregnant, that changed everything."

"You covered your shock well the night I told you," she said with a slight smile.

"Solid training, believe me. I'm not sure what was the bigger shock, the fact that you actually called me after all that time, or your reason for calling."

"You sounded very calm. I expected you to at least ask if you were the father."

He wrapped his arms around her and hugged her to him. "Laura?" he finally said near her ear before kissing her there. "I knew you'd never been with a man before. I knew that you must have felt something for me—something very strong—or you wouldn't have made love with me. There was never a doubt in my mind that I was the father."

He kissed her with a passion that took her breath away. When he finally released her, he said, "Once I got over the unexpected news, I realized I'd been given the chance to have it all—you, the baby, a family—and I made up my mind I wasn't going to take no for an answer."

Her stomach growled. She couldn't believe it. Not now, not at this most intimate time. Then it growled again.

He released her, laughing. "All right, all right. I get the message. Why don't you slip into something comfortable and I'll take you to eat. Believe it or not, that was my reason for waking you up in the first place." He leaned over and kissed her cheek. "When we get back, we will talk about the next step in our relationship."

Rob stood and walked out of the room, disappearing into the other bedroom.

She glanced over and saw that he'd placed her bag on the bench at the end of the bed. Laura opened her suitcase and pulled out a pair of slacks with an elastic waist and a blouse that could be worn loose.

She knew what the next step would be. She just needed the courage to tell him that she wanted him—in her bed, in her arms, in her life.

Chapter 9

The restaurant had an Old World charm with a beautiful view of the river. They chose to be seated on the terrace so that they could hear the water flowing over the rocks that formed a small waterfall.

"I'm so glad you decided on our getting away for the weekend. I hadn't realized what a rut I've been in until you showed up." Laura lifted her glass of tea and toasted him.

"Is that your polite way of saying that I have single-handedly ruined your routine?"

"Well, yes, as a matter of fact. But in the very nicest way. And you've spoiled me rotten this past week, as you well know."

After giving their order to the waiter, Rob said, "Enjoy it while you can. Unfortunately, I'm going to have to leave on Monday. I'm not certain when I'll get back here."

"Monday. I thought you said you had a month."

"That's what I requested. Initially it was granted, but I spoke to my supervisor this morning. Something has developed on a case I've been on and they need me back there. I begged the weekend off. He figured that getting married was good enough of an excuse, but I have to leave first thing Monday morning."

She took her time picking up her glass and sipping on her tea before she replied. "Of course. I understand."

He reached over and took her hand. "I'll get back as soon as I can. Please know that."

She smiled. "I'm not helpless, you know. I'll be fine."

"You can spend your weekends at the ranch. I know Mom would love to have you."

"That really isn't necessary, Rob. I've been taking care of myself for a long time, you know." She smiled.

"But you've never had to go through a pregnancy." He straightened when the waiter returned with their salads, set them down and disappeared. "I'll call you every night—and please!" He held up his hand. "Please don't tell me it isn't necessary. It is to me. I need to hear your voice. I'm going to miss you like crazy. You know that, I hope."

She picked up her fork. Concentrating her attention on her salad, she replied, "I'll miss you, too."

Rob couldn't remember a time when he had felt as frustrated with a situation as he did now. There for a little while she had begun to open up to him, to share a little of her feelings. But as soon as he'd mentioned he was leaving earlier than planned he could practically see the walls rising around her, guarding her against hurt or disappointment or something similar. He wasn't sure.

He took solace in the fact that she had admitted having a crush on him all those years ago. He wanted to coax her outside of those walls as soon as possible...which meant he would be asking for a transfer as soon as he got back to Washington.

The sun was setting when they pulled into the lane that led to the cottage that evening. Rob was pleased that Laura had relaxed more as the meal progressed. She'd asked him about his job, which, unfortunately, he couldn't discuss with her, but he had managed to keep her entertained with stories he could tell. The sparkle had returned to her eyes as she'd laughed at some of the tales he's shared.

Now it was time for him to be noble and leave her alone tonight.

Their wedding night.

Okay, so maybe he'd better think about something else. There was no reason to make a big deal out of the fact that since they were married there was no reason in the world for them to sleep apart.

The problem was that he didn't want to push her and set his cause back even more. So. He would show her that she had married a gentleman.

Even if it meant spending another restless night alone.

"Shall we sit out here and watch the sunset?" he asked when they walked onto the porch.

Laura smiled and sat down in the swing that was attached to the porch ceiling.

He sat down beside her and casually draped his arm along the back of the swing, his fingers brushing against her hair. As though it were the most natural thing in the world, Laura rested her head on his shoulder and sighed. "This is so nice, Rob. Thank you."

He rubbed the back of his hand against her cheek. "My pleasure."

They sat there until dark before going inside. When Laura said, "If you'll excuse me, I think I'll get my shower. I'm feeling like one of my cats— feed me and all I want to do is curl up and go to sleep."

"Sure," he said, shoving his hands in his pockets. "I won't be long."

They hadn't bothered with a light in the sitting room. Laura turned on a lamp in the bedroom, and it wasn't long before he heard the water from the shower.

Rob paced restlessly, trying not to picture her in the shower, stroking soap along her body—her beautifully rounded body—her delectably delicious and sexy body.

When he heard the water stop, he figured he

should gather his gear for his shower. But he didn't. Instead, he continued to pace.

He heard the bathroom door open, then she called his name.

He strode to the door of the bedroom. "Do you need something?" he managed to say before coming to a complete halt just inside the doorway.

He'd picked out the gown she wore now from her lingerie drawer. It was white satin and he figured it looked like something a bride might wear on her wedding night. But he'd had no idea it would be so revealing, and so perfect for her.

She tilted her head slightly and smiled. "Actually, there is something I need, if you don't mind."

"Of course—" He stopped and cleared his throat. "Of course not. Name it."

"I want you to sleep with me tonight. I want to start out our marriage in the way I hope it will go. I want you to make love to me." She finished in a whisper, her cheeks glowing.

Rob was beside her in three steps. "I hope you aren't teasing me, honey. I'm dying here."

She went up on tiptoe and brushed her lips across his mouth before she leaned against him. "I want you very much," she said between tiny kisses to his cheek, chin and mouth.

He closed his eyes in a quick prayer of gratitude, then he scooped her up in his arms and placed her on the bed. "Hold that thought, love. I'll be right back."

He went into the other bedroom and grabbed his

bag, brought it back to the bathroom. When he needed to he could shower and shave in minutes. It didn't take him long before he was back in the bedroom with a towel draped precariously around his waist.

She watched him with glowing eyes as he tossed the towel aside and crawled into bed beside her. "I can't remember the number of nights I've dreamed of this since last February," he said.

She turned toward him so that she was lying on her side. With her free hand, she stroked his chest, his shoulders and his upper arms. "So have I," she admitted.

There were no more words. Instead, they expressed their feelings with touches and sighs, exploring, memorizing and treasuring what they had found together.

They turned to each other during the night, sleepily caressing until both were aroused once more, then taking their time satisfying their needs.

When Rob opened his eyes the next morning, he was gratified to find Laura fast asleep beside him. This was their real first time together. He didn't have to worry about her darting away to catch a plane, to return to her safe haven, to hide from him once again.

The words spoken earlier had helped, but it was their nonverbal communication that assured him there was more than enough love to share between them and for their baby.

He pulled her into the curl of his body and contentedly went back to sleep.

Chapter 10

A Friday in September

Laura finished her telephone conversation and returned to the report she was trying to get finished before the end of the day. It would help tremendously if her energetic guest would take a break from his kickboxing and consider taking a nap.

She rubbed her swollen abdomen and shook her head. The miracles of science had informed her that she was carrying a boy, who she secretly thought of as Rob Jr. Like his father, Rob Jr. had a great deal of energy. She'd heard of other unborn babies sucking their thumbs, getting the hiccups, stretching, shifting and occasionally throwing a punch.

Not Rob Jr. From the time she felt the first flutter

of movement, he'd made it clear that he was training as a combination gymnast, pole-vaulter and kick-boxer with a little kung fu thrown in.

Her ribs stayed sore from his very proficient left-right jabs. He'd already communicated the positions he preferred her to be—flat on her back was highly appreciated. Just when she thought she could get some sleep at night, he started his sit-ups, jumping jacks and somersaults.

He did not like her sitting at the office. At home she sprawled in her comfortable recliner. Here she was in a captain's chair where she worked at her computer.

He was already vigorously registering his protests and she'd barely been at work an hour.

She rubbed her forehead and wondered if her bladder was going to be able to take another direct hit by a minuscule heel before she would be forced to waddle down the hall to the bathroom.

No one had truly explained to her the sensation of sharing her body with another person. She could understand that because it was almost indescribable. She already had a clue to her son's personality and she'd never seen his face.

Whenever she thought about his birth, the assorted emotions that swept over her almost swamped her. She already knew that childbirth was painful…how could it not be? So she had to deal with her fear of certain pain and how she might tolerate it as well as the fear of the unknown.

She also had a giddy feeling of anticipation—like her birthday and Christmas all wrapped up in one.

Or...like hearing Rob's voice unexpectedly on the phone every time he called.

She hadn't seen Rob since the weekend they got married. Once he left, she made up her mind to put all of her feelings about him in some safe compartment so she didn't have to deal with them. After all, they had done everything they could as responsible adults. They had married for their son's sake. So she could get on with her life—her job, her routine, her plans for her future.

Only it hadn't worked out that way.

Just as she hadn't understood what it would be like to be pregnant, she hadn't understood what it would be like to commit herself to a relationship with another person.

Even though she had finally accepted, at least intellectually, that Robert Whitfield Langston was in love with her, it had taken weeks before she could understand and accept his love in her heart and soul. She had actually fought the knowledge, insisting to herself that he was only doing all of this because he was a good man, a moral man, a mature man.

But as she had grown to know him better, even she could see that his behavior toward her, even his tone of voice, was different with her than he was with anyone else.

More loving.

He made no attempt to hide how much he missed her whenever he called.

Rob had been optimistic when he'd told her that he would call her every night. Sometimes he managed a call once a week. When she heard from him she knew he couldn't tell her where he was or what he was doing. Sometimes the calls were rushed.

No matter. Because every call showed his love and concern for her and their baby.

Therefore, there was no way she had been able to go back to the way her life had been before. She'd gradually adjusted to her ever-expanding waistline, her periodic cravings for the strangest food combinations, and to the inquiries and raised eyebrows regarding the coming event.

Yes, she was pregnant. Yes, the due date was in October. She left it to those who were interested in such things to do the math and draw their own conclusions.

As the weeks and months passed, she discovered that she missed Rob more than she'd ever believed possible. However, another insight came to her that she would never have expected: she realized that even if she never saw him again, loving him was nothing to be feared.

What an epiphany. She didn't have to be afraid of loving someone. She didn't have to fear the loss of that love. Because the love would continue with her and be expressed by the living reminder of their love—their son—regardless of what might happen in the future.

Despite her weight gain, Laura had never felt as light or as free as she did when she let go of her

fear. It was as though she'd been living in a prison—
one of her own making, but no less real for that—
and had found the key to step out of the prison.

Another sharp kick to her bladder immediately
brought her back to the present. She pushed herself
up from the chair by leaning on the desk and hurried
down the hallway.

When she returned to her office she found Judge
Hernandez waiting for her.

"Good morning," she said. "Were you looking
for me?"

Arthur had been standing with his back to the
room, looking out the window when she walked in.
Now he turned and looked at her. "How are you
feeling these days?"

"About what you'd expect. My toes make rare
appearances in my life and I get my exercise trotting
back and forth down the hallway." She noticed that
he was holding a paper in his hand.

He waved her to her chair and took the one across
the desk from her. "I received your request for a
maternity leave. It says here that you want to begin
effective October eighth."

She smiled. "That's right."

"Isn't your baby due sometime that week?"

She nodded.

"Is there some specific reason you want to work
right up until the birth of this child?"

"Well, I thought it was fairly obvious that we're
all carrying a heavy load these days. I know that my
leaving is going to create a hardship on everyone

else. So I thought I'd be here for as long as possible.''

"What if the baby comes early? Do we need to keep trained personnel on the premises just in case?" His dark eyes danced and she relaxed somewhat.

"I'm open to suggestions," she replied, watching him.

"I don't want you to think that we don't appreciate everything you do here. You've got the place more organized than it has been in years, but I think it's time for you to consider cutting back, slowing down, and enjoying your new family."

"Are you firing me?"

He smiled. "No. What I'm suggesting is that you take the next year off and stay home with your baby."

"I can't do that. Who would—?"

"I've already found someone who can come in, who has experience working in a county larger than Travis and who is willing to start immediately."

"You *are* firing me."

"Laura, I've known you for a long time. I sometimes think I know you better than you know yourself, at least about some things. This job has been your life. But your priorities are changing. They have to. This baby is going to need you. We can hire people to take over some of the responsibilities you carry here at the office. But you are the only person who can be this baby's mother. I also think that when the time comes and your maternity leave is over, you won't be able to go off and leave your baby with someone else.''

She stared at him in shock.

She'd never once thought about giving up her job. This was who she was. This was what she did. She would be lost without her professional self. She was good at it. She didn't know a thing about being a mother, or caring for a baby. She had planned to hire a nanny to take care of him after the first few months.

But Judge Hernandez was right.

All of her views had been changing lately, her ideas about pregnancy, about being a wife, a mother. Why would she think that she could blithely walk away from her infant son each day after having carried him beneath her heart for all those months?

"You don't have to make any decisions about this today,'' Arthur continued. "Talk to Rob. Think about it. See what the two of you come up with. In the meantime, we're bringing the new man on board Monday. You're welcome to come in and work with him...or not. Your choice. Personally, I think you could use the extra rest for the next three weeks just staying home.''

"If I decide I want to come back?'' she had to ask. She needed to know.

"Then your job will be here for you.''

"But what about my replacement?''

"He understands that he may only be here for six months. That gives him a chance to decide if he wants to move here permanently.''

She let out a sigh of relief. "Oh. Okay." She looked at her desk, at the work waiting to be done, then grinned. "Sure you couldn't get him to come in now? There's nothing I'd like better than to go home and put my feet up."

He stood and leaned over, patting her hand. "Then do it. I'm sure Sebastian can take care of any emergencies. I want you to take care of yourself, you hear me?"

She stood. "Loud and clear, sir." She looked around the office and realized that she no longer had any real attachment to the place. She knew she was good at what she did, but she was exhausted. For the first time she didn't feel guilty admitting it to herself.

By the time she pulled into the driveway, Laura knew what she would do. Of course she would talk to Rob about it. But it wasn't as if she needed to work for the money. She worked for the fulfillment of being good at something. But she reminded herself that she hadn't been all that accomplished when she took the job. She had learned, practiced and honed her skills.

Right now she knew nothing about being a mother. But now that she knew this was going to be the next step in her life, she was suddenly excited by the prospect of learning about parenting and child rearing. She wanted to be there for her son from the time he first greeted the world until she waved him off to school.

The idea continued to grow and blossom in her

mind as she parked the car and went inside the quiet house. She knew how lonely she'd been growing up alone. Maybe in a couple of years she and Rob could discuss another child, maybe two more.

She smiled at the thought.

Both cats looked at her, startled by her unscheduled appearance in what was their exclusive daytime domain. "Don't let me bother your naps. In fact, I think that's an excellent idea."

She walked down the hallway to the bedroom removing her top and working at the waistband of her skirt. When she stepped inside the room, she came to an abrupt halt.

A darkly tanned, nude man lay sprawled across her bed, a sheet barely preserving his modesty. His arms were flung out as though he might be reaching for someone and his head was half-buried in a pillow.

Laura could barely contain herself at the sight. She wanted to leap on the bed and hug and kiss the oblivious man, but she restrained herself. He looked exhausted.

She glanced around the room and saw several pieces of luggage over in the corner.

Rob was home. And from the looks of things, he was staying for longer than a weekend.

It was then that she remembered that Rob hadn't seen her since she'd turned into a lumbering whale. Or did whales lumber? Whatever.

With sudden overwhelming modesty she went into the bathroom and got undressed, then slipped on her summer nightgown that was large enough to be used as the Big Top at a circus.

But it did camouflage her ungainly figure. She returned to the bedroom and carefully crawled onto her side of the bed, grateful for the king-sized mattress. She and Rob Jr. would rest and allow Rob to sleep. His face looked drawn, and there were shadows beneath his eyes, but he'd never looked better to her.

Yep. The anticipation was even better than Christmas and birthdays.

Rob shifted, aware on some level that he needed to wake up. There was a reason he needed to get up and shower and be ready for something.

Laura. He had to get up before Laura got home from work.

But he was so tired. He couldn't remember the last full night's sleep he'd gotten during the past few months. He'd worked around the clock. But it had been worth it.

He was home now. That was all that mattered. And he needed to get acquainted with his new bride all over again.

He stretched and yawned, then turned over and brushed against something soft nearby. That was enough to make him open his eyes, even as he recalled there were a couple of cats in the house.

Only this wasn't Shadow or Vagabond. Laura lay beside him in a sound sleep, looking more beautiful than he'd ever seen her. His hand had brushed against her breast. He lifted his finger and lightly stroked, watching with delight as the nipple hardened beneath the soft cotton material.

He pulled away and looked at her rounded middle which had the most interesting shape, the material shifting and moving as though a couple of puppies romped beneath it.

He leaned over and kissed her stomach. "Hi there, hot shot. I understand you've been giving your mom fits lately," he murmured.

At the sound of his voice, Laura's eyes flew open. "Rob!" she whispered, lifting her head.

He leaned back from her stomach so that he could see her. "Hello, gorgeous. What a surprise to find you here. When did you get home?"

She yawned. "A little after ten. I'm officially relieved of all my duties, it seems. How about you? When did *you* get here?"

"Must have been about nine. I had a chance to hitch a ride on a flight coming in overnight, but we were delayed landing. I'd hoped to get here before you left for work, but didn't make it. I figured I could get a few hours sleep and have dinner waiting when you got home." He glanced at his watch. "Guess I blew that. It's already after six."

She pushed up on her elbows. "It can't be! I've never been able to sleep that long at a time." She patted her tummy. "What a good boy he's been, letting me sleep."

Rob leaned over and gave her a leisurely kiss. When he finally raised his head, they were both flushed and short of breath.

"Wow," she managed to say.

"What can I say," he said with a grin. "You're a very sexy lady."

"Yeah, right."

He placed his hand on her stomach. "You are, you know. Being pregnant obviously agrees with you." As though unable to resist, he kissed her again before he finally pulled away and said, "I have missed you more than you can possibly imagine."

"Same here."

He grinned. "That's good, because you're going to have to put up with me around from now on. My transfer is official, but first I get the next six weeks off to stay here and tackle that bedroom before the baby arrives, and to look after you."

"Then we're going to have plenty of time together. Today was probably my last day at work."

"Until when?"

"Oh, I don't know, until this young man starts to school, maybe, unless he has another brother or a sister who might need my full attention."

"Are you serious?"

"Very. My life is taking a brand new turn and I intend to enjoy every moment of it."

"Mrs. Langston. Have I mentioned how very much I love you?" he asked, his hand continuing to caress her.

"Both of us?" she asked with a grin.

"You betcha. I intend to be right here from now on."

"Even if we aren't producing a granddaughter for Emma?"

"Well, you know what they say—if at first you don't succeed, try, try again."

Dear Reader,

Usually I write stories about the hills and hollers and small towns of America at the beginning of the last century, but when I got the opportunity to help Annette Broadrick and Ann Major create the story of the Langston brothers, I jumped at the chance.

Our choice of setting was inspired. I love the ranch land around the Devil's Backbone area of the Texas Hill Country. And the library at Southwest Texas State University with its beautiful vistas is about as romantic as a library can be.

And then there was Clu Langston. He is the kind of man that appeals to me and the kind of hero I love to write. The tremendous obstacles he's overcome have left their mark, and those who are unaware of his battles misinterpret what they see. Clu is brilliant, inventive and empathetic. He has fabulous potential as both a scientist and teacher, but his career path gets stopped in its tracks when he meets Zizi.

What can you do when you love someone who treats you like a best friend? If you make a move you could lose him or her from your life forever! What could make you take such a risk? Could a meddling mom and a competition among siblings give you that needed push?

I hope you enjoy *With Marriage in Mind*.

Sincerely,

Pamela Morsi

WITH MARRIAGE IN MIND
Pamela Morsi

For Easton.

The little guy who's going to teach me
what grandmothering is all about.

Chapter 1

No one expected him to win. Not his brothers, not his mother, not even himself. Clu Langston had never won anything in his life. Certainly he'd never beat out Rob or Gabe on anything. Unless it was "most medication taken in any given year." Or maybe, "Langston brother most readily recognized by anyone employed in south Texas hospitals." From childhood, Clu was "the sick one" of the Langston boys.

"Don't romp around with Clu!" Mom would warn them. "His bones are brittle, they might break. Don't grab his arm like that! His platelets are low, you'll bruise him."

In the rough and tumble home life of the Langston boys, Clu was set carefully on the shelf like a piece of spun glass, kept at a safe distance from everything fun or lively or even vaguely competitive. Clu had never suffered the humiliation of being last chosen for the team. He never got to play at all.

But that was all behind him now. Most of the people who knew him weren't even aware of the sickly, set-apart Clu. They weren't aware that his five-year-old vocabulary had included words like lymphoblastic, chloroma and pseudodiploid. He kept himself in shape, ate right and had been in remission for twenty years. Still, he'd never imagined beating his brothers at anything. And Mom's little competition wasn't going to be any different.

Clu pulled his ocean-blue Porsche Boxster into the employees' entrance of the multilevel garage beneath the library at Southwest Texas State University. The Boxster was the undisputed prince of staff parking. Among the scratched-up Chevys and economy sedans, it stood out like a cup of latte at a Mexican beer joint.

Clu loved the powerful machine. It was a marvel of engineering, a perfect melding of the style and the science. That it cost more than a small house here in San Marcos was a fact he forgave.

He passed up several perfectly good parking places as he searched for the vehicle that he most wanted the Boxster to be up close and personal with. Finally, near the elevator, he saw the unpretentious white Corolla he was looking for. It had a worn and fading "Puro San Antonio" bumper sticker and the license plate read Z Z 2U. Clu eased the Boxster in beside it.

He allowed himself just a couple of sweet moments of pure fantasy. He imagined himself standing beside the Boxster as a curvy, exotic, flashing-eyed brunette hesitated at her car, listening to him talk and laughing at his jokes. Ahh…that would be heaven.

Clu glanced down at his watch. It was five minutes to nine. Heaven could wait, but his work probably couldn't. He grabbed his laptop, its case doubling as a carryall for his notes and memos, locked the Boxster and headed across the garage and up the three flights of stairs to the lobby level of the library.

He could have simply taken the elevator into the building's front door, but that would make his trip through the Circulation Department hectic and hurried. It was much better to get to his desk, sort everything else and then, assured that things were running smoothly, he could leisurely go check his mailbox and take his time speaking to a certain interesting Corolla owner who worked in that department.

He'd been at Southwest Texas for three years. Three years of learning the ins and outs of library work. Three years of commuting from his mother's ranch. Three years of being close to the woman he loved. Close, but never close enough.

The phone at the reference desk was ringing. He could hear it from the stairwell. It was ringing and ringing and ringing and ringing. Nobody was answering it. He hurried through the back office area, not even hesitating at his own cubicle. The main lobby was expansive and open and amazingly quiet, except for the incessant telephone at the reference desk. Clu made his way past the copy machines and the carrels of computer terminals. He grimaced unpleasantly, understanding that nobody was answering his phone, because, once again, nobody was there to answer it.

He stepped behind the reference counter and jerked the receiver to his ear.

"Langston, Math-Science Reference."

"Uh...yeah...hi," the voice at the other end began tentatively. "I...uh...I'm doing a paper on this guy, Isaac Newton right."

"Yes," Clu answered.

"Right and well...uh, I know that he like created gravity, like when that apple fell on him, or fig or whatever, right."

"An apple," Clu told him. "At least that's the myth."

"Myth, yeah, well right, but this guy in my frat house told me that his prof said that Newton invented the calculator. I thought that like IBM invented the calculator. Could that prof have been wrong about that?"

Clu tried to keep the long-suffering sigh out of his voice. Basic Science 101: Intro to Scientific Thought brought the huddled masses into Clu's realm of the library every time.

"Newton didn't invent the calculator," he told the uncertain young man gently. "He invented calculus. Your frat brother just misheard the professor. I'm sure he said that Newton invented calculus."

"Oh yeah right..." the voice sounded pleased. "That's like some kind of math, right?"

"Right," Clu agreed.

He was explaining to the caller where and how to find the material for his paper when the elevator doors popped open. His co-worker, Bonnie Tugman, stepped out. Fat, fiftyish with frizzy hair, Bonnie was the poster child for the failings of the tenure system. She'd gotten hers more than a decade earlier and hadn't put in a good day's work since.

She made her way across the lobby, only passing by the reference desk on the way to her office. She gave him a cursory glance and then waved to him dismissively.

"Don't even say good morning to me," she told him. "I'm just not in the mood for small talk. I had a terrible night. Terrible. Jim and I fought all evening, so I know I'm a little late."

Clu was still giving directions on the phone and couldn't offer a response. Bonnie, however, didn't require one. She was loaded down with bags of all kinds, a purse, a briefcase, a backpack, a canvas booksack and a big brightly colored shopping bag emblazoned with the name of the local outlet mall. They hung upon her like an American Medusa, capable of keeping the world in her grip.

"That man is just living in some other century

and I'm just getting completely sick of it. I don't have to put up with that, you know. I could have married anybody I liked. I had my choice. Unfortunately, I chose him.''

Finally Clu was able to hang up the phone.

"You're late," he said. "You should have been manning the reference desk since seven-thirty!"

"I told you, Jim and I had a fight."

"You said you had that fight last night," Clu pointed out.

"So I'm running a little late this morning."

"An hour and a half is more than 'a little late.'"

"Well, I'm here now," Bonnie said. "And look around. It's not like we're swamped."

"We don't know how many reference calls were missed," he said.

Bonnie shrugged. "Oh, they'll call back. They always call back."

Clu couldn't argue with that. And he really didn't want to. He didn't want to argue with her. He didn't even want to talk with her if he didn't have to.

Bonnie Tugman was his cross to bear. They had worked together almost since Clu's first day. Since the decline of her work ethic, she'd been transferred from section to section. It never panned out and she was moved again. And again. And again.

Unfortunately, she seemed to like Reference. Or at least she didn't complain about it any more than other departments in the library. She and Clu shared the same job level, though she never hesitated to remind him that she was a *real* librarian, as in having a master's degree in library science. All of Clu's education, from undergraduate through his Ph.D. had been in the hard sciences. The library was about the only place on campus that such a thing could be considered a detriment. Clu tried to think of Bonnie as a kind of generalized unpleasantness that made all the little petty annoyances of the day unnoticeable.

It was another fifteen minutes before she leisurely made her way to relieve Clu at her work station. He went into his office and divested himself of his jacket, hanging it on the hook behind the door. He booted up his laptop and began checking messages. Sometimes it seemed as if his job was simply checking messages. Phone messages and e-mail messages, faxes and bright blue notes printed with the words While You Were Out, little yellow Post-it notes with two-word reminders, all represented complex problems someone was hoping Clu could work out. Somehow he always did.

He'd spent most of his life figuring things out with test tubes and lab data, experiments and equations. Among the scientific elite of the nation's finest universities, he broke new ground and scaled the frontiers of objective knowledge.

Now he answered reference questions in a small, south Texas state university, reputed to be the "best party school" in the region.

He was taking a short hiatus, he reminded himself. It wasn't as if he were going to do this forever. He was taking a few years break from the pressure of a life of science. He was on a sabbatical of the heart.

There was an e-mail from Mom. It read simply "Go after what you want." Clu shook his head. That was Mom. Pushing, even when she had no idea where he was headed. She'd never asked him why he'd given up his research grant. Why he'd turned his back on a promising career. Never questioned his reasons for staying at the ranch. Or what drew him to his job every day.

His love life, or lack of it, was not a thing that he ever discussed with his mother. He was no different from most men on that score. The two were very close, but there were some things that a man could never share.

Since the discussion about the horse on Mother's Day, Clu had been thinking more than he liked about where his life was headed and whether he was going to spend it alone.

Zafir, that glorious Arabian, meant a lot to him. He'd taken care of him since Dad died. He didn't really want to give him up, but he was willing to let one of his brothers have the horse. The competition, however, had stirred something inside him. The reality of his situation hit him square in the face. He was thirty-four years old. He was living with his mother. He couldn't remember the last time he'd had a date. And he was in love with a woman who seemed to think that he was only her best friend.

Clu left his cubicle for the lobby once more. With Bonnie seated at her post behind the reference desk counter and his work laid out for the morning, he decided that the department was at least under control and it was reasonable for him to make a quick trip across the library.

Bonnie had picked up the phone and was rehashing the story she'd just related to Clu to an unknown friend at the end of the line.

"I'm going down to check my mail," he told her.

She nodded and waved him away. Clu headed for the glassed-in area perpendicular to the elevators.

The mail room was on the far side of the Circulation Department next to the interlibrary loan office. Clu quickly retrieved his mail. Memos about staff meetings, routed library journals and the occasional scientific review of books. He tucked the pile neatly under his arm and headed back through the rows of desktop computers to the glass fronted corner office. Painted in neat block letters upon the door it read Aziza Josephs, Director, Circulation Of Library Materials.

He could see her inside. She was dressed in the red silk business suit that always seemed to brighten her eyes and enhance the bronze in her olive complexion. Her thick dark hair was pulled back from her face and as fastidiously coiled as that of a ballet dancer. As she studied the image upon her computer screen, her brow was furrowed intently.

Clu tapped on the door. She looked up and her expression changed immediately. Her eyes were bright and narrowed at the edges where her smile reached its zenith. She eagerly waved him in.

"Good morning, Miss Josephs," he said.

"Not particularly," she answered, laughing. "But getting better whenever you drop by."

Clu stepped inside allowing the door to close behind them, affording them as much privacy as a glassed-in corner office could manage.

"Anything I can help you with?" he asked.

She shook her head. "Just the usual stress du jour," she answered. "What about you?"

"I just got here," Clu answered. "There hasn't been time for much to go wrong. Of course, Bonnie was an hour and a half late, but I can't let that get to me."

She laughed. He loved the sound of how she laughed.

"What was it this time? The ungrateful children or the bad choice of husband?"

"The husband," Clu answered.

She tutted. "Poor Jim," she said. "He is such a sweet and understanding guy. I don't know how he puts up with her."

"Maybe he's like me and just keeps hoping she'll transfer out."

"Shame on you," she said.

"Zizi," he began with feigned consideration. "I'm thinking that you could really use Bonnie's experience down here in Circulation."

"You are wicked," she told him. "Besides, I've done my time with Bonnie. She was in my department nearly a year before she became convinced that what we do is really as hard and thankless as we've always said it is.''

"A mere eleven months with you," Clu pointed out. "I've already had her as a scourge in my life for nearly three years. You'd think I'd get a reduced sentence for time served."

She giggled once again and leaned back in her chair, affording him a better view of her. Zizi wasn't merely dark and exotic, with a bright mind and a wonderful laugh. She was, in scientific terms, a .7. Her waist-to-hip ratio was that preferred by human males across all cultural barriers. Size twelve Marilyn Monroe had been a .7, skinny supermodel Kate Moss was as well. Bushmen in Borneo, shown drawings of the female form, described the women with the .7 ratio, whether fat or thin, as more attractive and better able to bear children than other body types. Clu wasn't sure that the childbearing thing held true—Zizi was thirty-three and had never been a mother—but as for the attraction part, well she certainly attracted Clu.

"So how was your weekend?" he asked her.

"I went to San Antonio to be with my family," she answered. "My sister's having another baby."

"Terrific!"

She nodded. "Her third. You'd think that would pacify my mother, but no. She wants *me* to get married. She wants *me* to have children."

"Your mother must have been talking to my mother," Clu suggested. "What did you tell her?"

"I said that I have Byron. He's all the offspring I need."

"What did she say to that?"

Zizi raised her eyebrow and looked down her nose, mimicking her mother's disdain.

"A woman with a cat. It's pathetic!"

Clu laughed.

"Well, your brother and sister have toed the mark," he said. "And it looks like mine might, too. My brother, Rob, got married at the ranch this weekend."

Zizi's jaw dropped open in shock.

"You didn't say a word."

"I didn't know," he admitted. "She's from Austin, someone he knew from college. They just showed up here for the wedding."

"Well, that's certainly romantic," Zizi said.

Clu shrugged. "Or expedient," he answered. "Rumor is there's a little Langston already on the way."

Zizi raised an expressive eyebrow, but her tone was without censure.

"Quick work," she said.

"Yeah," Clu agreed. "And Rob acted like he wasn't even interested in the competition."

"The competition?" Zizi looked puzzled.

"Didn't I tell you about Mom's little Mother's Day competition?" he asked.

She shook her head.

"She's concocted a plan to lure her childless sons into fatherhood," he said.

"Lure you how?" Zizi asked.

"With a horse."

"A horse?"

Clu nodded. "Dad had a horse that he rescued from wedding carriage duty on the streets of Houston. It's a beautiful white Arabian, wonderful head. Fabulous gait. Dad named him Zafir. Broke him to the saddle. My brothers and I all love that horse. Mom decided to use Zafir for leverage."

"Uh-oh, this sounds like a serious meddling-mom plan."

Clu nodded. "She says that an animal can't be divided three ways. So the first of her sons to give her a granddaughter gets the horse."

"Does she really think something like that will work?"

Clu shrugged. "I wouldn't think so," he said. "But I wouldn't think that Rob would suddenly up and marry. And Gabe brought his old girlfriend to the wedding."

"Gabe has always got a girl on his arm," she pointed out.

"Not like this one," Clu told her. "Normally he goes for the short-term bimbo brand of female companionship. Now he shows up with Sam, who has four little girls she's adopted. This is a woman with marriage and family in mind."

"Your mother must know you guys better than you think," Zizi said.

"Looks like it," Clu said. "In any case, I took Zafir for a brisk canter at dawn this morning. I figure

I have several months before I have to hand him over to one of my brothers.''

Zizi was shaking her head.

"Are you saying that the pitter-patter of little feet is not in your immediate future?"

Clu shook his head. "It's not likely."

"You can't be tempted with a horse?"

"Well, it's quite a pretty special animal," he admitted. "I wouldn't mind having him."

"Ah…" she teased knowingly. "The gentleman has a weakness for beautiful white Arabians."

Clu was thoughtful for a moment, he could have easily met her humor with more of his own, but somehow he wanted to share the truth with her, he wanted to share his feelings, though he wasn't sure quite how he could explain without revealing too much of his heart.

"Growing up I…well, I spent a lot of time with my mother," he began. "Dad played sports with the other boys and took them for overnight rides and all that sort of thing. I didn't do much of that."

He recalled one long ago day seeing Rob and Gabe in their Little League uniforms. They'd stopped by the hospital with Dad to visit him. Rob's team wore red. Gabe's blue. The chemo drug dripping from Clu's IV bottle was yellow.

"Just about the time he brought home the Arabian, I developed an interest in riding." It was his second remission. He'd been scared and vulnerable and too wounded by his past to even think of his future.

"Dad let me ride Zafir," he said simply, not conveying any of the absolute incongruity of allowing the worst rider in the family upon the horse that his father loved so much.

Clu smiled. "Those are the times I remember most with my father," he said. "And it was also the first time I ever remember feeling freedom. It was my chance to be like my brothers."

Clu recalled with distinct clarity, the great height of a young boy on a full-grown horse, the surging muscles between his knees, the wind in his face and the absolute and exquisite pleasure of being normal, being healthy. After years of desperate hope followed by wrenching setbacks, those things that he'd most longed for had come to pass. Riding Zafir at his father's side had been the first time he'd been able to accept that his wishes had indeed come true; he was going to live.

Something must have shown on his face, because when he glanced at Zizi again her expression was puzzled and showed concern.

"So you really would be willing to fall into your mother's scheme?" she asked.

Clu had momentarily forgot his mom's machinations and the likelihood that Zafir would soon be the personal property of Rob or Gabe.

He shook his head. "If I could put together a nontraditional genetic replication project I might end up being the good guy on the white horse."

Zizi laughed lightly at his lame attempt at humor, but in truth, there was really nothing funny about it.

Clu genuinely worried that he might never marry
and have a family. He was in love with a woman
who saw him only as a friend. And he was afraid to
risk losing her entirely by trying to be more.

Chapter 2

The sun was almost directly overhead when Zizi managed to sneak away for her lunch break. She found a place out on the second floor terrace of the LBJ Student Center to eat the chicken salad and crackers. This time of year was the very best in south Texas. Warm and breezy, the chill of winter behind them and the sweltering summer still weeks ahead. It was important for her to take a few moments to be outside. The picturesque hill country vista was as beautiful as any vacation spot on earth. Her work inevitably kept her indoors, but a break like this was a welcome reminder that her life need not be restricted to the narrow confines of the library walls.

She was a woman in touch with nature. Her weekends and vacations were peppered with long hikes. And she prided herself on being able to identify the flora, fauna and rock strata that crossed her path.

The morning had been hectic, as Mondays often were. But in truth, she loved the job. She loved the chaos and craziness of it. Circulation management was considered by most in library science to be the doghouse job. The least desirable position in the discipline. For Zizi it was the heart of the library. Her specialty in the master's program had been public administration. She'd come to San Marcos to take her job as a step toward that goal. And then discovered surprisingly that this *in the trenches* work was much more to her liking than the bureaucratic behind-kissing of the library director's world.

Zizi was relaxed as she breathed the fresh air and spread her crackers with chicken salad. In the distance down the hillside she could see the city of San Marcos laid out before her. It was a pretty town with fine old buildings and a marvelous courthouse square. Beyond the city was the curve of majestic pecans and sprawling cypress that edged the river as it passed under Interstate 35. It was restful, relaxing, a view evoking contentment. But Zizi was not totally content. Every time the door to the food court opened, she looked up. She was hoping that it would be Clu. She was hoping that he would join her. That was unlikely, of course. Their busy schedules rarely allowed for a coincidence of that proportion. Though they usually had a quick word together at the end of the workday.

Clu was so smart and funny and engaging. He had a way of seeing the world that was vivid and full of depth. But he had a clever wit and an eye for the absurd that always had her looking at things differently.

He was also the most attractive man she'd ever seen in her life. That thick brown hair and those unexpectedly pale blue eyes could catch attention of women everywhere. The fact that they were combined with a lean, muscular body and the face of a matinee idol just seemed almost unfair. The first time she'd met him, almost three years ago, Zizi's heart had skipped a beat. She could have suffered a tremendous crush on the man. Fortunately, the rumors got to her pretty quickly. Maybe that was for the better. She'd stopped being calf-eyed crazy around him, a long-term victim of unrequited love, and had been able to discover Clu Langston as a genuinely interesting person.

The door opened and Bonnie Tugman stepped outside. She'd obviously been over to the Tejas Café. She carried a taco salad in a covered plastic container that was nearly as big as a laundry basket.

Zizi resisted the impulse to duck under the table. Bonnie spotted her and waved as she hurried over. Zizi's heart sank. Bonnie's presence would certainly be the end of her soul-filling commune with the midday breezes.

"I'm so glad you're here," Bonnie said. "I just can't stand to eat alone. And now that they don't allow smoking in the cafeteria, I'm forced onto this godforsaken porch!''

Bonnie set her salad on the black metal picnic table and lit up her ultraslim cigarette before she even sat down. She took a deep drag and then let the smoke out in a long grateful sigh.

''All these nonsmoking rules around here,'' she said. ''They think they're going to force me to quit. But I'm not giving up my smokes for anything or anybody.''

She pulled off the top of her salad, and then opened the plastic packet of salsa dressing with her teeth.

''Are you going out with that guy from the bursar's office again?'' she asked.

Zizi felt her face flame. She knew that her dating failures had become a subject for entertainment and speculation among the staff. Zizi-One-Date is what they called her. Nobody had said it to her face, but it had been impossible not to overhear it eventually. That fact that it was more true than cruel didn't make it any easier for her.

''Oh, no, he and I decided we didn't have all that much in common,'' she said evenly.

''Dumped another one, huh,'' Bonnie inferred sympathetically. ''You sure do go through 'em, don't you.''

''It was a mutual breakup,'' Zizi assured her.

''Well, you're going to have to stop being so picky,'' Bonnie continued. ''There aren't that many single men, not in your age group anyway, and if you keep running off every eligible fellow you meet, you're going to end up as an old maid librarian for a certainty. Don't you hear that biological clock ticking?''

Her mother might get away with whining about her daughter's declining options, but Zizi had no intention of discussing her biological clock with Bonnie Tugman.

''Has your department been busy this morning?'' she asked, determinedly changing the subject.

Bonnie filled her fork as she took a drag on her cigarette.

''Oh, the usual,'' she answered. ''One of the physics professors is giving extra credit to his class for finding and reading a ten-year-old article that he wrote after his dissertation. It's completely outdated and irrelevant, but the students are practically coming to blows over that roll of microfilm.''

Bonnie exhaled a cloud of smoke before filling her mouth with food. She continued talking through both actions.

''The freshmen in Intro to Scientific Thought are all starting to work on their term papers. And that group of mealymouthed kids, you know the Dorksters or whatever they are called...''

''I think they call themselves Geekoids,'' Zizi corrected.

''Dorksters, Geekoids, whatever, a group of those pimply-faced science nerds has been monopolizing Clu all morning with some Internet-chaos theory supposition they've come up with.''

Zizi nodded. Clu would undoubtedly not be down for lunch then. But at least she didn't regret it. He truly enjoyed the Geekoids and their bright minds and wild ideas. He seemed to relate to them in a very special way, as if he knew what it was like to live almost completely within your own head and could appreciate the gift of having another person who was knowledgeable enough to share. He was such a natural teacher. He was a good librarian, of course. But Zizi couldn't help but think it was a shame that he'd given up his professorship back east.

Beside her Bonnie sat within a billow of white smoke as she alternately puffed her cigarette and chewed her salad. Determinedly, Zizi tried to concentrate upon the restful view once more.

"Poor Clu Langston," Bonnie said, somewhat abruptly. "Now that is a dad-gummed shame if I ever saw one."

Zizi couldn't imagine what the woman was talking about. "That he enjoys sparring with the Geekoids?"

"No, not that," she answered, flicking an ash. "It's the rest of it that just makes a woman want to cry in her tea."

"What do you mean?"

Bonnie cocked her head to one side and gave Zizi an impatient look before shaking her head sadly.

"When a man is as smart, rich and good-looking as Clu Langston," she said, "it just seems danged unfair that he would have to be gay."

Zizi felt a flush color her cheeks.

"That's only a rumor," she told Bonnie adamantly. "You shouldn't be spreading that around. None of us knows if it's true."

"Of course it's true," Bonnie insisted, eyeing her with incredulity. "You always defend him. Even though it's obvious."

"I don't defend him," Zizi said firmly. "He doesn't require defending. And what is obvious is that he doesn't think his sexual orientation is anybody's business. I can't help but think he's right about that."

Bonnie took a deep draw on her cigarette.

"Now don't get all self-righteous on me, Zizi Josephs. You act like I'm gay bashing or something," she said. "I'm glad he's gay. Gay men make the best co-workers. I'd state that fact under oath. And believe me, I know. I've had just about every kind there is."

"Why can't you simply say that Clu is your best co-worker," Zizi suggested. "That would be completely factual and wouldn't presume any of the rumors you seem so keen to spread about him."

Bonnie put another forkful of salad in her mouth. She puffed on her cigarette as she chewed.

"I don't spread rumors," she said. "And I don't presume anything. I just call them like I see them."

"And you see Clu as being gay," Zizi said.

Bonnie nodded. "It's as clear as if he'd come out of the closet and told me so," she answered.

Zizi had heard the whispers before. Practically

from the day Clu began working, there was speculation. A number of openly gay men were already on staff and wondered aloud if he was of them. Somehow it was suspect when an MIT graduate from a wealthy and powerful local family chose library work over any of the more macho scientific disciplines at which he excelled. And it was unfathomable to the library gossips that any man with a gentle heart, a handsome face and stylish clothes could be anything but homosexual.

"You can't proclaim a man to be gay just because he doesn't hit on every pretty freshman in a crop tee," Zizi said.

"Not that alone," Bonnie admitted. "But that and everything else about him."

"What everything else?" Zizi asked.

"His name is gay," Bonnie said.

"Clu? That sounds gay to you?" Zizi shook her head. "There is no such thing as a gay name."

"Of course there is, though Clu isn't really a gay name," Bonnie admitted. "What kind of name it is, I have no idea. But his middle name is Montgomery and that's as gay as a three-dollar bill."

"How so?"

"Montgomery Clift, of course. He's a gay icon. You couldn't have a more gay name."

"A boy is named when he's only a day or two old," Zizi pointed out. "His mother couldn't possibly know his sexual orientation."

"There are no coincidences," Bonnie declared firmly. "She gave him the middle name Montgomery and that's gay. Whether that's what made him gay or his mother instinctively knew it already doesn't matter. It is what it is."

Zizi rolled her eyes.

"So what about Field Marshall Montgomery?" Zizi asked. "Are you suggesting that the hero of El Alamein was gay as well?"

Bonnie shrugged. "They don't call homosexuality the *British disease* for nothing."

There was no reasoning with complete and confident lunacy.

"This is positively stupid," Zizi said. "There is no such thing as a gay name."

"So, if you don't believe the name," Bonnie asked. "Surely from your own experience you know he's in a gay job."

"A gay job?"

Bonnie nodded with absolute certainty. "Of course. Everybody knows that men who are chefs, interior decorators, florists or librarians are always gay."

"You didn't mention hairdressers."

Bonnie shrugged. "That goes without saying."

Zizi was annoyed and spoke up sharply. "A man may choose any occupation that he likes from professional wrestler to female impersonator, it is absolutely no indication of his sexual preference, it only indicates his vocational preference."

Taking another deep drag of tar and nicotine, Bonnie was unconvinced. "Maybe it doesn't indicate anything to you."

"Think of all the men on the staff that you know are straight," Zizi said. "Bob Benson in Rare Books has nineteen grandchildren. Larry and Millie Schertz are the most happily married heterosexuals in America. And Happy Gonzales in Serial Acquisitions, do you think Happy is gay?

Bonnie didn't attempt to argue that.

"There are some exceptions, of course," she said. "But Clu Langston isn't one of them."

"I don't think that you can judge that one way or another," Zizi said.

"How do you explain the car?" Bonnie asked.

"The car?"

"Have you ever in your life seen a more gay car than that blue thing that Langston drives."

"The Boxster?" Zizi was incredulous. "Don't tell me you think that a car can make you gay."

"A car can't make you gay, but choosing to drive a certain car can tell you a lot about a person."

"Like my Corolla says something about me," Zizi suggested facetiously.

Bonnie nodded. "It's sporty and neat with that little spoiler on the back," she told her. "It says that you're lively and outgoing, even if you're getting older, a bit rusty and rundown."

"Thanks a lot," Zizi said, refusing to be sidetracked into another argument. "And a Porsche sports car would broadcast my sexual preference."

"Absolutely."

Zizi shook her head in disbelief.

"So everybody who drives a Boxster is gay?"

"Everybody in Texas," Bonnie assured her. "This is the land of the double-cab diesel and the four-wheel SUV. A man who chooses a fancy European sports car definitely marches to a different drummer."

Zizi sighed heavily. Her tone was long-suffering. "So he's a very handsome librarian, his middle name is Montgomery and he drives a sports car. That's your evidence that Clu is gay."

"You tell me?" Bonnie replied. "Why does a man in his mid-thirties still live with his mother? Why have we never seen or heard of him having a date? You've met his brothers. He's a lot smaller and less rugged than either of them. Why is that? And while he's got all that education and teaching experience, why does he work here as a reference librarian?"

"I don't know the answers to any of those questions," Zizi admitted. "But I've got a question for you. Why do you think that a man who is so open, up-front and honest about everything would keep something like this such a secret?"

Bonnie shrugged. "There is still a lot of prejudice against a lifestyle like this. People are touchy about state-funded education. Maybe he doesn't want to embarrass his family or cause any kind of confrontation with his church."

"I don't believe it," Zizi said. "He just isn't the secretive type."

"He isn't?" Bonnie asked, raising a skeptical eyebrow. "What about his annual vacation."

Zizi was stopped cold. She knew immediately to what Bonnie referred. It was strange, very strange. She'd been curious herself. Every year Clu took the first week of June for vacation. He never said where he was going and deflected any queries in that direction. He always returned sun-browned but curiously subdued, as if his time off had been less restful than disturbing."

"What about his vacations?" Zizi asked defensively.

"You know what happens the first week of June, don't you?"

Zizi thought for a moment and then shook her head. "No, what?"

"That's gay pride week in Key West."

"What?"

"It's not like an official thing," Bonnie explained. "The Chamber of Commerce has nothing to do with it or anything. But gays all over the country know that they can show up there that week in Key West and meet gays from all over the world."

Zizi was dumbfounded.

"I've never heard of such a thing," she declared.

"Then you have obviously not been attending the Southern Baptist Convention," Bonnie said. "They were all up in arms about it a few years ago. Clu Langston goes to Key West for gay week and meets men. That's why he's so quiet when he gets back and never talks to anyone about where he's been and what he's done."

"Do you know for a fact that he goes there?" Zizi asked, her heart caught painfully in her throat.

"I don't *have* to know for a fact," Bonnie said. "If it looks like a duck and quacks like a duck and takes the first week of June for vacation…"

Bonnie let the rest of her comment go unsaid. She rose to her feet and threw her now empty salad container in the nearest garbage bin. She lit another cigarette and dragged upon it heavily as if desperate to get one more smoked on her way to the stairwell.

"I've got to get back to the library," she said. "I was a teeny bit late this morning and Clu probably expects me to make my break short."

Zizi felt strangely bereft. Her heart was beating a little too quickly and her emotions shifted from defensiveness to disappointment.

"Despite all your wild ideas," she told Bonnie flatly, "I don't think you've proven anything about Clu and I don't think you should be speculating on things that are none of your business."

Bonnie shook her head. "Truthfully Zizi," she said. "I don't give Clu Langston much thought one way or another. But I like you a lot and I hate to see you mooning over a fellow that you can never have."

"What!"

"It's as plain as the nose on my face that you're crazy about that man," she said. "Maybe you should face the fact that since he hasn't so much as escorted you to a movie in all the years you two have been friends, then for sure his romantic interests run in another direction."

Chapter 3

A young man made his way to the reference counter. His jeans were worn and dirty, and his hair was plastered to one side of his head.

"Hey...ah..." the student said to Clu as he looked around curiously. "Is...ah...is this where I was last night?"

Clu considered informing the kid, in his best reference librarian tone, that since they'd never laid eyes upon each other and Clu was not adept at fortune-telling there was really no way that he could accurately answer that question. But the guy was clearly not the sharpest knife in the drawer, so Clu took pity upon him.

"Third floor, maybe," he suggested.

The T-shirted fellow nodded gratefully and gave a thumbs up. "Cool, thanks dude."

Clu acknowledged the gesture and then glanced down at his watch. It was two minutes to six o'clock, the hour when his workday ended. Guymon Jones, who was working the desk until ten, was already at his station. Immediately Clu began to pick up his notes and memos. Although he had no plans for the evening except dinner alone and a few innings of ESPN to put him to sleep, he was anxious to make his getaway. He wanted to be conveniently standing next to the Boxster when Zizi got to her car. He'd ask her about her day, make a lame joke or two and listen to her laughter. It was a special part of his evening, full of expectation and hope.

Every day he wanted to ask her to grab a bite, or go for a drink, or see a flick. Every day, however he got into his own car and let her get into hers. They parted company and he spent his evening alone.

He was shy, of course, but that wasn't the problem. Nobody was *that* shy. He wasn't afraid of women. He was comfortable with them and always had been. His college days always found him with a pretty coed at his side.

He'd been younger than his classmates. Younger than all the Wellesley girls at the Tower Court Mixer. But he'd dated his share nonetheless. With his good looks he'd attracted plenty of attention from the opposite sex. Clu had enjoyed the stimulation of female minds as scientifically bent as his own. And the titillation of female bodies that were his perfect biological opposite. Later when he'd taken the assistant professorship at Vanderbilt, he'd even had a couple of serious relationships. He'd thought he wanted to marry and have a family. But the women in his life were never quite what he'd hoped.

That was until the day that he'd first walked into this library. The day he'd first met Aziza Josephs. Bright, funny, outgoing, empathetic, Zizi was, in his studied estimation, the most desirable woman on planet earth.

He'd really just come to interview for a temporary job. His father's unexpected death had brought him home to Texas and he wanted to stay close to his mother for a few months, to make sure she was all right. But he couldn't sit at home all day doing nothing. He'd come to the university for a short term diversion. He hadn't opted for a teaching position; that would have entailed a commitment for a full semester. He was just staying a few months, then he'd go back to Nashville, back to his life. That was his plan.

Meeting Zizi had changed all that. He knew almost from the first moment that she was the woman of his heart, everything that he had longed for in his lonely life.

He went to his cubicle, slipped his laptop into its case and pulled on his jacket. He wanted to see her, talk to her, just for a moment. Without that moment, the night would seem unfathomably long.

Clu's trip to the garage did not take him down the back stairs, but across the main lobby through

Circulation. He made his way through the current periodicals section and past the banks of computer terminals. He smiled and waved at students he knew and people on the staff. Clu had made a lot of friends here at the library. He loved the work and wasn't sorry that he took the job. It was about the only thing that had worked out for him, though.

He and Zizi had so much in common, but she was also everything that he was not. Outgoing and vivacious, she had men after her like green on guacamole. It was the first thing he'd found out about Zizi. She had more than her fair share of admirers. None of them ever lasted that long. It was a joke among the staff that Zizi could find fault with a fellow at five hundred yards. She always had dates. And they were most often first—and last—dates.

Clu realized immediately that the quickest way to end up as her most recent broken heart was to make a play for her. As long as they were buddies, friends, confidants, they could spend time together. The minute he tried for something more, he might well find himself out of her world forever.

As he neared the library's front entrance, he spotted her. She had her jacket on and her briefcase in hand. She was standing in discussion with a female student next to the ancient photocopy machine known affectionately as Old Buffalo. Old Buffalo was the first coin-operated copier on campus. An experiment the library administration tried out with the new technology, Old Buffalo was now older than most of the students who used it. Certainly it was a couple of decades older than the pink-haired young woman who stood next to it now, her silky slick black blouse, with one lone button fastened, fitting tightly across her bosom.

As he neared the two, Clu heard the coed's question.

"Does this machine take copy cards?"

Zizi pointed to the sign directly behind the girl and read the words printed there in eight-inch letters aloud.

"Nickels Only."

The pink-haired one glanced at the sign herself and then turned to Zizi once more.

"Does it take quarters?" she asked.

"No," Zizi said. "It only takes nickels."

Clu was grinning as he wrapped a friendly arm around Zizi's waist and edged her through the door.

The student was assessing the change in her hand and looked up once more, intent upon further inquiry.

"Dimes?"

"No," Clu said, forestalling Zizi's answer. Smiling at the girl he added, "No drachmas, no pfennigs, shillings or three-cent pieces. The change machine is at vending downstairs."

He just managed to get Zizi whisked through the elevator door before it closed and they both burst out laughing.

"You are terrible," she accused.

"Answering student questions about Old Buffalo has led many librarians to a lost weekend."

His arm was still around her waist. He dropped it abruptly. They were friends, he reminded himself. They were friends and only friends. Any push for more and she might simply push him away. That he couldn't risk.

"I've been thinking about the story that you told me," Zizi said.

"Story?"

"About the horse, Zafir. I assume from the name that he's a boy."

"Yes, he's a horse," he told her. "The word horse is masculine. A girl would be a mare."

Zizi raised an eyebrow. "Excuse me," she said, feigning criticism. "I believe *horse* to be a species and therefore gender neutral."

Clu shrugged.

"It should be. And maybe in the English language it is," he agreed, then added in a deep cowboy drawl. "But in Texas, ma'am, horse means male just like man means male."

"Unless one is speaking in terms of mankind," she said.

"Or horsekind, as the case may be."

She groaned.

He grinned at her. "Does this machine take nickels?"

"Only the plug variety," she shot back.

He loved sparring with her, making up puns and having private jokes. She was his partner in a way that no other woman had ever been. They liked the same movies, read the same books and appreciated each other's sense of humor. It was a perfect relationship, except that it was no relationship at all.

"What have you been thinking about Zafir?" he asked.

"Oh, about you and your father," she said. "How he just happened to see that horse pulling the buggy in Houston. How he felt compelled to buy him. And you remember those times with him and Zafir as the best."

Clu nodded.

"Big things often turn on such small decisions," she said.

"More than you even know," he told her.

They reached the parking garage and their voices seemed to be amplified by the concrete emptiness. Clu modulated his tone, making his words more intimate.

"Truthfully, I had always wanted to ride," he confessed. "I pretended not to have an interest in horses, but when I saw Zafir, I couldn't keep it to myself anymore."

"You wanted to ride, but didn't?"

He nodded silently.

"Why not? A young boy raised on a ranch, surely you were almost expected to ride."

"Nope, my brothers were, but not me. I wasn't expected to do much of anything," Clu told her. "Robbie and Gabe were riding practically as soon as they could walk and helping out with the stock when they still needed a stepladder to reach the stirrups. I was kind of a mama's boy, I suppose. I was in the house a lot. I watched them from the window."

They walked into the space between the Boxster and the white Corolla. Zizi leaned against her car and looked at him, her brow furrowed thoughtfully.

"Why didn't you just go out and join them?" she asked.

"At first because I knew Mama didn't want me to," he said. "She was afraid I would be thrown or get stepped on or just fall and hurt myself."

Clu leaned against his own car. He was directly across from her, looking into those wide, dark eyes.

"I didn't want to add to the worries that she already had," he said. "I'm sure I told you, I was sickly as a kid."

Zizi nodded vaguely, as if it were no explanation at all.

"By the time she quit being scared about me, I figured I wouldn't be any good at it," he continued. "I was big enough to be self-conscious. I was awkward and clumsy. I thought that if I tried and failed, Dad would be disappointed in me. I knew Dad loved me, but it was easier to let him love the little nerdy kid with the chemistry set. I was afraid that if I tried to ride and failed, he would be so disappointed."

"But you took the risk anyway."

Clu chuckled as he nodded. "I'm so glad I did. I'll never really be the cowboy type," he said. "But I love being on horseback. It's relaxing, pleasurable and a real challenge to be of one mind with a well-trained, intelligent animal."

"Sounds like a Vulcan mind-meld," she said.

Clu raised one hand and made a V between the middle and ring fingers.

"Live long and prosper," he said. "Do you ride?"

"Oh, yeah," she told him. "I was one of those pubescent twelve-year-olds who went completely horse crazy. I begged my parents every day to buy me a horse. They never succumbed to the pressure, but they did see that I got a ride out to the stables every Saturday morning."

"English saddle or Western Pleasure?"

"I've done both," she answered. "But I really wanted English. I dreamed of doing steeplechase like *National Velvet.*"

Clu grinned and nodded. "The best Hollywood horse movie."

Zizi agreed.

"How long did that last?" Clu asked her.

"A few years," she answered. "I think Mom and Dad were praying I'd get interested in boys. I did finally, but I never thought they were as interesting to talk to as horses."

Clu clutched his heart as if he'd been stabbed.

"I'm wounded," he cried. "Medic!"

She laughed again. She laughed that wonderful laugh that he loved hearing so much.

"So you're not into equestrian pursuits these days."

She shook her head. "A couple of times a year I'll get a hankering for the saddle," she said. "When

I'm at the park or the beach, I'll pay for a mount for a few hours. But, it's just not the same with a spiritless rental horse on an established trail.''

Clu nodded in agreement.

''Well, some Saturday you should come out to the ranch,'' he said. ''Mom's got eleven hundred acres that we can wander across. I'd even let you put Zafir through his paces.''

As soon as Clu said the words he wanted to take them back. He'd actually asked her to the ranch. It was almost like asking her out. It might even be construed like that and she might even back away from him. Big things turn on small decisions, she'd said. He couldn't risk that this one might turn out to be a disaster.

''I didn't mean that like it sounded,'' he said quickly. ''I wasn't suggesting it like…like a date.''

He saw the expression on her face and realized he'd made it worse.

''I…ah…don't let me hold you up,'' he muttered. ''See you tomorrow.''

He slid into the Boxster and angrily jerked the gear shift into reverse.

''Idiot!'' he whispered to himself under his breath.

From the rearview mirror he could still see her watching him as he drove away.

Chapter 4

Zizi sat listening patiently to the young man seated on the other side of her desk. He was dressed in the worn and ragged concert shirt of a now defunct rock band, Birkenstock sandals and a pair of very baggy short pants that only came down to about midcalf, leaving a pair of hairy lower legs and feet exposed to unblinded eyes. His beard was actually getting a bit past the stubble stage, but his hair was very neatly and closely cropped. The word Rock was visible on the left side of his skull. Zizi scolded herself silently for the little private thought that he must be advertising his cranial density, as in: head as hard as a...

"I am a citizen of this country and the state of Texas," he declared, his voice rising to an unnecessary level. "As such, I own all the books in this library. They are my property. So I can't be fined or reprimanded in any way for having them in my possession."

Zizi kept her expression noncommittal, determinedly hiding the little giggle that she felt inside. Of all the modes of explanation for overdue library books—I forgot I had it; my roommate took it; I was using it as a leg for my couch—her favorite excuse, by far, was the enraged patriot who has every right to keep books as long as he pleases. It was a justification offered a couple of times every semester and invariably the would-be lawyer thought himself to be the very first to think up such a defense.

"The purpose of a public institution is to serve the public," he continued. "Onerous regulations limiting my use of materials to a specific length of time do not serve me, they restrict my personal liberties as well as the free flow of information."

Any second now he was going to trot out the Constitution and the Bill of Rights.

Zizi glanced up to see Clu peeking in through the glass. When their eyes met, he winked and waved, conveying the silent message that he had stopped by to see her, but it was nothing important enough to disturb her at work. She couldn't acknowledge his presence, but folded her hands together and concentrated more intently upon what was being said to her, knowing that Clu would understand.

Clu always understood. And she had always

thought she understood him. It seemed she was coming to understand him more than ever.

She didn't for a moment believe Bonnie's contention that there existed such a thing as gay looks or gay professions or a gay car. That was half stereotype, half silliness. But the secretiveness of his annual vacation did strike a chord with her. There was obviously something going on that he was not willing to share. And then yesterday, he'd given his invitation to the ranch to ride. An invitation that he made sure she understood to be completely nonromantic.

Not a date.

He'd made sure that she understood that perfectly. He wanted to be her friend and nothing more. A sickly mama's boy, he'd called himself. Different from his brothers, he'd said. Bonnie might have her reasons all wrong, but she was right, Zizi feared. Clu Langston was undoubtedly gay.

Why did that fact, something she had suspected herself for a long time, make her feel so hurt and lost? Her best friend was gay. So what?

So maybe he'd become more than a best friend to her.

Zizi continued to listen to the long-winded rhetoric coming across her desk. Patiently, she heard the young student out completely, allowing him to run out of steam on his own without any comment or encouragement from her. That was the most important aspect of complaints, Zizi had discovered long ago. Just hearing people out, letting them voice their frustrations. This was especially true, she thought, of students who were always caught between their necessity to the school and their powerlessness within it.

Finally, after using up all the words that he knew, the young man fell silent. Zizi allowed that silence to grow until there was room for both of them to be relaxed in it.

"So, Mr. Simington," she asked finally. "Can you pay the fines you owe today, or do we need to set up some sort of payment schedule?"

His answer was soft-spoken in comparison to his earlier harangue.

"I probably have about half of it," he said.

Zizi nodded.

"Can you pay the rest by the end of the semester?"

The young man agreed politely. "Yeah, I think so."

"Then let me get Marianne to write you a receipt."

She led him out of her office and into the main hub of the Circulation Department and turned him over to her assistant. Marianne was all smiles, as if the guy's boorish behavior when he showed up at this office a few moments ago had gone completely unnoticed.

"I leave you in good hands," she told Simington and then glanced toward her assistant to add, "I'll be in Reference if you need me."

Marianne nodded and Zizi made her way through

the department. The library wasn't all that busy this morning. Three of the four positions at the checkout counter were being manned. Two student assistants were loading returned books on carts to take to the stacks. An anthropology professor was attempting to have all the recommended readings for his class held on reserve. She gave an approving smile to her staff and headed for the north side offices of the reference staff.

Clu was not in his office or at the reference desk. Guymon suggested he might be in the sixth floor stacks. With a hasty thank you, she headed for the elevators.

Zizi had spent last evening strangely saddened and depressed. She'd eaten a low-calorie frozen entrée and sat in front of the TV watching reruns of a World War II documentary on the history channel. Even Byron crawling around on the back of the couch and putting a paw on her shoulder like a long lost friend hadn't been enough to shake her from the blues. Somehow yesterday she'd felt as if she had lost something. And she hadn't even known that she wanted it until it was gone.

The sixth-floor stacks were a maze of shelving. A mass repository for all of the literature and the bulk of the sciences. Finding one lone person should not have been an easy task. But Zizi knew where Clu was most likely to be even before she ventured near. In the area outside the reading room she could hear excited voices and good-natured joking. Not unusual sounds for this time of the semester.

"If a cloned mammoth could be carried by a modern elephant," a teasing tone suggested. "Then I guess that explains why such a nice woman as Mrs. Walsh could have a son like Harley."

The statement evoked a good deal of snickering.

"I'll tell Mom you said that," another voice countered. "I bet she's wondered herself."

His words raised the laughter to the level of guffaw. Amid the sounds, Zizi heard a familiar chuckle.

"Brian, if you're truly interested in Harley's origins, we've got a lot of really interesting new material on genetics."

"Brian and bioscience? Not likely," a girl piped in.

Zizi came around the stacks to see Clu in his element, surrounded by young, enthusiastic students with a hunger for knowledge. The smart kids easily recognized Clu as one of their own.

"When you get right down to it," Clu told them. "Genetics is the link between the disciplines."

"Say what?" was the skeptical reply.

"The DNA molecule is the foundation of biological existence," Clu said. "And nothing could be more mathematical than the double helix."

The statement was greeted with a moment of thoughtful silence.

"Hey, that might not be too far from right," Brian agreed finally.

"I wonder if you could break the genetic code down into binary?" someone asked.

"I think they've already done it," Harley said.

They all looked toward Clu, questioning without words.

"Check out Matson," he suggested. "QH438, somewhere around there."

The students hurried in that direction, Clu looked ready to go with them, until Zizi caught his eye. He grinned broadly and hurried over in her direction. As always, the sight of him could take a woman's breath away. Certainly Zizi's breath, anyway. And when he smiled, as he was doing now, he was irresistible.

"Miss Josephs," he said. "What brings you to math/science stacks, or as we call it, the Geekoid Homeland?"

She grinned at him.

"Just checking up on my favorite reference librarian, also known as the High Priest of the Society of Students on Science Scholarship."

He laughed. "I love being around the kids," he admitted. "Their brains are processing in overdrive and it forces you to keep thinking, to keep examining what you know."

Zizi nodded. "Do you miss teaching?"

"Oh, yeah, some days I miss it terribly," he said, a wistful tone evident in his voice. "I could have probably set up my career so that it would have been mostly lab work. I loved doing that, but I missed the contact, the excitement that you can share when an idea is presented to a growing mind for the first time. I get a lot of that here, and it's the very best kind of interaction. It's because it's not a formal setting where I lecture, I get to hear what they have to say. And they can say anything that they want, because they aren't being assessed or graded by me on anything at all.''

Clu picked up the pile of opened books on the table. He checked the Library of Congress numbers on the spine and handed one to Zizi. She looked at it as well and saw that it belonged a couple of shelves down from the other two he was putting up. As they were getting everything back in place, she wondered about his life, the choices that he'd made. In the back of her mind, she could hear Bonnie Tugman's rampant speculation.

''Shelving library books is probably not what the little kid with the chemistry set imagined himself doing with his life,'' she said.

Clu shrugged. ''He just wanted to grow up to do something,'' he answered.

''But something different than this,'' she said. ''I guess I've always wondered why you left Vanderbilt.''

''When Dad died, I just felt like Mom needed me,'' he said. ''We've always been especially close, though she really wanted Rob. It was Rob who she hoped would stay. But...I guess we all have our demons. I was the one who got a sabbatical and I...well I just stayed.''

''Why aren't you teaching?'' she asked. ''Why didn't you apply for a position on the faculty?''

Clu's brow furrowed and his expression became wary. He was obviously not as gifted at dissembling as he should be. He was hiding something. Zizi was afraid that she knew what it was.

"You know how academia is," he said. "You don't just walk into a university and fill out a job application. When a position opens up they appoint a search committee and they recruit and screen candidates nationwide."

Zizi shook her head. "Don't try to convince me that you couldn't get hired," she said. "You have a more impressive curriculum vitae than half of the tenured faculty."

"Credentials aren't everything," he said. "Besides I wasn't interested in a professorship. I could have stayed in Nashville."

Once more Zizi wondered worriedly why he had not.

"In science we try to expand the boundaries of knowledge," he said. "Sometimes you can do that best with research. Sometimes aiding or inspiring the work of others is more important."

"I'm sure that many scientists can be excellent teachers while not being especially talented or creative in a lab," she said. "But most would pick one or the other. And the way I see it, you seem to be pretty good a both."

Clu was half-turned away from her, seemingly studying the book spines on a nearby shelf.

"Let's just say that I like it here in the library," he told her finally. "I like the work and I like the people I work with."

He was looking at her intently as if he were asking her to read between the lines, asking her to understand without him saying it, that he was saying more.

Zizi swallowed the lump in her throat.

The hard sciences, especially math and physics in academic venues, were well-known macho preserves. She'd heard plenty of bright young women, even a few of Clu's Geekoids, complain that the resistance to women was tremendous and pervasive. Even with universities actively trying to recruit females, the structures and hierarchy within the disciplines continue to make gender a troubling issue. If the climate was unwelcoming to women, Zizi speculated, it might be even more so toward gays. Had that been what had happened? Had his sexual preference made his career impossible?

She didn't ask that question. She was afraid of the answer.

What must it be like, she wondered, to be denied the opportunity to use your God-given talents and abilities because of something innate in you that others didn't want to accept? At least there were laws to protect people from bias based on race or gender or disability. Those prejudices hadn't yet been purged from society, but at least they were growing very unacceptable. But excluding or relegating people because of sexual preference or mental health were intolerances still held in good opinion by a lot of people who really ought to know better.

"You do miss it," she said.

It was a statement. It required no response, but Clu nodded his head all the same.

"An idea will pop into my head and I'll start thinking about the possibilities and I'll start planning how to set it up in the lab and then I'll remember, *hey Langston, you don't have a lab.*" He offered a little chuckle. "Maybe I should get Mom to let me set one up in one of the barns."

Zizi smiled at his determinedly sunny attitude.

"Do you think she'll let you?"

"Maybe," he replied. "For sure if I tell her it's a cloning experiment to get her those granddaughters she wants so badly."

She laughed with him, but thought to herself that the granddaughters wouldn't be such a bad idea. Being a father would make him look straight to his colleagues. That would open those doors that had once closed so unfairly upon him.

Of course cloning was not the only way to be a father.

Zizi turned to him. He was so familiar to her, yet she was beginning to look at him in a way that was totally new. Clu Langston was warm, friendly, good-looking and upbeat. He was her best friend, she reminded herself, and the best kind of friend to have.

"I wanted to take you up on your invitation."

"Invitation?" There was a sudden wariness about him.

"Horseback riding. Remember? You invited me out to the ranch."

"Yes, of course I remember."

"Are you still on for it?"

"Sure, anytime."

"How about Saturday?" she asked. "Would Saturday work for you?"

"Absolutely," he said. "Saturday would be great."

"Do I get to ride Zafir?"

"Of course you can," Clu said. He was smiling now. Smiling as if he were delighted that she was coming.

Zizi hoped that it was true. She hated to force herself upon him. But they were friends, best friends. Best friends ought to be able to spend time together, shouldn't they?

Chapter 5

Clu didn't understand his good luck, but he certainly didn't want to question it, either. Zizi Josephs was coming out to the ranch to spend her Saturday alone with him. It was like something he might have come up with in an idle daydream. When he'd asked her it had been a slip of the tongue. A slip which he backed away from quickly and rather clumsily as well. But she had taken him up on his accidental invitation and he was going to try to make the best of it.

"Earth to Clu. Come in Clu."

He glanced up to see his mother, fork raised, staring at him from across the table.

"Did you say something?" he asked.

She gave him her infamous raised eyebrow.

"I've been carrying on a one-sided conversation here for ten minutes," she told him. "Maura called me today and she's just full of speculation about Gabe and Sam."

"Oh yeah," Clu responded vaguely.

Apparently his mother and Sam's aunt were conspiring to push his brother and her niece together.

"It could be the best thing that's happened to Gabe," Emma Langston predicted.

"I've always liked Sam," Clu agreed. "I never understood what happened between those two."

"Is something wrong with that pork chop?" his mother asked, pointing to his plate.

Clu glanced down and realized that he hadn't even touched his dinner. Immediately he proceeded to cut it up and take a quick bite.

"Mmm, it's great, Mom," he assured her.

Clu and his mother shared the cooking chores. At least that was the way they would have described it. The truth was that on Clu's night to cook they routinely had hamburgers, pizza or spaghetti. It was his mother who fixed healthy well-balanced meals, and all that she required of him was that he eat.

"I've just got a lot on my mind," he explained.

"Apparently so," she answered.

"Are you going to be home tomorrow?" he asked.

"Tomorrow? I didn't have any specific plans," she said. "Why?"

Clu hesitated. He almost hated to even say it aloud.

"I have a friend coming out to ride," he said. "I...well I was hoping for a little privacy."

His mother feigned complete disinterest, concentrating upon her squash and tomatoes.

"I've been meaning to go into Wimberley," she said. "The merchandise in the little antique shops there comes and goes so quickly, I'm always worried I might miss something."

The truth was, Emma Langston hated shopping and tolerated antique stores as a necessary evil. Choosing to make a day of it was a big concession on her part.

"Thank you," Clu said. "I do want you to meet her, but after we know each other better."

His mother smiled. "Eat your dinner," she admonished.

Clu did as he was told. His thoughts were still in a terrible whirl. It was his chance with Zizi. At long last he was getting his chance. But he knew well the risk that he was taking. If he moved too fast or maybe too slow or just plain wrong, he could find himself in the heaping pile of cast-off admirers. She never stayed with anyone very long. And most of the men of her acquaintance never made it to the second date. Clu hadn't waited this long to become one of those discarded.

"So, is this the one?" his mom asked, startling him from his rumination.

"The one what?"

"The one who has held you here in Texas all this time."

Clu hedged. "I like Texas," he answered.

His mother chuckled, as if finding his attempt to keep his private life private amusing.

"I know you like Texas," she said. "It's a great place with lots of good people and lots of good memories. That's how I feel about Mexico. We went down there every summer of my girlhood and I could pack a few clothes in the car and head in that direction right now with a happy heart."

She paused, leaning forward slightly to emphasize her point.

"I like Mexico, but it would take something pretty special to keep me down there for years on end when I had a ranch up here going to seed for want of my attention."

Clu didn't respond.

"It seems to me that when a man who has spent most of his life thinking to expand the boundaries of scientific knowledge is suddenly stopped in his tracks with the opportunity to work at a library reference desk, there has got to be some explanation."

The excuse that he gave to others—that he was there to help his mother—was not about to fly at Emma Langston's dinner table. She might be still grieving, but it was a private thing, requiring neither assistance or witness. And she had thrown herself into the management of the ranch with a good deal of fervor and excitement. She'd been raised around the cattle business and had always been an equal partner in the ranch with her husband. Just as she was in their marriage. She actually seemed to take on the job as a challenge.

"Library work is important work," he told her defensively.

"It is important work, essential work, valuable work," she agreed, a little bit too quietly. "It's just not your work."

"It's my work now," Clu insisted. "And, you know, I get more direct contact with students now than I did in lectures or labs."

His mother waved away his words. "I've heard that sorry excuse more times than I care to," she answered. "And it's about the smelliest truckload of organic fertilizer I've ever been presented."

She gave him a hard, critical look. The truth it expressed made Clu glance away.

"You're a scientist," she told him. "You have been since you were a little boy. Now I'm confident that this little detour eventually leads back to the main road, but you can't just keep weaving in and out, assuming that somehow you'll get there. On the highway of life, son, there comes a time to pick a lane."

"I can't, not yet," he told her.

She continued to look at him expectantly.

Clu was thoughtful for a moment. Wanting to explain how he felt, how things were, but not sure exactly how to do so.

"Do you remember how I was after the bone marrow transplant?" he asked her.

For a second he saw a haunted look in her eyes.

He knew the memory he evoked was not a pleasant one.

"Of course I remember," she said. "You were as weak as a kitten. You hadn't quite got your strength back from the last chemo when the donor became available. The surgery sapped every drop of energy from you."

Clu nodded. "I had to choose what I could do very carefully," he said. "Just holding a book up was exhausting. Trying to read a few pages would tire me out so bad that when they brought lunch I couldn't muster the strength to raise the spoon to my mouth."

His mother nodded and smiled. It was a bitter-sweet smile.

"You had to decide which was worse," she recalled. "Going without your beloved books or suffering the indignity of having your mother feed you."

"I had to set my priorities," he said. "I had to figure out what was most important to me and go after it."

"I remember," she said. "If you thought your father was coming to visit you would rest so that you could feed yourself. If it was just the two of us you'd read yourself to exhaustion and let me shovel in the chicken broth and jello."

Clu shook his head, a bit chagrined. "You figured that out, huh?"

"You were a sick little boy," she said. "But never a complicated one. You loved us and wanted to please us. We both knew how much effort it took you to pretend that everything was all right when it wasn't. I worry that's what you're doing now."

"No, Mom," he assured her. "I'm not really unhappy. But it is like it was back then. I've figured out what is really important to me and that's what I'm going after."

"And this woman that is *really important* is coming out here tomorrow?"

He nodded.

"So how long have you two been dating?" she asked. "I never see you going anywhere."

"We haven't been dating," Clu answered. "And her visit tomorrow isn't a date. I'm...I'm a little hesitant to actually ask her out."

His mother's eyes widened and she looked worried.

"Clu, this woman isn't married, is she? Tell me you haven't gotten yourself mixed up in something like that."

"Oh, no, Mom," he assured her. "She's absolutely single, never been married, no kids or anything like that."

"So why aren't you dating her?"

"Because...because she doesn't like the men she dates much," he said.

Her brow furrowed and she eyed him curiously.

"You've lost me," she said.

"Every man she goes out with, and believe me there are a lot of them that are interested in a woman as bright and attractive as she is," he began. "Every one of them ends up getting dumped. Usually after only one date. The people at work make a big joke of it. That she can reject any man in Texas at fifty paces.''

His mother laughed delightedly. "I think I'm going to like this girl.''

"You will like her," Clu agreed. "She's just the kind of woman that you'd like to see me with. She's warm and funny and empathetic. And…well…I'm in love with her.''

"Does she know that?''

"Of course not," he answered. "I told you I can't be one of the million guys that are after her. I'd just end up in the rejects pile with the rest of them. We are friends. That's why we get to spend time together. That's why she's coming out here to go horseback riding.''

His mother was thoughtful. "I don't think that's the right way to go about it, Clu. With women, I believe that honesty is pretty much always the best policy. It's so unexpected it catches them off guard.''

Clu shook his head. "I can't just blurt out, *I'm in love with you.*''

"I don't know why not," his mother said. "Eventually you're going to have to say it. You think it will be easier when she's already got some other man's ring on her finger?''

Her words caught Clu up short. In that his mother was right. Zizi was destined to be someone's wife, someone's lover. Things wouldn't stay as they were. And he couldn't wait forever.

Chapter 6

At the last moment Zizi had hoped it might be rainy and stormy and their day together cancelled. It was a stupid idea to spend more time with Clu. Even dumber than the ridiculous plan she had been formulating in the back of her mind. If she had any sense at all, she should take off running in the opposite direction. But a woman in love rarely has any sense at all.

She should never have suggested it. She wasn't even sure why she had. But she was not about to get out of it easily. Saturday dawned bright and beautiful. Zizi could not summon up even the slightest sore throat or vague muscle ache. She had said she would spend the day at his ranch. So, dressed in a button-down shirt and a soft, well-worn pair of jeans, Zizi pulled on her boots and headed up Ranch Road 12 toward the area known locally as Devil's Backbone.

With her hair in one long tail pulled through the back of her Spurs: NBA Champions cap, she was able to roll down the windows and let the fresh country air pour in to meet her.

The profusion of bluebonnets that colored the landscape in the last few weeks was giving way to the brighter hues of Indian Paintbrush and Mexican Hat. The roadside blossoms contrasted starkly against the rocky white limestone of the Texas Hill Country. Stands of live oak trees grew among the stubborn cedars and prickly pears.

The area, once the sole province of rugged ranch-folk and their grazing cattle was now being bought up and subdivided by retirees and wealthy young Austinites who wanted their little country acreage and hilltop views away from the hectic rush of the city.

The road twisted and turned as it wound itself through the hills making the forty-five mile an hour speed limit seem fast and exciting as if she were driving a powerful sports car. Zizi thought of the Boxster. She was smiling as she imagined Clu putting that road-hugging machine through its paces on the morning commute.

She found the turnoff easily enough. There was no grandiose pillared entry or wrought-iron gateway depicting the herd's brand. Just a large country mail-box that read simply: Langston.

Zizi eased the Corolla across the cattleguard and onto the solidly packed caliche drive. The road curved around the side of the hill near the river and then back upward. The ranch house and outbuildings were tin-roofed weathered cedar and sat upon a ridge with a wide vista of rolling hills snaked by the Blanco River. Zizi's heart melted. She'd seen her share of ranch palaces, houses so impressive and costly they made the J. R. Ewing's of Southfork look like sharecroppers. This was not one of those. Tucked away from the sight of the road, the Langston homestead did not scream, "hey, we've got money!" but rather whispered softly, "this is a place meant for family and children."

Shaded by towering pecans, the house was an old-style, one-and-a-half story country home with a steep sloping tin roof. The main entryway was on the corner and wide porches fanned out the full length of the adjoining sides. From the number of bent wicker lounge chairs and benches it was obvious that a lot of time was spent outside.

Beyond the house a dozen buildings of various ages and uses could be seen. A tall open-sided hay barn nearly matched the height of the grain silo. Most of the buildings were a mix of mortared white limestone and grayed cedar siding. Though the boundary fences were metal post and barb wire, the lots around the breeding barns and horse corrals were weathered stake and rail, dating the ranch decades earlier than the shiny machinery in the equipment sheds might suggest.

Zizi's intent was to stop in front of the house. She hated to go up and knock on the man's door, possibly encountering his mother. But she had invited herself on this fool's errand and there was nothing else to be done about it.

As she drove past an open ramada within a quarter acre fenced corral she noticed a cowboy with a couple of horses. The big, shiny bay was saddled and standing docilely as the cowboy readied the milk-white horse beside him. Zizi looked the animal over carefully, curious if this was Zafir. She knew a little bit about Arabians, but she wasn't sure if she knew enough to recognize one over another breed. Perhaps this was the gelding. He was smaller than the bay and a lot less brawny. Those were definitely traits of the Arabian. And he was unquestionably beautiful. His mane and tail were both grown long and sleek. They were pure white as well, but didn't have the same undertone hue that was near blue. His head was small and dished faced, the sides elegantly scooped inward giving him a handsome sculpted look. Even during the saddling he held himself *collected* as the horse trainers would say, his nose straight down so that he could more alertly observe those things happening both in front and to the sides. This had to be Zafir, Zizi decided. She could easily see Mr. Langston choosing to rescue this animal from a wedding carriage duty. And she could see Clu, the meek little mama's boy, tamping down his own fear and risking his father's disappointment for the need to ride him.

The cowboy had thrown the saddle across the horse's back and was buckling the girth as Zizi approached. She considered stopping to question the man as to where Clu might be, but decided against it. She would politely drive up to the house like any invited guest.

The cowboy turned and she offered a wave. This was the country and waving at those you pass, dear friends or complete strangers was the acceptable social convention. He waved back, familiar and welcoming.

Zizi did a doubletake. That *cowboy* was actually Clu Langston, her Clu Langston.

She hit the brakes.

The Corolla skidded slightly on the caliche and a cloud of dust enveloped both her and the car completely. Through the chalky haze, she looked at him, awestruck. His worn and faded gingham snap shirt clung to his lean sculpted frame faultlessly. Wranglers, as snug as skin, tapered from narrow hips down powerful thighs and long legs. His boots were scuffed and authentic. He wore a smoky gray Stetson.

He was handsome, powerful, masculine. Her heart lurched. There is something about a cowboy, Zizi thought, that just sets the blood of Texas women pounding. Her own was certainly surging. He was smiling at her, that open, caring smile. She wanted to throw herself at his feet.

"Careful Zizi," she cautioned herself, then she called out to him. "Good morning."

He patted the horse's rump as if to reassure him and then sauntered over to Zizi. His looks, his gestures, his walk, everything about him was incredibly sexy. She swallowed back the sensation of drowning.

Deliberately she took a deep breath, clicked off the lock and pulled back on the door handle.

Clu was there opening the door. He offered his hand to her in the gentle unassuming way he had that made exceptional manners seem easygoing.

"So I see you made it," he said.

"I didn't recognize you in your western duds," she admitted. "It's like a whole new you."

He laughed lightly. "Yeah, all I have to do is put a slug of tobacco in my jaw and drive Dad's old pickup down to the beer joint and I pretend I'm just one of the good ol' boys."

Clu's words were lighthearted and there was no evidence of pain upon his face. But Zizi's heart went out to him, nonetheless. Clu Langston would never really be one of the boys. What a heartbreak and a burden for him. And what a tragic secret.

Without consideration of her action, Zizi reached out to lay a sympathetic hand upon his chest.

Clu seemed momentarily startled by the gesture, but then laid his hand atop hers. She could feel the beating of his heart. Her own was pounding inside her. She was looking directly into his searching gaze. Inexplicably, she trembled.

"Zizi?"

Her name was a question.

She pulled away.

"Is this Zafir?" she asked quickly, moving away from the man who was able to touch her so deeply.

She walked up to the horse and ran her hand along his flank. Normally she would have given a strange animal a moment to get used to her, but she was so anxious to get away from the intimacy of her moment with Clu that she was foolhardy. Fortunately the Arabian was an even-tempered and accepting animal. He gave her a long assessing look, but didn't even sidestep.

"He's not the nervous type," she observed aloud.

Clu came up behind her. He was standing a little close, she thought.

"Zafir is amazingly self-possessed," he agreed. "I guess it's from those years pulling a carriage in downtown Houston. He was used to all those tourists and traffic. An occasional unfamiliar presence is not going to scare him."

Zizi turned to face Clu once more, but stepped back, deliberately reasserting that comfortable distance the two of them had always maintained.

"It's hard to imagine him pulling a buggy," she said.

Clu nodded. "It is, until you see him hitched to it. The little white two-seater was actually constructed with his proportions in mind. He originally belonged to a genteel old lady from Galveston. She loved horses, but didn't ride. She kept Zafir in her carriage house until she died. When her estate came up for auction, well, there's not much demand for draft horses of any variety."

"I suppose not," Zizi agreed.

"People believe their eyes," Clu added. "They make decisions based on appearance and just fit things into categories and dismiss them. It's a mistake my father was not prone to make."

She shook her head. "But Zafir looks so right with that saddle on him."

"Yeah," he agreed. "It seems so obvious. It's amazing sometimes what we can't see."

He patted the horse on the rump and moved closer to Zizi once more, smiling.

"So are you ready to ride him?"

"Me? Oh, I'd love to," Zizi said excitedly.

"I've packed us a lunch," he said, indicating a pair of saddlebags already hanging from the sides of the bay. "I thought I'd take you down the river to where the creek flows in. There's a nice little spot there. Cool and romantic."

"Romantic?"

"Picturesque, might be a better description," he amended quickly. "I think you might like it."

Zizi smiled at him. "I'm sure I will," she said.

Clu tightened the girth on Zafir once more and offered Zizi a leg up.

She giggled, grinning at him.

"I said I *prefer* English, but it doesn't mean I can't ride western," she said, demurring his cupped hands. She placed her booted foot into the stirrup and grasping a hank of milk-white mane, raised herself into the saddle in one fluid motion.

Clu gave her a nod of approval. "For a lady with odd preferences, you sure do that like you're familiar with it."

"I'm like Zafir here," she said. "You've looked at me too long as a librarian. It's just hard to imagine me as a cowgirl."

Chuckling, Clu mounted up and directed them toward a worn pathway. They rode single file between two stake-and-rail fences. Though it was clearly a one-horse trail, he walked the bay through the tall grass in order to be beside her.

The Arabian had an easy gait. He was alert and aware, every step careful. But there was no hesitance or jerkiness in his movements. As if he knew his job and had confidence in the combined intellect of himself and his rider. Zizi relaxed almost immediately. She remembered why she had liked riding so much. The height and strength and majesty of movement, man and animal. Even with her thoughts in such confusion as they had been the last few days, she couldn't help but enjoy herself.

"The Blanco runs across the northern edge of the property," Clu explained to her, gesturing toward the distant landscape. "It's a beautiful river, but it flooded pretty badly a couple of years ago and the land hasn't completely recovered. Still, it's a nice well-worn path, not too challenging for a rusty rider on an unfamiliar mount."

Zizi made a face at him. "I resemble that remark."

"I thought so, at least," he agreed.

As they made their way through the maze of shed and barns and outbuildings, Zizi got to see up close remnants of a way of life with which she was mostly unfamiliar. Huge barrels still set beneath the corners of the roof slopes to collect water. A tall windmill turned lazily in the morning breeze. Flocks of chickens and guineas cackled and pecked as they roamed freely from pen to pasture. The Langston ranch still bore the traces of a time gone by, a time when long distances and bad roads made the wagon trip into town an infrequent occurrence. And the Langstons who had lived here had, of necessity, been dependant upon themselves.

"I love this ranch," she told him. "It's so solid, like it's been here forever."

Clu nodded. "Because it has been," he told her. "As my old granddad used to say, 'Langstons have been camping on the side of this hill since the Alamo was just another church.'"

"Really?"

He laughed and shook his head. "My old granddad was famous for his exaggeration," he said. "But our family has been here close to a hundred and fifty years. That's still a long time and a lot of generations."

Zizi whistled appreciatively.

"It's like some great Texas dynasty novel," she

said. "I can see it now—*The Langston Legacy,* now available in paperback."

"That's undoubtedly how Mom sees it," Clu agreed. "Only her version has a soap opera element. None of her sons produce sons. So now she's wishing she'd have granddaughters."

"It is sad somehow," Zizi told him. "It looks like such a wonderful place to grow up, such a wonderful place to be a child."

"I think it was," Clu said. "For my brothers especially, but for me too. I didn't have the run of the place like they did, but I had a lot of good times as well."

She saw that he was lost for a moment in some thought that was almost melancholy. But then he was back with her, smiling.

"Of course, it's not like there will never be any more kids around here," he said. "Mom's just not the most patient type."

"So you think your brothers will get busy starting families?"

"Rob and Gabe?" He seemed surprised at the question. "Sure they will, sooner or later." he said. "Very few fellows stay bachelors forever."

"Eight percent of the population," she blurted out without thought.

Clu was momentarily taken aback and then shrugged.

"Yeah, I guess so."

Zizi hoped she hadn't embarrassed him. He hadn't

shared his secret with her. And she didn't want to push him into doing so.

"I always planned to have a family," he said.

It was all she could do to keep her jaw from yawning open in stunned surprise.

"I just haven't got around to it," he said. "But I love kids and I do hope to have a couple of them one of these days."

Zizi hadn't any idea of what to say. It was not completely surprising. Clu obviously liked younger people. He got along well with students. It was only natural that he would want the same family experience that other people had. Gay adoption was not unheard of. But that was for gay couples. Could a lone gay man adopt? Zizi had no idea.

But perhaps that was not what he was saying. Was he thinking to have a biological child? Test tube baby? Surrogate mother? A million questions swirled inside her head, but she wouldn't, she couldn't ask them. If he wanted her to know, he would tell her on his own. But that crazy scheme in the back of her mind was becoming more concrete in her thoughts.

Up ahead, cattle rested in the shade beneath the branches of a massive live oak, their white hides shown clearly against the background of earth and sky.

"Are those your cows?" she asked, deliberately changing the subject.

"The Charolaises are my mother's," Clu answered. "I just live here, remember, same as they do."

"I hope you have less Spartan accommodations," she teased.

"I have a nice room and my own office, filled with computers and fossils and books of all description," he answered. "Perfect science guy digs, not a cowboy's bunkhouse."

"Was your father disappointed that none of his sons followed in his footsteps?" Zizi asked.

Clu shook his head.

"My dad loved this place," he said. "He thought for a time that Rob might want to run it. But he counseled us all from an early age to find a better way to make a living."

"He didn't want you to raise cattle?" Zizi asked surprised.

"Oh, no."

"Why not?"

Clu was thoughtful for a moment as if forming his answer. Surprisingly, he turned to her with a mischievous grin.

"What does a rancher do when he wins the lottery?"

His abrupt change of subject caught Zizi up short, but she recovered quickly.

"A joke, huh," she said. "All right, I give. What does a rancher do when he wins the lottery?"

"Nothing," Clu answered. "He just keeps on ranching 'til the money's all gone."

Zizi groaned amiably.

"Do you know how ranching is like cocaine addiction?" he asked.

"How?" she responded, enjoying his grin.

"They both cost a fortune and never make a dime. But do you know why cocaine addiction is better than ranching?"

"Better? Why?"

"You can go into treatment for cocaine," he said. "With ranching, you just keep ranching 'til it kills you."

She groaned again.

"Where do you get these jokes?"

"I told you," he replied. "When I hang out at the beer joint, I'm just another one of the guys."

Zizi really didn't enjoy being reminded that he wasn't.

"So ranching is not a paying concern," she said, more seriously.

"Not ranching on this scale," he said. "Agribusiness is big business with huge investments and global markets. Mom raises a few cows and takes them to auction a couple of times a year. That's more of a hobby than a profit venture. She gets a tax break by keeping the farm exemption on the land. In a good year she breaks even."

"But she still does it," Zizi pointed out.

Clu nodded. "Because she still loves it. After all these years, she's still a ranchwoman at heart."

"I guess it's in her blood," Zizi agreed.

"Or rather her gene pool," he said.

"That means it's in yours too."

He chuckled and shook his head.

"I must be some kind of throwback," he said. "Or maybe a mutation."

Zizi didn't like hearing that either. He made so light of it, his choice, his preference, his inclination of nature. As if what it meant to his life, to his future, were no big deal. But it marked everything, changed everything from what might have been. And for her, that truth was weighed heavily with disappointment.

They rode along together in silence. The idea that had been niggling upon the edge of her mind for days now began to grow in her mind. It was unwise. It was injudicious. It was fraught with inherent difficulties. The more she thought about it, the more she found herself drawn to what was, absolutely, the most surprising turn her life had ever taken.

Chapter 7

His spirit buoyed, his thoughts sunny, Clu couldn't quite believe that Zizi was at the ranch, by his side, for at least a good portion of his Saturday. And he hadn't needed to risk a thing by asking her. She'd volunteered.

She looked good. She looked really good. It was amazing how some women were at their best in fancy evening clothes, bright jewelry and big hair while others looked so very good in faded blue jeans and a baseball cap. Squint-eyed he tried to picture her wearing that alone and then pulled back on his own reins. He'd have a better chance of not blowing things between them if he didn't let his mind wander in that direction.

If this wonderful gift, this day alone with her, had

any chance of being long remembered as golden-hued and romantic, then he definitely needed to squelch all thoughts that might lead to graceless groping. This was an opportunity, a very unique opportunity to perhaps let her glimpse, from a safe distance, another side of her best buddy, Clu. His natural tendencies to just grab her and kiss her would be like mixing highly unstable compounds under pressure. There was just no telling what might result.

His mother had encouraged him to try honesty. That certainly sounded like a good idea. But after hiding his feelings for so long, it was daunting to think that he might have to express them. It was thrilling as well. It was a lot like walking into a casino and putting everything you own on twenty-three red. It was exciting to do, entertaining to watch, but the aftermath could take a lifetime for recovery.

As he rode down the river trail beside Zizi, exchanging their usual light banter and esoteric word play, he knew that he needed to make a decision of some kind. He'd put his life on hold for so long, he'd nearly forgotten that he had one. One good thing about the silly granddaughter competition for Zafir, was that it reminded Clu of all that he was missing in his life. The things that he had so wanted to live for, no longer were part of his life. He'd truly wanted his career. He was a man of science and he wanted to live that way, immersed in a world of the creative analytical.

Those weren't the only dreams he'd been giving up. He wanted a future that included a wife he loved and children to nurture. He'd cast those hopes aside as well, just for the pleasure of being near Zizi.

If he risked it all and told her what was in his heart, he might lose her. That was equally untenable. The situation had paralyzed him for three years. He couldn't let that go on forever. It was like dividing by zero. The longer he did it, the more fragile the problem became.

"What is that over there?" Zizi asked, pointing to a clearing upon a distant hill. "It looks like log cabins and Indian tepees."

Clu followed her gaze and nodded. "That's what it is," he said. "The log cabins are prefab and the tepees are made of fiberglass, but that's what they are. It's a summer camp."

"I thought you owned all this land," she said.

"My mother does," he corrected. "The camp is one of her projects."

Zizi nodded.

Clu watched as the woman at his side put the Arabian through his paces. She was a good rider, not tentative or unsure. With her back straight and her hands at ease upon the reins, Zizi looked as if she rode every day. And Zafir took each step like he was leading a grand parade, almost as if he knew how well the two of them looked together.

"You're doing great," Clu told her.

She laughed, pleased with his praise.

"I guess it's just like riding a bicycle," she said.

Clu nodded and replied, teasing, "Except that you don't have to pedal."

When they reached the edge of the river it was necessary to travel single file. Clu took the lead.

The silence that settled around them was both companionable and somehow isolating. It was like their whole relationship. He got to be with her, but never one with her. She was always close, but never quite close enough.

The sound of rushing water could be heard in the distance. The Blanco, at one of its widest points, moved lazily along, calm enough that the reflection of both horses and riders were discernable. But the noise up ahead was a reliable portent of the troubled waters to come. The horses began to pick their way more carefully.

The river snaked back and forth through the Langston property, swelled by spring-fed creeks that had spilled for five hundred years cool and clean out of the limestone hills. As they approached this one the draw widened and undergrowth flourished. At the congruence of the two flows ancient cypress trees grew tall and majestic, casting broad swaths of dark shade over the stone-strewn surface. The spring branch came in on the far side, falling about three feet onto a standing piece of sandstone so long eroded it had a hole the size of a stovepipe in the center of it. The two waterways mingled and swirled together before falling over a narrow ledge and rushing through the rocky narrows downstream.

Clu stopped and dismounted, dropping the reins

to the bay in the tall grass at the edge of the draw. He untied the saddlebags with their trail picnic and slung them over his shoulder before turning to help Zizi.

She was pointing across the water to a thick length of heavy rope that draped low out of the branches of a cottonwood tree.

"Is that what I think it is?" she asked him. "Is this the swimming hole for the Langston brothers?"

He followed her gaze.

"That belongs to Rob and Gabe," he told her. "I didn't learn to swim until I started going to camp. Come, I want you to see my place."

Clu stood beside Zafir as Zizi got down. From his position he couldn't help but notice the enticing way her backside filled her blue jeans. He swallowed and deliberately looked away. Patience, he reminded himself sternly, was not only a virtue, but also the most valuable asset of the scientific mind.

It was curious how an analytical brain like his own, given this privacy and proximity, abandoned all thoughts of science for thoughts of sex.

He didn't trust himself to help her down, but once she was there and Zafir contentedly chomping at grass, he held out his hand. She took it. It was soft and warm and seemed small inside his own, but it was powerful as well. Shards of static electricity jolted through his veins. The force of it nearly stopped his heart. Yet, he kept smiling at her. How could any man help but smile at her?

He led Zizi though the accumulation of smooth

worn rock and cypress knees to the wide sandstone platform just beyond the little waterfall.

"This is my place," he said, softly almost reverently, as if he was sharing a special part of himself.

Clu glanced around and saw that it was only a big flat rock next to the river. It wasn't amazing or magical. Yet, it had always seemed so to him. When his parents had brought him down to the river to watch his brothers swim and play, this ringside seat on the beauty of nature had seemed the grandest and finest spot on the ranch. His brothers swimming, diving, and generally running wild, would bring him leaves and locust, caterpillars and frogs. He always carried a huge magnifying glass for closer observation and a journal for taking notes. His days at the water hole was the botany and zoology that rounded out the chemistry experiments in the playroom and the math he did in his head.

He turned to Zizi.

"It was a lot bigger and...impressive...I mean when I was a kid," he explained.

"It's great," she said, with unmistakable sincerity. "The trees and the water, the solemnity and the peace...I love it. Is this where we get our picnic?"

"Absolutely."

Clu felt buoyed by her enthusiasm.

They spread the red-check tablecloth upon the rock, sitting on opposite corners to anchor it. He began unpacking the romantic repast.

"Did you make lunch yourself?" she asked him.

With a grin he nodded affirmatively. "I've been up cooking since dawn," he lied with a wink.

He set the bread board between them. The blade of its knife was stored safely and neatly in one side.

"Ah...for the special entrée of the day," Clu announced in an affected voice an indeterminately foreign accent. "We have a lovely wedge of aged Manchego cheese imported from distant Spain to our local grocery store, just for madam."

He laid it on the board.

"On the side we present a browned creation of wheat, salt and yeast. Mixed and kneaded and allowed to rise, we call it bread, madam, baked fresh, right here in south Texas, but inspired by the great breads of France."

Holding the loaf by its ends, he set it next to the cheese with great ceremony.

Zizi was giggling now. It egged him on.

"Add to this, madam, a bottle of soft California merlot," he said showing her the label as if to get her approval.

"Mmm, very nice," she said, joining in the game.

"Indeed," he said. "Nine ninety-nine a bottle, but nothing is too expensive for madam."

She laughed out loud at that.

He began rifling through the saddlebag looking for the corkscrew.

"Bread and wine and cheese and...thou," she said.

There was something about the way that she

looked at him, that caused Clu nearly to stab himself as he attempted to open the wine.

"Yes," he said. "A picnic, just you and me."

He looked at her then, loving her, wanting her. What might it be like to touch her skin, to taste her lips, to...

"Whoa cowboy," he muttered to himself under his breath. That was a dangerous direction for his thoughts to be headed.

"What did you say?" Zizi asked.

"I...ah...we also have strawberries and apricots for dessert."

Clu pulled out the glasses and poured the wine. The long-stemmed goblets looked especially elegant in the rustic surroundings. And Zizi looked so natural, so perfect in the setting. It was an idyllic dream. As Clu sipped his wine and gazed at the woman he loved, he slipped into the dream and revelled.

"This must have been such a wonderful place to grow up," she said.

He nodded. "It was," he told her. "It's a real family kind of ranch. A great place to raise kids."

"If I squint just right," she said. "I think I can almost see the three Langston boys."

Clu laughed. "You can probably hear them before you can see them."

"Noisy bunch?"

"Very."

"Me and my siblings, too," she said. "Lots of arguments and accusations. Do you three fight?"

"Occasionally," Clu admitted. "But as brothers go, I think we had just about the right amount of closeness and competitive spirit."

"Is that why your mother put up Zafir as bait?"

Clu chuckled and then shrugged. "It was a feeble attempt," he said. "She's getting desperate."

Zizi was sympathetic. "I've only been here a couple of hours and I can see how much this ranch *ought* to have children on it. Think how that lack must frustrate her."

Clu nodded. "I guess when you raise three kids, you believe they'll raise kids of their own," he said. "After losing my dad, I think she really feels like life is short. It's much too important to waste on things like careers or capital accumulation."

She drank down the dregs of her wine and held out her glass for more.

"That's what she thinks my brothers have done," Clu continued. "Rob's all wrapped up in his job with Secret Service and Gabe wants to make so much money multi-millionaires will have to come to him for a loan. Until now, neither of them have indicated any interest in a permanent man-woman relationship."

"So what about you?" Zizi said.

She was looking a him. Not just looking, she was assessing him. Sizing him up as she slowly tilted her glass back and forth, the dark red liquid inside it rolling languidly.

"Yeah, I guess that leaves me," he admitted. "I certainly have thought about it."

"You have?"

"Well, of course," he said. "I love kids."

She took another sip of her wine never taking her eyes off him.

"In the right situation, with the right woman," he went on. "I've...well, I've always known that I would want that someday."

It felt strange having her watch him this way, strange, but somehow exciting. He could almost see her mind at work. He had no idea what she was thinking, but something was up, something was changing between them. He could feel the break-through coming and he wanted it. He desperately wanted it.

Zizi drank her wine.

The silence between them began to run long. Clu strained for something more to say.

"Mom told us that she wished she'd had girls," he said. "She said that at least women want to get married and start a family."

The minute the words were out of his mouth, Clu could have cut his tongue out.

"I don't mean all women, of course," he back-pedled hurriedly. "There are lots that are totally ful-filled by their careers and their...their friends. I'm not one of those guys that believe a female has to have a husband and babies in order to have a mean-ingful life."

"Of course not," Zizi agreed. "And I didn't think for a moment that you meant anything like that."

She held out her glass again.

Clu relaxed gratefully and filled it.

The bread and cheese was practically tasteless to him, but he ate it nonetheless. Zizi had yet to even take a bite.

"To some degree, I think your mother is right," she said.

He swallowed. "Really?"

"While I think both sexes do want family and children, women have their biological clocks. Men can still be fathers when they are in their nineties. If we're going to be mothers, forty is a late start. So we've got to begin thinking and planning earlier."

He nodded. "Yeah, I guess so."

"I certainly want children," Zizi stated with absolute conviction. "And I wonder how much longer I can wait."

"Oh, you've got lots of time," Clu assured her quickly. "You are young and beautiful. Every man in town wants to go out with you."

She shrugged away his compliment. "Oh that," she said. "That's just the competition, I think."

"The competition?"

Zizi smiled at him and then shook her head and gave a long-suffering sigh.

"I guess you would be the one guy in town who doesn't know about it," she said.

She took another sip of wine and moved to sit cross-legged on the tablecloth.

"When I came to San Marcos it was my first big job," she said. "I wasn't really thinking about dating or getting involved with anyone."

Clu nodded. That made sense. Most people approached a new position just that way.

"I went out with a few guys," she continued. "It was just casual dating, I thought. I didn't feel like I had anything in common with any of them. So after a couple of dates, I'd suggest that they just move on."

She gazed at sunlight shining through her glass for a moment as if lost in contemplation.

"I didn't think much about it," she said. "Until suddenly it seemed like I had this reputation for being unattainable."

A knot tied in Clu's stomach.

"Now when men ask me out, half the time it's on bets or dares or just for the challenge of seeing if they can be the one to get me, even if they don't want me."

There was no bitterness in her voice, only sadness and resignation.

"It's like some terrible self-perpetuating cycle," she said. "The more I wind up dating these bozos who are trying to show off to their friends, the more rejections I seem to pile up and the more my notoriety as Zizi-One-Date grows."

Of course that was the way it was, Clu thought to himself. He should have realized long ago that what people believed about Zizi could never be true. What an idiot he was! Maybe his mother was right. Maybe honesty was the best policy.

"I've heard you called that," he said. "Truthfully, I've wondered myself about all those guys."

She smiled and nodded.

"I never meet men who are genuinely interested in me," she said. "*You* are the only man in my life who seems genuinely interested in me."

Clu's heart began to pound.

She looked up at him. Something in the intensity of her gaze subdued him. This was no lighthearted conversation. Her words were clearly thought out and deeply meant.

"Maybe I don't have to wait," she said.

"What?"

"For a family, for children," she said. "Maybe we don't have to wait."

Clu eyed her, speechless. He didn't know what she was thinking. He didn't know what she was saying. He didn't know if he could breathe.

Zizi downed her wine in one long gulp and held out the empty glass to him once more. He gave her the last of the bottle.

"I cannot imagine any man in the world that I feel closer to or more comfortable with than you," she said. "And I don't know anyone who would make a better father."

"Ah...thanks," he managed to get out.

"Here we are, two close friends, two people who adore each other, two people who both want family," she said. "Doesn't it seem sort of stupid that when looking for someone to share a life with, we've never bothered to look at each other."

"Oh, my God, Zizi, I—"

"I want to have a family," she interrupted. "I

can't imagine anyone I would rather have it with than you, my best friend.''

"You want to have a baby with me?''

Carefully he set his wine down, afraid that the glass might slip through his fingers.

"Not just a baby,'' she clarified. "My parents are very traditional and I suppose I am myself. I'd want marriage. Mommy and Daddy together until death do us part.''

As the truth of her words filtered through, his mind warred with adulation and disbelief. It was happening. It was really happening. After all this time of waiting, his dreams were coming true. Zizi wanted him. She wanted to be his. How could it be true? How could this have happened? How could it be this easy?

Clu didn't bother to answer his own questions. Immediately he was beside her pulling her into his arms. He brought his mouth down to hers, eager to taste those lips that he had longed for so long.

At the last second she turned her head and his kiss landed upon her jaw. She held herself stiffly in his arms, as if she were uncomfortable, uncertain. Perhaps she was. This was their first kiss, their first moment of romantic affection. It was all new to them. Maybe it was completely new to her. And he hadn't even declared himself.

"Zizi, my Zizi,'' he said to her with all the tenderness in his heart. "I would love to marry you. I want to be the father of your children. I'm so surprised. You can't know…''

Clu wanted to declare his heart, he wanted to tell her how long he had loved her and how often he had dreamed of this moment. Valiantly he tried to put the words together.

"You know I think that honesty is the best policy, for friends and especially for couples. There are things about me that you don't know. Things I've never said. I have to tell you—"

She placed her fingers atop his lips.

"Shh," she said. "You don't have to say it. I already know."

"You know?" Clu was stunned. "How long have you known? Did you know from the first?"

"I suspected, I guess, from the very first," she told him. "People talk. But I didn't really believe it until the last few days. Bonnie was speculating about it and then there was some things you said."

"Bonnie knew?"

It was unbelievable.

"Oh, she doesn't know, but she thinks she does," Zizi said. "I didn't encourage her, I can assure you of that."

"Well, I don't care who knows it," Clu said, laughing.

He pulled her tightly into his embrace once more.

"Zizi, I'm going to be the best husband you could ever imagine," he promised. "I'm going to spend my life making you the happiest woman in the world. No wait, I want to do this right."

He pulled away. He was already on his knees, so he took her hand and brought it to his lips.

"Aziza Josephs," he said. "Will you marry me?"

Chapter 8

Monday morning she woke up feeling queasy. But that was no surprise. Zizi had felt that way for two days. It wasn't morning sickness, though that welcome but miserable malady was still a possibility in her future. This unpleasant nausea could be better described as *marriage sickness*.

Zizi was getting married to a man that she loved, a man who was her best friend, a man who was intelligent, interesting, good-looking and wealthy, a man who very much wanted a family. She had forced the issue, but he had proposed with enthusiasm. The two of them were going to be wed. And the prospect of it made her sick to her stomach.

It had seemed so reasonable. She could be with the man she loved. She would have his name and bear his children. But now, faced with the reality of it, she found that wanting a man who, by his very nature, did not want her was somehow deflating.

Clu was so happy. He was as excited as if it were a real marriage. He'd wanted her to stay for dinner Saturday night and meet his mother. The prospect was daunting. Zizi just couldn't meet the woman. She just couldn't look her in the eye. It didn't matter that she was willing to give Mrs. Langston the grandchildren she obviously wanted, it felt wrong and Zizi didn't want the close scrutiny of anyone.

But it was not like she could keep it a secret. Clu came into San Marcos on Sunday to take her to church. Zizi first thought to use her sick stomach as a reason to stay home. But Clu's newfound interest in putting his arms around her and trying to kiss her was even less appealing than facing five hundred eyes at the church.

It was all well and good for him to hug and smooch her like a best buddy, but she could not remain unmoved by his nearness. Intellectually she knew that his hand at her waist was just a touch, but her senses called it a caress and it stirred powerful feelings within her.

Did he feel anything? Could he feel anything? Would he be capable of performing sexually with her? Or would their children be conceived with a turkey baster? And either way, could her own heart bear the incongruity?

She arrived at work, her thoughts in a whirl. So much so that the bouquet of red roses sitting upon her desk took her completely by surprise. Marianne scurried in right behind her.

"They just came," she said. "Aren't they gorgeous!"

"Yes," Zizi answered, feeling strangely as if she'd gotten the wind knocked out of her.

"There's a note," Marianne pointed out excitedly. "See what he says."

"He?"

"Well, of course it has to be him. Clu," she said. "What's wrong with you? You sound like you just had a major attack of the stupidities. Oh and ah…congratulations! I'm so thrilled. And I love weddings."

"You heard?"

Marianne nodded. "Millie Winkleman…Dave's wife, saw you two together in church yesterday. She thought it looked like something was up and called Bonnie. You know Bonnie, she dragged it out of Clu this morning. By now everybody on campus must know."

Her enthusiasm was almost overwhelming. Zizi felt inadequate to respond to it.

"You two were so sly," Marianne continued. "None of us suspected. Everybody thought you were just friends. In fact, some people, Bonnie especially, thought…well never mind about that. I'm so happy!"

Edgy and uncomfortable, Zizi reached for the little card. She fumbled with it clumsily for a moment before getting it open. She just stared at the words written there. She heard a long, heartfelt sigh and turned to see her assistant behind her, peering over her shoulder.

"Langston's Law of Astronomy and Physics for the bride-to-be," Marianne read aloud. "A Geekoid moving towards a heavenly body will generate floral display in warning of imminent encounter. You and me. Lunch. The Palmer House. One o'clock."

Zizi continued to stare at the card. The phrase bride-to-be seemed almost burned onto her retina. She'd agreed to marry this man. No, *agreed* was not a fair term. She had proposed that this man marry her. With an unrequited romance in her heart and a couple of glasses of wine in her head, she'd thrown caution, and what common sense she had, to the wind. She'd asked him to be her husband.

"This must really be love," Marianne said beside her.

"What?"

"I see you here in the flesh, but your thoughts are a billion miles away," she said. "Or maybe they are just across the building."

Marianne giggled delightedly. Zizi tried valiantly to smile along with her. Apparently she was unable to mask her real feelings.

"Hey, it's okay to be nervous," her assistant said reassuringly. "When Dale and I got engaged I went back and forth between sighs of rapture and tears of anguish. And I was so young, I was still too dumb to know how scary happily-ever-after can be."

Zizi did her best to put a brave face on it. "I

suppose I have those pre-wedding jitters everybody talks about," she said.

Marianne nodded. "I'll fix your schedule so that you can have the late lunch," she said. "And I just want to say how very happy I am for you. Everyone is. We all thought that you two were just friends, but it's unanimous here in the department that you and Clu are going to be great together."

Zizi thanked her and determinedly tried to generate that same level of confidence. They would be perfect, she reminded herself. They had so much in common. Felt mutual respect. They both wanted children. They were the best of friends. Those things had convinced her on Saturday. Monday morning, however, such justifications were lame.

Gratefully, this particular Monday was as hectic as usual. Zizi was so loaded down with matters requiring her attention that she had hardly a moment to think about her frightening future. In fact, she could, and would, easily have put it from her mind completely if every employee she saw hadn't taken the opportunity to offer best wishes.

Apparently Marianne was right. Planting a piece of gossip with Bonnie Tugman was better than radio advertising and billboard combined. Everyone who worked in the building seemed to know. And she got calls from friends and acquaintances all across campus who had heard the news.

Even a young student, stringy-haired and thin enough to make the malnourished seem pudgy, made her way past Marianne and into her office.

"Is it true you're going to marry Dr. Langston?"

Her bottom lip was quivering and her eyes, huge behind thick lens glasses, were welling with tears.

"Yes, it's true," Zizi answered.

"He's the nicest man in the library, the nicest man in this school. He's...he's... You better treat him good!"

The little girl fled in tears.

Zizi went to the doorway, looking questioningly at Marianne.

"Who was that?"

"Her name's Brittany, I think," her assistant answered. "She's a freshman, one of the Geekoids."

"Crush, I guess," Zizi said.

Marianne nodded. "You'd best be prepared for that. There's probably a hundred baby broken hearts just like hers."

"Yeah, I guess so."

"Makes me glad I'm not so young," Marianne said. "I'd hate to spend all that emotional energy loving someone who will just simply never even think to love you back."

Her words stabbed Zizi like a knife. She and young Brittany had more in common than anyone would ever know.

"It's almost one," Marianne said, glancing down at her watch. "The eager bridegroom should be here to whisk you away momentarily."

"Oh, right," Zizi said.

She went back into her office. She checked the mirror in her compact and thought she looked pale.

She put on some lipstick, but that only seemed to make it worse. She was digging through her purse for blush when Clu showed up. He was all smiles.

"You ready?" he asked.

"I was trying to fix my face," she told him.

"You don't need fixing," Clu said moving toward her. "You are the most beautiful woman I know."

He leaned forward to kiss her. Zizi turned her head defensively and his lips landed safely upon her cheek.

She stood up. They were close, too close Zizi thought. But with the chair at the back of her legs there was no room to retreat, only to sit back down. Having him lean over her seemed even more intense than being within arm's length.

"Let's go," she said.

Clu nodded and stepped back, gesturing toward the glass wall that separated them from the rest of her department. "I guess this isn't the place, is it?"

He took her hand in his. It felt strange to walk with him this way. He was smiling broadly, proudly. When he was offered congratulations, Clu beamed with pleasure. He spoke to everyone they passed, obviously proud to have her at his side.

But why wouldn't he be, Zizi thought. He was displaying a deliberate deceit. He wanted the world to think that he was in love with a woman, so no one would believe that his preference was men.

When the elevator door closed in front of them, he loosed her hand. She'd expected that. What she had not expected was that he would wrap his arm around her waist and pull her tight against him.

"Alone at last," he said.

Startled, Zizi stiffened.

Clu's brow furrowed. "It's okay, Zizi," he said comfortingly as he put some distance between them. "I didn't mean to scare you. It's me, Clu, remember? I'm your best friend."

He reached for her hand again. He held it in his own and patted it reassuringly.

"How was your morning?" he asked, gently changing the subject to neutral ground.

"Busy," she answered.

She related the story of Brittany's visit to her office.

As the elevator door opened, Clu escorted Zizi out into the parking garage with a hand at the small of her back.

"You must have misunderstood," he said. "I can't imagine that little Brittany has a crush on me. She's one of the Geekoid kids, just eighteen. I'm sure she was just wanting to meet you. She probably thinks of me as one of the guys, a sort of big brother."

Zizi didn't dispute his interpretation, though she knew it to be wrong. She didn't want Clu to have any more insight into women's hearts. He might learn to look into her own.

He opened the passenger door of his Porsche.

"I've never ridden in your car before," Zizi pointed out.

"I know," Clu answered. "So we'd better enjoy it while we can."

He closed the door and walked around to his side and got in.

"What do you mean, 'enjoy it while we can?'" she asked as they strapped on their seat belts.

"A two-seater is not exactly ideal for a family," Clu answered. "What do you think? Should we trade it in for some conservative family sedan or should we go the whole nine yards and get us a minivan?"

"You'd give up this car?" Zizi was genuinely surprised.

"Do you see a place for a car seat in here?" he asked.

The question was obviously rhetorical. Zizi didn't bother to answer. Of course getting married, having a baby, would involve changes. She knew that. And yet somehow she thought they could do this without everybody knowing, without making a big deal of it, without really doing anything different.

Clu started up the engine and they zipped out of the parking space, through the rows of cars in the garage and out onto the street. He wasn't driving at all fast, but the tiny road-hugging sports car made ordinary driving seem more fun, more like a carnival ride than a commute. In a few moments they were off campus just outside of downtown, turning into the parking lot of the Palmer House.

"Did you call your parents yet?" he asked.

Zizi felt a flood of unexpected guilt.

"No, not yet," she answered. "What about you?"

Clu nodded. "I told Mom last night. She is so thrilled. She can hardly wait to meet you. I had to make her promise not to drive into town this morning to introduce herself."

"Oh, dear," Zizi said, her courage failing her.

Clu opened the door for her and led her into the restaurant. "Don't worry," he told her. "She's going to love you. Seeing me happy is enough to make her love you already."

Zizi nodded. She wondered if his mother knew the truth about him. She wondered if she was going to have to live their lie in front of everyone. She certainly could never tell her own parents. They'd never understand it. And his mother probably wouldn't either.

"Two?" the hostess inquired of Clu.

"Can we have a quiet corner," he said. "How about here on the patio?"

He glanced toward Zizi for her to concur.

"That would be fine," she said. "Something private."

Clu smiled at her approvingly.

The patio tables of Palmer House were separated from each other by vibrant green foliage, palm fans, copper plant and dieffenbachia. They were seated beneath a broad low limb of an ancient oak. The hostess set menus in front of them. Clu ordered raspberry iced tea for two.

"I wish that it could be champagne," he told Zizi

the minute they were alone. "But that would make this afternoon a long one."

"It's certainly best to have a clear head," she agreed.

From his pocket, Clu pulled out a small velvet box. He opened it and set it on the table next to her.

"I thought that before we face our parents, you'd want to have something on your hand to show."

The *something* he referred to was a dome-cut star ruby set amid a crescent moon of sparkling diamonds. Zizi just stared at it.

"I know it's not traditional," Clu said. "But red is definitely your color and I wanted a symbol that was special and unique. Like us."

Zizi wanted to cry. She wanted to scream to the heavens. She wanted to sob and moan with anguish.

"What are you thinking?" he asked her.

"I'm thinking it is the most beautiful engagement ring I've ever seen," she answered truthfully.

She heard Clu's sigh of relief.

"Let's try it on," he said. "I had to guess at the size."

He took her hand in his. She looked down to see that she was trembling. Clu was slightly clumsy, but managed without too much trouble to slip the gorgeous piece of jewelry onto the third finger of her left hand.

It looked beautiful. It was a perfect size and style for her long, narrow hand. Somehow, he had known that.

With the dazzling ruby in place, Clu looked into

her eyes and Zizi saw something there, an intensity that she didn't understand. He leaned forward to kiss her. Immediately she sat back in her chair and brought her hand up as if admiring the sight of the ring on her finger.

"It's very beautiful," she told him. "And so thoughtful of you. Thanks so much."

To her own ears the words sounded strained and detached. Zizi wanted to cry. All those years she had rejected one likely guy after another because she had not wanted to settle. She had not wanted to marry for any reason other than mindless, passionate, all-consuming true love. She had all those things to give. And she could give them to the wonderful man who had just put a ring upon her finger. But she had come at last to settle for less than perhaps she might have gotten from the men she had cast aside.

Clu smiled at her, apparently determined not to be put off by her ambivalence.

"I saw it and bought it," he explained. "And then I thought that I should have allowed you to pick it out or at least hint to me what you might like."

"I didn't even think about an engagement ring," she admitted. "I mean, I just didn't think we'd have a long enough engagement to need one."

Clu looked surprised. "You don't want a long engagement?"

"Well, no," she said. "I don't see any reason for it. And if you want to win Zafir, we need to…to get started."

"Zafir?" Clu shook his head and chuckled. "Neither that horse nor my mother's little brotherly competition has any part in this decision. I hope you don't think that is why I want to marry you?''

"Oh, no, I know why," she said.

"So there is really no reason to rush, if you don't want to," Clu assured her. "I realize that women can't plan a fancy wedding in a few days. I'm resigned to waiting."

"You want a big wedding?"

"I want whatever you want," he said. "I would assume your mother would have some ideas as well. My mom was already speculating this morning about your parents' church in San Antonio and how far ahead one has to book the St. Anthony Hotel for a reception."

"Oh, no, we can't get married in church," Zizi said, horrified.

Clu looked puzzled. "Why not?"

Zizi didn't want to answer. She didn't want to tell him that she could never make vows before God based on lies about who they were and what their relationship would be.

"I just...I just don't want to wait that long," she said. "I want to run off. Las Vegas, I guess or the county courthouse. Something quick and...and private."

Clu's brow was furrowed in concern, but he nodded. "All right," he said. "Whatever you want."

The waitress came and they gave their orders. The tortilla soup was renowned as the best in town. Zizi was too nervous to try to eat anything more substantial.

"The only way we are going to be able to keep my mother away," Clu said, "is to run off and not tell her. So I guess we're talking Vegas."

"That sounds good to me," Zizi said. "The sooner the better."

Clu nodded vaguely and reached into his pocket for his Daytimer.

"We could do it over a weekend," she said. "Fly up on Friday night and back on Sunday afternoon."

He agreed vaguely as he studied his calendar.

"The next two weekends are out," he said. "I'm taking vacation time next week. I already have a commitment that it's too late to get out of."

"Next week?" Zizi swallowed. "You mean the first week of June?"

He looked up at her. "Yeah, I have someplace that I go every year. I guess you'd say it's become sort of an annual tradition with me. I see old friends, meet new ones. People count on me to be there."

Zizi's heart was in her throat. That's one thing she hadn't thought of. She hadn't thought about him continuing his secret life. It was a world that was alien and therefore frightening to her. And definitely dangerous to her peace of mind.

"Every year I go to—"

"Don't tell me," she interrupted. "I don't want to know. We're not married yet and your life is your own."

"I wouldn't want to keep anything from you,"

he said. "Maybe someday you'd want to come with me."

"No, I don't think so," she answered with certainty. "Clu, I have to tell you something."

"What is it?" he asked.

"I don't know what your expectations are for this marriage," Zizi said to him. "I don't know how you want to play it or what we will be like together, but I have to insist, and there is no room for compromise on this, I have to insist that you be faithful to me."

Clu's eyes narrowed and he studied her as if he had never seen her before.

"Zizi, sweetheart, of course I will," he said. "How could you think anything less?"

"All right then," she said, raising her chin bravely. "I want us to be married this week. We can get our blood test today after work and our license at the end of the week. We can say our vows at the courthouse. I want you to be my legal, faithful husband before you go off on your…your *vacation*."

Chapter 9

"It just doesn't make a lot of sense," Clu mumbled to himself as he sat at the reference desk attempting to post the weekly statistics on his laptop.

"Of course it doesn't make sense," Bonnie Tugman piped in. "The statistics never make sense in this library. Is this the first day you've noticed that?"

Clu was momentarily startled at her comment. He hadn't realized that he'd spoken aloud. And he hadn't been thinking about the numbers he was filling into the little boxes upon the screen.

"I'm sorry, Bonnie," he said. "I was talking to myself."

"You get more like my husband every day," she answered. "That man is about to drive me completely insane, you know. I don't know why I even put up with him.''

Clu was no longer listening. He was thinking about Zizi Josephs, the only thing that made sense in his world, and marveling how the two of them suddenly didn't make any sense at all.

He looked up and gazed longingly toward the Circulation Department. He couldn't see her, but he knew that she was there. Was she smiling, happy, upbeat as she always had been? Or was she the way she'd been at lunch, solemn, thoughtful, somehow almost wounded.

His Zizi was officially to become *his* Zizi. They were to be married, husband and wife, one flesh, the seeds of a family looking toward the future together. And he had never felt so distant from her since the day they'd met.

None of it made sense. Out of the clear blue she'd offered to marry him. And not in some far off happily-ever-after. She wanted a wedding right away. If in his most hopeful fantasies he'd ever imagined this, he would have said it would make him the happiest man in the world. But it *had* suddenly happened and as far as he could tell, he wasn't all that happy.

''I certainly had my choices, let me tell you. I could have married any man in this town,'' Bonnie rambled on.

Clu ignored her. He was thinking about Zizi. He was unhappy. She was unhappy. There was something wrong here. Something fundamentally wrong.

For one thing, they hadn't said that they loved each other. That afternoon down at the river, he had tried.

She had stopped him, saying that she knew it. And since then, it was as if she didn't want to hear it. Didn't most women want "the words"? Wasn't that what the talk shows and radio advisors were always telling men, to "say the words." He wanted to say them. In truth, he wanted to hear them. But apparently she didn't.

Don't worry about it! he admonished himself. She wanted to be his wife, so she must care about him, even if she couldn't say so. *Don't look for a problem where there isn't one.*

And if her nonspoken love were not strange enough, the woman who wanted to be the mother of his children didn't seem to want to kiss him. That really confused him.

He knew that there were all different kinds of relationships. He prided himself on openness and acceptance. He didn't think that certain intimate milestones must be passed by a specific time. But he did imagine that most men who were officially engaged and had a wedding secretly scheduled at the end of the week had at least shared a kiss with their bride.

He'd tried to meet her lips with his own at least a dozen times in the last three days. She always stiffened up and pulled away, or turned her head at the last moment. It was as if she didn't want him to touch her, though he'd felt her pulse racing. He might not be the most experienced Romeo in Texas, but he could tell if a woman was excited. There was nothing inherently cold in Zizi, yet she deliberately shied away from physical contact.

He had not pushed her, nor would he. Still, Clu was hurt and felt confused.

Don't dwell on the negatives, he told himself. Perhaps she was simply nervous and inexperienced. My God, could she be that inexperienced? How did you ask a thirty-three year old woman if she was a virgin? You didn't. At least Clu didn't. He hadn't asked that question of anyone.

Just leave it alone, don't mess up the good that you've got, he warned himself once more. Their sex life was something they could work out together. It was the sort of thing where infinite practice was no hardship.

Bonnie had moved from her diatribe upon the faults and shortcomings of her spouse and partner to the deficiencies in her lazy, thankless offspring.

Clu continued to ponder his wedding and his bride-to-be. She wanted to marry quickly, tomorrow if possible. She didn't want their families, their friends, to share in their joy. He didn't mind a private ceremony at the county courthouse, though it wasn't his first choice. But he had the distinct impression that she chose it specifically as if she were ashamed of what she was doing.

And then there was that strange statement about being faithful. Since when did a bride have to tell the groom that she expected that?

"Quit worrying!" he ordered himself aloud.

"How can I stop it?" Bonnie answered him. "It's my nature."

Clu was startled from his musings once more, surprised that again he'd spoken aloud. Zizi was going to be his wife. Maybe she was acting strange and unhappy about it, but she was wearing that ring on her finger. He'd won. So why couldn't he just accept his good luck and go on?

"It's not *my* nature," he said.

He was not the type of man who worried about nothing. He was a man of science. In science, questions were never ignored and nothing unproved was ever just accepted.

Clu rose to his feet.

"Where are you going?" Bonnie asked him.

"To work out some problems," he answered.

He crossed the main floor of the library in long strides. If people spoke to him, he paid them no mind. He walked directly through the Circulation Department and into Zizi's office.

She was in discussion with Marianne, but he refused to turn around and wait for a better time. They were going to talk this out, the way they should have the day it came up.

He couldn't just accept his good luck and go on, because lives are not lived from thrill to thrill, joy to joy, miracle to miracle. Lives are lived from day to day. That was what childhood cancer had taught him. That is what he tried to share with the struggling everyday survivors that he met.

He knew it was a risk. *She wants you now. She'll marry you now. If you push, you might lose her.*

Strangely his mind wandered to Zafir. He remembered how drawn he was to ride the white Arabian. And how frightened he was that he would make a mess of it, embarrass himself in front of his family, risk the love and respect that his father had for him. But he had risked it. He had risked it all. And he had gained far more than he'd ever imagined.

"We have to talk...now."

The last word was directed at Marianne, whose eyes had suddenly become big as saucers.

"You're right," Zizi agreed. "We do need to talk."

Marianne scurried out of the room, shutting the door behind her. Still, the glass wall gave little sense of privacy.

"Not here," Clu said. "Come on."

He didn't even look behind as he led her through the back of the library, through Acquisitions and Cataloging, up the stairway, through a door marked Staff Only and into Microfilm Storage.

The windowless cavern was filled with row after row of shoulder-high cabinets of gleaming pea-green metal. Clu walked down three rows before he saw the empty filer's chair. He rolled it up next to the nearest cabinet and offered Zizi a seat. She politely declined.

"Something is going on here that I'm not completely sure about," Clu began. "I think that I should speak plainly."

"No, wait," Zizi said. "I should go first. I'm the one who needs to apologize."

"Apologize?"

"Well maybe not apologize," she said. "But at least I should try to explain how I feel. I want to go through with this. I want to be your wife. I have...I have genuine feelings for you that perhaps you are unaware of. I know that I've pressured you to do this at a faster pace than you would have. And I understand that you would like to have your family with you. I'm just...I just can't even think about you going off on that...that vacation. I know I shouldn't feel like this, I know I shouldn't take it personally, but the idea of you there...in Key West...it bothers me. I have to tell you that it bothers me."

"Key West?"

"I know that you're going to Key West."

Clu just stared at her for a long moment, surprised. Eventually he managed a chuckle. "Well, I suppose the kids would love that," he said. "But the Langston Foundation just can't afford it."

"The Langston Foundation?"

"We've got kids coming from all over south Texas and with the competition for cancer resource dollars, well, Camp Can-Do couldn't even make it through the summer without all of us volunteers."

"Camp Can-Do? What is Camp Can-Do?"

"That's the camp my mother founded," he answered. "You saw it. With the prefab log cabins and the fiberglass tepees."

She continued to look confused.

"Mom wanted to send me to camp like my brothers," he explained. "But back then there weren't any places that took kids with cancer. So she simply started one, just for cancer kids and their brothers and sisters. It's the first week of June every year."

"I didn't know you had cancer," Zizi said the words in almost a whisper.

Clu shrugged. "I told you that I was sick all the time as a kid."

"You said sick," Zizi insisted. "You *never* said cancer."

"Probably not," Clu admitted. "It's a really powerful word. It scares people or makes them feel pity. Neither reaction is particularly helpful."

Zizi's eyes were wide, her expression incredulous.

"I hope that this is not scaring you," he said. "I've been free of disease for twenty years. I shouldn't have any problem becoming a father and my children are no more likely to get cancer than any other children."

"You were sick? Through your childhood?"

"On and off about nine years."

"So that's why you spent so much time with your mother," she said.

Clu nodded. "Yeah, Mom did most of the running back and forth to the hospital. Dad had a ranch and a business to run and my two brothers to take care of as well. When I was home, everybody helped, but Mom was pretty much in charge of my care."

"And that's why you were *different* from your brothers."

"Cancer made me different as a kid," he said. "Back then, different was the worst thing to be. Now, it doesn't matter so much and I'm just me, Clu Langston."

"Clu Montgomery Langston," she said.

He nodded. "Awful, huh. My mother's maiden name."

Zizi was looking at him strangely. "Is there another way in which you are different from your brothers?" she asked.

Clu couldn't figure out what she was getting at.

"You mean, like I'm a science nerd, a Ph.D., ah…ah…what?"

She didn't help him out.

"Clu," she asked quietly. "Why do you want to marry me? Is it for the horse?"

"The horse? I told you I wouldn't marry anyone over a horse."

"Then why?"

This was his moment. The moment that he had wanted and the moment that he had dreaded. The moment when he told her everything that was in his heart, everything that she had been unwilling to hear.

"Are you going to let me say it?" he asked.

"Say what?"

He smiled. "Zizi, I love you. I have loved you, since forever. I…I am a man of science and one of the wonderful things about science is that the more that you learn, the more that you realize you don't understand. I thought that I knew what I wanted in life. I wanted a busy, active career and an agreeable wife who could be a lover and a partner. I thought I knew exactly how to find that. Until the day I walked into this library and met you. At that moment, somewhere inside me I felt a special bond between us. A bond that was more spiritual than physical, but held me more tightly than anything in my world so far. I couldn't leave here. I couldn't leave you. I gave up my life, my career, my future in science to sit across a library from you and dream that someday you might be mine. I want to marry you, Zizi, because I love you. I don't know what your feelings are for me. But I hope they are, in some way, like my own.''

She was looking up at him. Her eyes were wide with wonder and her expression more joyful than he'd seen it in days.

''Oh, Clu, I love you, too!''

''You do?''

''I kept looking for a man to love and none of them were that man, then you walk into my life and you're perfect except...except...oh Clu, we've been so stupid. We've waited so long.''

He didn't want to wait anymore. He wanted to kiss her, just one little kiss. He would try not to press her, not to frighten her, but he had to taste her. He had to taste those lips that spoke such sweet, sweet words.

Clu pulled her to him gently. There was no hesitation in her. Zizi wrapped her arms around his neck and when he brought his mouth down to hers, she was open and eager.

It was a lovers' kiss. Seeking and revealing as they lingered over lips and teeth and tongues. It was an elemental sharing, filling his heart with aching tenderness and his body with sizzling fire. He tried to restrain himself. He didn't want to scare her, but suddenly he knew this was no frightened fawn in his arms. His Zizi was a true, complete and physical being as well as a spritely spirit and soul mate. She returned his affection full force and without inhibition.

Clu ran a hand down her spine, along the concave of her .7 waist and the alluring curve of her well-shaped backside. Her flesh was firm and responsive. His own was rising to the occasion as well. He ached to rub himself against her, but politely broke off the kiss and put a little distance between them.

Zizi would have none of that. She pressed herself against him. Clu moaned aloud as the firm roundness of her bosom flattened against his chest and the top of her pelvis fit snugly at his groin. They were kissing once more, deeply, intimately.

Her dark, silky hair had come loose from its conservative confines and the soft strands fell in their faces. The scent of it lured Clu's mouth from her lips down the length of her jaw to the sensitive skin at the nape of her neck and behind her ear. He wanted to bury himself in that sensual feminine softness. He wanted to explore her, subdue her, devour

her, lose himself in her. He allowed himself one
tender love bite on her throat as he felt her own
small, delicate teeth nipping playfully at his earlobe.

Her hands were everywhere, measuring his shoulders, massaging his back. One set of questing fingers
mussed his hair. While the other slid over his ribs.

It was impossible to believe that they had never
touched before. He knew instinctively all her
sweetest, most vulnerable spots. And she, in turn,
caressed with a confidence that was without reserve.
She burrowed her hands inside his jacket and eased
it from his back. It slipped unnoticed to the floor.

He returned his mouth to her own once more, tast-
ing her pleasurably. She made tiny, hungry sounds
in her throat and wiggled her hips suggestively. The
combination nearly drove Clu over the edge. Unable
to resist, he stroked her bottom and brought his other
hand up to cup her left breast. It was firm, larger
than he would have thought, and at its peak he could
feel a thick, pouty nipple.

He felt a quick stab of frustration. There were far
too many clothes between him and the prize that he
sought. His fingers flew to the neckline of her two-
piece suit.

"Let me just open this," he said. "Let me just
open it a little."

Zizi didn't bother to answer, but while he fumbled
apart the top button, she undid the other three. He
pulled the sides of fabric apart and his breath caught
in his throat. The bra she was wearing was some
sort of red diaphanous material that was virtually

see-through. Those nipples that he had wanted so much to inspect more closely were in complete view. Lovingly, almost reverently he caressed her. He dragged his gaze from the sight to glimpse her face, eyes narrowed in dreamy fulfillment, lips parted in pleasured expectation.

The fevered energy inside was flowing between them as well and Clu didn't try to fight it. He lowered his mouth to her breast, teasing her with his tongue and suckling her proud, hardened nipples.

Zizi was not at all passive in this. She made swift work of discarding his tie and loosing his shirt. One stubborn button that held fast was jerked free and shot against the pea-green metal with a distinctive ping.

Her neatly manicured fingernails scored his bare chest. The sensation heightened his need to near mindlessness. In a haze of blue desire all his senses were Zizi, all Zizi, totally Zizi.

She was in no better control. The sounds she made, part cry, part plea, were so sexual they nearly turned his legs to jelly. He wasn't sure if he could remain standing. Zizi didn't seem all that steady herself.

Grasping her below the ribs, Clu picked her up, intent upon propping them both against the filing cabinet. She didn't bother to put her feet back on the floor, but wrapped them around him. The action raised her skirt practically to the waistband. And the feel of her high heels against his buttocks was uniquely exciting, spurring him forward.

He clasped her bottom, a cheek in each hand, and raised her a couple of inches to make her fit against him more tightly, more intimately. She made a little startled sound.

"Oh! Oh, Clu, is all of that…is that you?" she asked in a startled whisper.

It took him a moment to find his voice. When he did, he tried to make a joke of it.

"Well, I'm not carrying a slide rule in my pocket, if that's your question," he answered modestly.

He punctuated his words with another kiss.

"Please don't worry, my Zizi," he reassured her tenderly. "I know how to be gentle. I know how to be patient. We'll take our time. We won't do anything until you're ready."

"I'm ready," she whispered. "I am so very, very ready."

The fact that it was the wrong time and the wrong place entered neither mind. Fortuitously, at that moment a curious Bonnie Tugman found her way to the Microfilm Storage to see what her co-worker was up to. She slipped into the door quietly. She could hear muffled voices, but it didn't sound much like a normal conversation. She surreptitiously snooped her way down the rows of pea-green metal cabinets, anxious to find out what was going on.

"Oh my God!" she screamed as she came around the corner and caught sight of the startled couple wrangling in flagrantly indecent amour.

Chapter 10

Zizi invited her fiancé over for dinner; kibbe and yogurt salad, her mother's recipe. But they hadn't even bothered to eat it. Their hello kiss had quickly escalated into raw, passion-filled and achingly loving sexual encounter. They lay together, naked, in her tousled white wicker bed, sated, satisfied and totally exhausted. Her cat, Byron, was snuggled up contentedly against Clu's other side.

He ran a gentle, loving hand from the curve of her throat, up across the tip of her breast down to the narrowness of her waist and then across her stomach to the attractive patch of damp dark curls at the crux of her thighs.

"Did I hurt you?" he asked her.

She shook her head. "I'll probably be sore tomorrow," she admitted. "But it was...mmm... wonderful."

"You are wonderful," he said. "You are everything I ever imagined and softer and sweeter and...and hotter than I ever dreamed."

They smiled at each other. She made a sound in her throat that might have been a purr. Their lips met. Just a touch at first and then again, more deeply. They were attuned now. They had kissed a thousand times through this day. They hoped the future would bring a thousand more a day for a thousand years.

"I love you, Zizi Josephs," he said.

"I know," she answered. "And I love you."

"We may have to wait until the end of the week, but I feel like today you became my wife, Zizi," he said. "Right now, I want to promise for better or worse and forsaking all others 'til death do us part."

"I promise too," she said. "But do you really think we should get married this week?"

"What do you mean?"

"I mean, don't we want our family and friends to be there with us?" she asked. "I'm sure that my mother will just be devastated if she can't have me in a white gown in this huge church wedding with an unreasonably expensive downtown reception."

Clu raised up on one elbow to look down at the woman he loved.

"So all this stuff about the Hays County Courthouse or flying to Las Vegas, you've changed your mind about that?"

Zizi nodded. "I guess I've changed my mind," she said.

"Okay," he said. "We'll give our mothers a chance to do it up big, but they'd better be quick about it."

Zizi giggled. "If what happened in the library this afternoon gets back to them I'm sure they'll be getting us to a very hasty 'I do.'"

Clu shook his head. "I am so sorry about that," he told her. "I can't believe I behaved so badly and embarrassed you so horribly."

Amazingly, Zizi didn't seem all that embarrassed. In fact she seemed in a downright jovial mood.

"I'm sure for Bonnie it was the gossip coup of the century," she said. "Can you imagine what must have gone through her mind when she realized that the hot young stud with the shirt practically torn from his back was Clu Langston, Ph.D. and the wild-haired, half-naked female with her legs around his waist was Aziza Josephs, Director of Library Circulation?"

Clu moaned, but was still smiling.

"Don't remind me," he said. "Two library professionals caught making out in the microfilm storage. What are our reputations going to be?"

Zizi smiled at him. "I don't think a little change in reputation is going to hurt either of us," she said.

He planted a tender kiss upon her brow.

"For sure the legend of Miss Zizi-One-Date is going to evaporate rather quickly when the men in this town have to start calling you Mrs. Langston."

"Well, there are some misconceptions about you that some folks are going to feel pretty foolish about," Zizi said.

"What misconceptions?"

"Oh, nothing too important," she said. "I'll tell you all about it some day."

"Why don't you tell me about it now?" he asked.

Zizi looked up into the eyes of the wonderful man she loved, a man who was gentle, sensitive, well groomed, close to his mother and incredibly handsome. In a roundabout way she answered his question.

"Let's just say that sometimes what looks to some to be a common carriage horse, could be a saddle-broke Arabian in disguise."

Epilogue

Mother's Day dawned cool and bright at the Langston ranch. Cool and bright and...well...noisy. A wet diaper awakened Robert Langston Jr., and he sent up a howl. That startled Ferdie, the girls' pet duck, and he began quacking to get out of the laundry room. Bea stumbled down to rescue him, waking Courtney and the twins in the process.

The minute Zizi opened her eyes she had to race to the bathroom.

Clu was right behind her, kneeling at her side to hold her long dark hair out of the way as she faced the new day over the rim of the toilet bowl. Since the front bedrooms of the ranch house were right next to each other, Sam heard the whole thing and got queasy as well, though she had thought her morning sickness was all behind her.

Emma shook her head and chuckled as she rolled out of bed. It had been quiet around the ranch for too many years. It seemed that was definitely a thing of the past.

She slid into her house slippers and tied on her chenille robe before heading to the kitchen to make coffee. Ferdie met her at the threshold.

"Get this bird out of my kitchen or I'm going to fry him up for breakfast!"

The girls all giggled and the twins began to ineffectively chase the animal around the room.

"You wouldn't fry Ferdie," Courtney stated with confidence. "He's your grandduck."

Emma couldn't quite hide the smile that curved up the edges of her mouth. Sam and Gabe's rainbow brood had come such a long way over the last year. It was amazing what a little happiness, stability and involved extended family could do.

"Well you girls better shoo him out in the yard just to be safe," she cautioned.

They did their best with the fractious fowl. Emma finally brought the broom to their aid. And the whole group swept outdoors.

Standing on the porch, Emma watched the little girls play. Admiring their youthful tenacity and grateful for their good health, she took a seat in one of the porch's bent wicker chairs, ruminating, as she often did these days, upon her great good fortune and what a difference a year could make. Three happily married sons, five grandchildren and two more on the way. She thought of her husband, her beloved

Robert, taken away from her too soon. He would have loved this family. She could think of him now without tearing up, without feeling hollow. She would always miss him, but her life had moved on.

The screen door opened. Sam and Gabe stepped out of the kitchen. He carried two cups of coffee and handed Emma one.

"Thank you," she said. "I hate to drink it in front of you, Sam. I know how hard it's been for you to stay away from caffeine."

"It's not hard this morning," she assured her mother-in-law. "It doesn't even smell good."

Carefully she lowered herself into the chair next to Emma. Yesterday, Bea had suggested that her mother looked like she'd swallowed a watermelon, and the description was not far from the truth.

Gabe seated himself on the arm of Sam's chair, as if he were loath to have any distance at all between them. They surveyed the game of "keep away duck" going on in the yard.

Sam shook her head. "I don't usually let them play outside in their pajamas," she said.

"Oh, but at Grandma's," Emma assured her, "all the rules are different."

"Not all the rules," Gabe corrected. "We heard you threatening the life of that duck."

Emma chuckled. "It was a sorry day when that noisy, useless critter wheedled his way into this family."

No one believed her. "You're as crazy about Ferdie as the girls," Gabe said.

"I must have been crazy to think when I bought the darn thing that he'd live outside like any other self-respecting duck in Texas."

From inside the house they heard the distinct sounds of a hard-bitten professional Secret Service agent speaking in baby-talk falsetto.

"Wet's go see Gwamma on da porch," Rob was saying. "Yes, Daddy and Rob Jr. all clean go see Gwamma on da porch, yea-us."

Gabe rolled his eyes. "When there's a baby in my house will I lose my dignity, too?" he asked.

Both his wife and mother nodded affirmatively.

Rob came out on the porch with Rob Jr. in his arms. The chubby, glowing little child had given them a scare at first. A difficult birth had injured his arm, resulting in a condition call Erb's Palsy. Fortunately Laura was able to be with the baby full-time and worked daily on physical therapy. Rob transferred to the regional Secret Service office in Austin so he was home almost every night to help. With their hard work and determined effort, little Rob Jr. showed no evidence of any lingering effects of the infirmity and had full use of the injured arm.

He held out both now to his grandmother and Emma gladly took the handsome young fellow onto her lap. The baby smiled up at her, proudly displaying his one little tooth.

The door swung open once more and Laura and Zizi came out arm in arm, followed by Clu.

"You think you're tired now," Laura was warning them. "Being pregnant is the easy part, it's after they're born that the real work starts."

Rob leaned against the porch railing and chuckled.

"Listen to her, will you," he said. "Last year she was a devoted career woman with absolutely no interest in children. Today, she's an authority on the subject."

"She's certainly earned her stripes," Emma pointed out.

Everybody agreed.

Clu dragged up a couple of chairs so the group was more like a circle than a line.

"How's the house coming?" Sam asked.

Clu and Zizi looked at each other and laughed. The two had purchased a stately old home in San Antonio's Monte Vista district that required a good deal of love, attention and refurbishing.

"May first was the renovation completion date," Zizi said. "Now we're not even asking when they'll be done, we're just hoping that the baby's room is finished before the baby comes!"

"Are you going to quit working when he gets here?" Laura asked.

Zizi shrugged. "I can't decide," she answered honestly. "I love my new job, but I really don't want to miss any of his baby moments."

"We're just going to play it by ear," Clu said. "Things have a way of working themselves out."

"That's for sure," Zizi agreed. "Who would have thought that Clu, sitting on the science sidelines at the library for three years, would be in the perfect position to pick up that basic sciences research grant at UTSA.''

Clu shook his head, amazed at his own good fortune. ''A brand-new lab, lots of resources and one upper-level course to teach per semester. Absolute heaven.''

''They're lucky to get you,'' Emma declared.

''Thanks, Mom.''

''I notice that you keep referring to your baby as him,'' Gabe said. ''Do you two know something we don't know?''

''No,'' Zizi answered. ''We're just using him sort of generically.''

''It might as well be a him,'' Clu said. ''I'm way out of the running to produce the first granddaughter. I still think it's unfair that Gabe wins the horse, Mom.''

''Yeah,'' Rob agreed. ''Acquiring four granddaughters for you by marriage, it smells like unfair advantage to me.''

Gabe snorted grandly. ''I know it's a big burden to you guys trying to keep up with me.''

''I think Sam was in cahoots with him,'' Laura said. ''All they wanted was to cheat you guys out of that horse.''

Zizi feigned total agreement. ''And now they've got the horse and a duck as well, is that fair?''

''I think Gabe should have to keep Zafir in the pool house with Ferdie,'' Clu said.

Emma was laughing.

"Okay, okay. I think you boys have made your point," she said. "I declare the granddaughter competition null and void."

"Gyp!" Gabe declared, good-natured.

"The Arabian is up for grabs again," Emma said. "To the first one who can guess what is going to happen next in this family."

There was silence on the porch for a long moment.

"We're all going to have more kids?" Rob suggested.

"It wouldn't take much imagination to guess that," Emma said, indicating her two pregnant daughter-in-laws. "Try harder."

"Gabe's going to buy out his competition," Rob said.

"From your mouth to God's ear!" he responded.

"Rob's going to run for public office," Clu said.

"Not in my worst nightmare," Rob assured them.

"Clu's going to win the Nobel Prize," Gabe said.

"I'm not sharing the money with you," he countered.

"You're all wrong," Emma said, chuckling secretively. "Every one of you is wrong, wrong, wrong. So I guess I get to keep the horse. I'd better go get dressed. We've got company coming."

She got up, handed young Robbie back to his mother and went inside.

The three brothers and their wives sat there looking at each other, puzzled.

"What was that all about?" Sam asked finally.

"Beats me," Rob answered. "Do you know?" He directed the question to Clu.

"I don't have any idea."

"Look," Zizi said. "Somebody's coming."

Glancing down the long caliche approach, they saw a rider on horseback.

"Who can that be?" Gabe asked.

"And why this time of the morning?" Laura piped in.

"Is it one of the cowboys?" Sam asked.

"Nobody would be working on Sunday," Rob answered.

"He looks kind of familiar," Laura said.

"Not to me," Gabe said.

"It must be the company Mom's expecting," Clu said.

"It's Judge Hernandez!" Laura exclaimed, surprised.

"Who?" Zizi asked.

"The man I used to work for. You guys remember, he was at our wedding."

"Oh, yeah," Clu agreed.

"What's he doing here?" Rob wondered.

There was no response to that query. They had to wait until horse and rider made their way to the porch.

"Good morning," Hernandez called out.

"Good morning," they answered in unison.

"You're looking great, Judge Hernandez," Laura said. "Have you lost weight?"

"Just a little bit around the middle," he confessed. "But please, call me Arthur. Guess all of you had better start calling me Arthur."

Six pairs of eyes stared at him, questioningly.

"Emma told you, didn't she?"

"Told us what?" Rob asked.

"She said she was going to tell you."

The judge suddenly appeared ill at ease and uncertain.

"Well...ah...she said she would tell you."

At that moment, Emma came out the door dressed in blue jeans, snap shirt and Stetson. She was a little bit breathless, obviously rushed.

"Morning, Arthur," she said. "I haven't got Zafir saddled yet, but I'm ready for a brisk canter this morning."

The judge's gaze seem to melt upon her like dairy butter in Texas sunshine.

"What is it that you haven't told us, Mom?" Clu asked her quietly.

She smiled at him. She smiled at them all.

"Guess what is going to happen next in this family?"

She repeated her earlier question and then answered it for them.

"It's a Mother's Day gift for all of us," Emma said. "A stepfather for my sons, a grandpa for the children and a wonderful, loving partner for me. Arthur and I are getting married."

The porch erupted in such delighted noisy celebration that the children playing in the yard actually

stopped and looked to see what the grown-ups were
up to.

And the grown-ups were up to a lot, judging by
all the hugs and smiles going around.

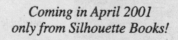

Silhouette
bestselling authors

KASEY MICHAELS

RUTH LANGAN

CAROLYN ZANE

*welcome you to a world
of family, privilege and power
with three brand-new love
stories about America's
most beloved dynasty,
the Coltons*

Brides of Privilege

Available May 2001

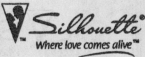

Silhouette®
Where love comes alive™

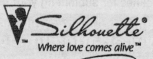

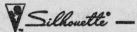